Black Petals

Mirella Sichirollo Patzer

History and Women Press
First Edition
Copyright © 2021 by Mirella Patzer
Internal design © 2021 by Mirella Patzer
Cover design © by Mirella Patzer
www.mirellapatzer.com

All rights reserved. No part of this publication may be reproduced, stored in, or introduced into a retrieval system, or transmitted, in any form, or by any means (electronic, mechanical, photocopying, recording, or otherwise) without the prior permission of the copyright owner.

This is a work of fiction. Names, characters, places, and incidents either are the product of the author's imagination or are used fictitiously and any resemblance to actual persons, living or dead, business establishments, events, or location is entirely coincidental. The characters and events portrayed in this book are fictitious and used factiously. Apart from well-known historical figures, any similarity to real persons, living or dead is purely coincidental and not intended by the author.

No part of this book may be reproduced, scanned, or distributed in any printed or electronic form without permission. The scanning, uploading, and distributing of this book via the Internet or via any other means without the permission of the copyright owner is illegal and punishable by law. Please do not participate in or encourage piracy of copyrighted materials in violation of the author's rights. Please purchase only authorized electronic editions, and do not participate in or encourage electronic piracy of copyrighted materials.

The author and publisher have provided this e-book to you for your personal use only. You may not make this e-book publicly available in any way. Copyright infringement is against the law. If you believe the copy of this ebook you are reading infringes on the author's copyright, please notify the publisher at www.mirellapatzer.com. Your support of the author's rights is appreciated. Thank You.

This is a publication of History and Women Press
www.historyandwomen.com
www.mirellapatzer.com

Books by Mirella Patzer

The Prophetic Queen
Orphan of the Olive Tree
The Contessa's Vendetta
Dangerous Betrothal
Perilous Love

Dedication

To my daughters

Amanda (Patzer) Braaksma
Genna (Patzer) Hawryluk

With an abundance of love

Chapter One

North Chelsea, Massachusetts
March 1875

AMELIA BELLEVILLE PAUSED at the top of the staircase. Her gaze roamed over the guests gathered below. She'd have to go down, but hesitating allowed her a few moments to compose herself.

Somewhere among those gathered was Regan Lockhart, the man her father had arranged for her to marry. It did not take long to spot him. The two stood together in the center of the hall, deep in conversation, crystal goblets of burgundy wine in hand.

Tonight's celebration was for her; the array of finely dressed guests, their laughter and buoyant chatter, candlelight dancing in candelabras and chandeliers, the luscious aromas flowing from the kitchen. Before the end of the evening, her father would announce her betrothal to Regan. All the reasons not to marry him flooded in. What if the kindness and respect he had shown her over the past few months disappeared once they married? Would they grow to love each other over time or find themselves trapped in a joyless marriage?

Her throat tightened. How could she marry a man she barely knew? Life was ever changing, shifting. What if he was not all he appeared to be? Or what if he turned out to be a better man than her father extolled? This was her chance. She could accept her fate and bravely face her future or succumb to these doubts plaguing her. Gripping the bannister, she resisted the urge to turn and flee. With shoulders back and chin held high, she inhaled a fortifying breath.

As if he sensed her gaze, Regan glanced up. Time stopped for her as she saw how he studied her, his eyes alight with admiration.

Amelia gathered the skirts of her silk gown, patterned with tea-roses, and went down the stairs.

"Ah, there she is, Thomas," she heard Regan say to her father.

All heads turned in her direction as she descended and cut through the clusters of people, nodding and greeting them as she strode forth.

Regan stepped forward to meet her. His warm gaze bathed her with appreciation. "You look beautiful. More enchanting than ever."

She returned his compliment with a nervous smile. "A woman announces her engagement only once in her life."

Regan lifted a glass of wine from a servant's tray and handed it to her.

She sipped the light, sweet white wine and studied him. He cut a suave figure in his midnight-blue frock coat and trousers. A light blue waistcoat and white shirt with a black cravat set off his lustrous, raven-colored hair and piercing ocean-blue eyes. His features were strong and well-defined, his lips fuller than those of most men.

In the beginning, she had resisted her father's entreaties to marry Regan, a man she had recently met and barely knew. But little by little, the more she came to know Regan, her heart had softened. Whenever they were together, he treated her with utmost respect and admiration. Nothing seemed untoward about him. She had finally relented to her father's powerful persuasions and agreed to marry him. Many couples grew to love each other. She hoped it would hold true for their marriage.

She stood by his side, mingling with the guests who seemed to take an instant liking to him. A nod here. A compliment there. Laughter and warmth filled the candlelit room, and Amelia relaxed amid the congeniality.

When Seeton, their butler, announced dinner, Regan offered his arm, and they led the guests into the dining room. Her father took his usual place at the head of the table. She and Regan sat facing each other. Her father had spared no expense for this meal; they dined on clam chowder and entrees of lobster and crab, roast beef, and vegetables.

Throughout dinner, she could barely concentrate on any of the conversation. The more serious talk focused on rebuilding shops, offices, and warehouses after the fire that had devastated Boston three years ago. Her father's shoe warehouse and offices among them. But she heard little of their talk. Tangled thoughts of her own future distracted her.

From across the table Regan occasionally glanced at her, offering a smile or a nod whenever she gathered her thoughts enough to speak, a mild distraction that helped ease her tension.

While they enjoyed their apple pudding dessert, her father tapped his wineglass with a fork and rose.

Amelia tensed.

The guests grew quiet.

Thomas dabbed the sweat from his brow with his napkin before beginning.

"Now that I have everyone's attention, I thank you all for joining us this evening. If you haven't met him yet, I'd like to introduce Mr. Regan Lockhart, a new business associate of mine, who hails from the nearby town of Winthrop. As you know, and like many of you gathered here tonight, the Boston fire burned down my entire business. I've been running it from a temporary location just outside of Boston. Recently, I asked Mr. Lockhart to invest in my company so I can rebuild. I'm pleased to say, he eagerly accepted, and my warehouse and factory will soon be ready for a grand reopening."

There was a round of applause, and Amelia couldn't help but be pleased. Every bit of good news brought on such a reaction. What had started as a small fire in the basement of a warehouse on Summer Street, spread quickly, demolishing sixty-five acres in the heart of Boston, and consuming nearly eight hundred buildings and the entire financial district. Thirteen people had died in the inferno, two of whom were firemen. Losses amounted to millions of dollars. Everyone in their social circle had experienced damages and financial defeats of one sort or another. It was no minor victory that his business had survived. He had not only rebuilt but also expanded. Her heart filled with pride at her father's business acumen and resiliency.

"And, of course, you all know my lovely daughter,

Amelia."

Amid the nods and smiles, Amelia held the stem of her wineglass, bracing herself for the forthcoming announcement. Everyone glanced expectantly from her to Regan. Secrets were impossible to keep among so many close friends.

Regan sat back in his chair; his head cocked to one side, as if waiting for her reaction.

The time had come. Her entire life was about to change. Could she marry a man she had known for only a few months? A man not of her choice but of her father's? Her mouth ran dry, and her stomach churned. She fought the impulse to kick her father under the table to halt the announcement. But it was too late. She must trust his judgement. He would never knowingly put her in an unhappy, tenuous situation. So, she formed an obligatory smile and pushed aside her unfounded doubts.

"Amelia has been the best of daughters, caring for me after my dear wife died two years ago. I'm proud of the lovely young woman you see here tonight. However, I'm not getting any younger, and I would be remiss if I didn't look toward her future. My greatest wish is to see her well settled instead of caring for me and running our home. I'm delighted to say I can now be at ease. Please stand and raise your glasses."

Utensils clinked against dishes, chairs scraped, and the rustle of silk and satin filled the room as everyone stood.

Her father paused. His face lost all color and his hand trembled. In a forced, jagged voice, he said, "I'm happy to announce the betrothal of my daughter, Miss Amelia Belleville, to Mr. Regan Lockhart." Again, he paused, and in a grinding voice, little more than a whisper, said, "The wedding is to take place in the spring."

The goblet tumbled from his hand and shattered when it struck the hardwood floor. He clutched his chest and struggled for breath. Swaying, he seemed about to lose his balance.

Panic welled in Amelia's chest.

Too late, she and Regan sprang forward to catch him as her beloved father crumpled to the ground.

A woman screamed.

By the time they rushed to his side, her father was dead.

⁓⚜⁓

STEADY RAIN POURED from a slate-colored sky. A bitter, wintery wind swirled and tossed dead leaves and debris over tombstones and graves. Somber mourners huddled beneath black umbrellas. She was utterly alone in this world, with no family or distant relatives. All who had gathered were friends and acquaintances of her father. Numb with grief, Amelia watched the gravediggers lower his coffin into the dark slot in the ground. Now was the time for her to toss the traditional handful of dirt onto the coffin, but the earth was too wet and muddy.

Regan stood beside her. He had been a constant presence over the past few days, helping her plan the funeral arrangements to the smallest detail.

He noticed her hesitation, placed his hand on her arm, and leaned his head closer. "Toss in the daffodil you're holding."

She dropped the flower into the grave, then sagged against him.

The inclement weather forced a hasty end to the service. The pastor stepped forward to comfort and provide her with his condolences for the last time. One by one, the mourners followed him, the downpour of icy rain hastening their steps.

Regan guided her into his coach. He closed the umbrella, followed her inside, and sat across from her. After removing his top hat, he offered her a warm rug to wrap around her legs. Then, with a tap of his cane on the ceiling, he signaled the driver to set off.

The vehicle jolted forward. His expression one of worry, Regan gazed at her.

"I'm grateful for all you've done, Regan. I couldn't have managed without you."

His deep blue eyes seemed to probe her soul, his expression soft and compassionate. "There's nothing I wouldn't do for you. And for your father, a dear friend and mentor, I could have done nothing less."

Amelia managed a weak smile. Too grieved to keep up a conversation, she retreated into silence.

When they arrived at the house, Sarah, her maid, welcomed them. In the parlor, a fire danced in the hearth. She led Amelia to a chair, reached for a blanket that had been warming near the blaze, and handed her a cup of hot, sweet tea.

Soon, the mourners arrived. With plates of food in hand, they lingered. They spoke in hushed tones about her father and came to her one by one to express their condolences.

Numb, every muscle in her body ached with exhaustion. She craved privacy and the comfort of her bedroom but had to persevere until the mourners left.

Though the dismal weather had kept some away, there were many more who had come. Thomas Belleville had been well-loved. She was grateful when the guests didn't tarry, eager to return home before the penetrating rain turned the roads into a sodden hazard.

Soon, only Regan and William Finnerty, the family attorney, remained. She led them to the library for a brief discussion. In the doorway, she halted. Her father's favorite sweater hung on the back of his chair. On the desk, a book lay open at the page he had last read. The sight of the objects, so personal, tore at her emotions. Here, in her father's private domain, she felt his presence. It was in the air she breathed and in every item she saw.

She crossed the room and stood behind the desk, resting her hand on the sweater before slowly lifting it and holding it to her face. Her throat clogged at his familiar scent that still lingered amid the threads—the aroma of his favorite pipe tobacco, the pungency of the liniment he used for his arthritic hands. Clutching it to her chest, the tears she had fought to keep at bay, now flowed unrestrained.

Regan's soft footsteps creaked on the wooden floor as he stood behind her and helped her to sit.

How small she felt in her father's chair. In all the years of her life, never once had she sat in it. It was odd to see the room from this unique perspective.

William, a balding, robust man in his fifties, poured brandy into a glass and offered it to her. "It's been a long day, Miss Belleville. You look chilled. This should help restore you."

Amelia took a long sip that burnt her mouth. Warmth trickled down her throat to her belly.

"Today isn't the right time, Miss Amelia," William said. "But there's the matter of the will. When do you think you might feel ready to have it read?"

She wiped her tears with the handkerchief Regan had handed to her. "Tomorrow afternoon?" she asked, hesitating.

"You're certain?" William asked.

"I can't see any reason to wait." It was good to have Regan and William looking after her interests.

He exhaled, as if relieved. "Then tomorrow it shall be. Until then, I offer you my sincerest condolences. I also grieve this loss of my childhood friend. The world is much diminished without him."

"I'll see you to the door," Regan offered, and the two left.

Amelia stared into the hearth's crackling wood and took another sip. The heat from the brandy and fire warmed her.

Regan returned. He sat and studied her from across the desk. "I'd like to talk to you about our wedding."

She had expected this. The topic had lingered silently between them since the night her father died. Was he going to call off the wedding now? It wouldn't surprise her. Amelia braced herself.

"I think we should postpone it, to respect the required mourning period of one year. You'll need time to adjust, to heal, especially when…" He paused, as if unsure of himself.

"Now that I'm alone in the world?" she added, surprised he still wanted to proceed with their nuptials. "You may say it. It's the truth, isn't it?"

He frowned. "I wouldn't have stated it in quite that

way, but yes. I'm worried about you living here all alone."

"Sarah is here, and so is Mrs. Appleton, our housekeeper. And Seeton, of course. Please don't worry, all will be well."

An awkward silence followed. He seemed to want to say something more, so she waited.

"I've been thinking." He stared down at his hands, then looked back up at her. "What would you say if I asked you to move into Edenstone with me and my family? As you know, my Aunt Beatrice and Cousin Clara live with me. It wouldn't be inappropriate. They can be your chaperones until we marry."

"Move into Edenstone with you?" For the briefest of moments, her heartache disappeared.

His brows rose when he noticed her expression. "The days to come will challenge you. There'll be many decisions to make, both big and small. Please consider it. Your future family would surround you. You needn't decide right away."

His offer was more than generous, but it felt improper for her to live with him in his house despite his cousin and aunt who would act as chaperones. Her stomach twisted. "I promise to consider it."

Sarah appeared in the doorway. "Would you care for a bath, miss?"

It was exactly what she needed, solitude and tranquility away from the attention and demands that had consumed her this past week. "Thank you, but I'm far too tired. All I crave is sleep. I'll bathe in the morning."

Regan rose and came around the desk to offer her his hand. "I agree. You need your rest. I'll leave and come back tomorrow."

She gave him a slight smile. "I look forward to it."

He walked with her to the staircase. She felt the hefty weight of his gaze upon her as she ascended. At the top, she turned to look at him. He smiled encouragingly and then walked out of sight. A moment later, she heard the front door click shut behind him.

With her hand on the bedroom doorknob, she paused. An eerie silence lingered in the house. It seemed empty, bereft of life and laughter. Sarah, who waited for her in her room, had already turned down the bedcovers and laid out a bed-gown.

"Let me help you undress." With deft fingers, she unlaced Amelia's gown. "There's chamomile tea in the pot on your nightstand to help you sleep."

"Chamomile tea is perfect," Amelia said with gratitude.

"A good sleep will serve you well. It's been a strenuous day. Everything may seem bleak, miss, but with a little time, you'll feel better. Besides, you have Mr. Regan. I've heard nothing but good things about him. A good catch, he is. More than one young lady has set their sights on him in the past."

Too exhausted to engage in further talk, Amelia let Sarah babble as she washed her face with a warm cloth. Soon, tucked in her bed and propped up on pillows, she sipped her tea. She let out a small breath as some tension eased from her body.

Sarah gathered the discarded clothes. "Will there be anything else, miss?"

"No, thank you, Sarah, you've thought of everything."

Sarah's smile was warm, but a little frown betrayed her worry as she left the room.

A sudden silence followed. After a few more sips, Amelia set her teacup on the nightstand and snuffed the candles. Nestling against the pillows, she burrowed beneath the warm covers.

An incoherent surge of grief surfaced. She'd lost both her parents and was alone in the world. Fears about what the future held swirled in her mind as she cried herself into a deep, exhausted sleep.

An increasing light stirred her slowly awake until she finally opened her eyes.

Her father stood at the foot of her bed. A dazzling glow of light surrounded him, its brilliance enveloping her in its warmth. He wore his burial clothes but looked different somehow. He no longer bore the signs of age. His bald head with its wisps of gray hair was now rich and thick with the chestnut-colored locks of his youth. The fine lines in his face had vanished, as had his portly belly. He gazed at her with soulful eyes that shined with a warmth which had not existed when he was alive.

"Father." Amelia reached out to him.

He frowned. "Forgive me, Amelia."

Myriad emotions coursed through her, yearning and sorrow among the strongest. "What could there be to forgive?" She crawled to the foot of her bed, reaching out with her hands, her heart aching to touch him.

But he backed away from her reach as a frown crossed his features. "Beware the black petals." Then his spirit, and the bright nimbus that engulfed him, faded into nothingness.

Chapter Two

Winthrop, Massachusetts

THE HEAVY RAIN ceased, and daylight waned into evening as Regan's carriage came to a halt in front of Edenstone. He entered the house where Edward Simpson, his butler, took his coat and hat. The rich aroma of roasted meat and vegetables wafted from the kitchen at the rear of the house. Simpson's wife, Mary, was housekeeper and cook. She proved her worth with every splendid meal she prepared. The couple had spent decades with the family and ran the household with precision.

"Miss Clara thought you would be much later, so she ordered dinner served. We were just about to bring it in. Your timing is perfect."

"Thank you, Edward." Regan strode toward the dining room but stopped and swung back around. "Please inform Mrs. Simpson to air and prepare my mother's bedroom for Miss Belleville. My fiancée may come to live here earlier than expected."

After Simpson nodded, Regan swept into the dining room.

"Aunt Beatrice," he exclaimed as he stopped to press a kiss on the old woman's cheek. "How lovely you look tonight." The day's events left him feeling drained. His leaden endearment sounded ingenuous rather than heartfelt.

His aunt didn't appear to notice, and her cheeks brightened like a rose in bloom. "Oh, hogwash, you rogue," she gushed. "Save those sweet words for your lady, not an old gal like me."

After a quick kiss on his cousin Clara's cheek, he took his seat at the head of the long candlelit table.

Clara scrutinized him as he reached for a bread roll and split it apart. "By the look of you, I take it the day was a grueling one?" She passed him a steaming dish of roast potatoes.

"You could say that," he muttered.

Aunt Beatrice sliced into her roast beef. "I hope you gave our condolences to your lady friend." She frowned with confusion. "Oh dear, her name escapes me." Shaking her head, she raised a forkful of meat to her mouth and chewed.

Lady friend. Poor forgetful Aunt Beatrice. He had told her Amelia's name many times. "I did, for which she asked me to thank you."

Aunt Beatrice smiled back at him, pleased.

"Your poor fiancée," Clara added. "Mother and I would have accompanied you today, but the weather refused to cooperate. You know how I hate to take Mother out in inclement weather."

"The day was bitterly cold from start to finish. The heavy rain made the roads nearly impassable with deep, mud-filled ruts. It's a miracle I arrived home without getting stuck. It was safer for you both to be here."

"That poor woman." Aunt Beatrice spread a rather large dollop of butter on her bread. "What will she do now?"

Regan reached for the roast and slid a few slices onto his plate. "I'm glad you asked. I've invited Amelia to come and live here right away before we marry. She is alone and I'm worried about her."

Clara set a forkful of food down on her plate. "You did? Goodness, where will we put her?"

"There's only one vacant bedroom in the house. Mother's old room. That's where she'll stay."

"But that's my sister's room." Aunt Beatrice's hand fluttered to her chest. "Where will you put Catherine then?"

Shock and dead silence fell over them.

Clara looked at her mother with alarm. "Mother, have you forgotten? Catherine's not with us anymore."

Aunt Beatrice wrung her hands, her expression grim. "But where did she go? And without a word to me."

Clara reached out for her mother's hand, and in the softest of voices said, "Mother, Catherine died a while ago. You remember, don't you?"

Aunt Beatrice's expression changed from confusion to distress. "Oh, yes, she did, didn't she?" Her eyes welled with tears. "How could I have forgotten such a thing?"

Pain was clear in his aunt's every word. He could understand her reaction. His mother and aunt had been identical twins, close their entire lives. A stranger occupying her sister's bedchamber would come as a shock to Aunt Beatrice. The two had spent much time in that room, reading, embroidering, and trying on their latest gowns. Their laughter once pealed freely and gloriously within its walls in the days before all the tragedies befell the family.

Clara remained silent for the moment. Typical of her, Regan thought. Even as a child she had been cautious about everything she said or did. Once she finished pondering what this would mean, her opinion would flow freely.

"The room will be perfect for Amelia," Regan said. "It faces the ocean and catches the sun in the mornings. I've already instructed Mrs. Simpson to prepare the room."

Clara sat back in her chair and stroked her chin. "Does she have no other family to care for her until the wedding? For her to be under our roof doesn't seem appropriate."

"Unfortunately, Amelia has no other living relatives. Besides, I don't give a damn what society thinks."

"Obviously," Clara said. "But there's much I have to do before the room is habitable. When is she arriving?"

"I don't know for certain, but I imagine it will be within a few days. You have an eye for decorating, Clara, and impeccable taste," Regan said. "A trip to Boston to buy some new furniture and bedding might be in order."

Regan knew his cousin well. There was nothing she liked better than to browse at some of Boston's finest shops. And judging by the heightened sparkle in her eyes, he knew he had guessed right.

"Of course, I would be happy to. And I know the perfect shop to purchase everything I need."

"Good. Tell the shopkeepers to send the invoices to me. If you can, go to Boston tomorrow. I suspect Amelia might arrive sooner than you think."

"I'll ask Mrs. Simpson to watch over Mother for me

and I'll head out first thing in the morning if the roads are passable, that is."

"The road between North Chelsea and Winthrop is not as well-traveled as the road from here to Boston, so I suspect it should be in decent shape."

"And I'll sort the linen cupboard with Mrs. Simpson," Aunt Beatrice chimed in.

Despite his morose mood, he raised a smile at the two. "I knew I could count on you both."

"Of course, you can, my dear," Aunt Beatrice said all abeam. "We help each other. That's what families are for."

REGAN INSERTED THE key into the lock of his mother's bedroom and paused before he gave it a twist. He hadn't been inside it since the day she died. He braced himself for the painful memories that were sure to assault him.

Amelia would be his wife, and as the future mistress of Edenstone, it was fitting she occupy his mother's old room. He inhaled a deep breath and turned the key. The lock clicked, and the door creaked open.

The room lay in darkness. Musty air, thick with dust, assailed him. Because of the dismal day, no rays of sunlight danced through the gap in the light blue velvet curtains like they once had. An absolute, morose silence reigned.

Regan stepped inside and crossed to the window. He drew the curtains aside with one strong motion. Beyond the window, rough waves crashed against the shore beneath the grey sky. When he turned back around to study the room, he could feel his mother's spirit here amid the grey-blue walls, oak floorboards, and painted ceiling. Memories of happier days flooded his senses. Embraces and laughter, bright colors, and singsong. Then came the memories of all the tragedies, and then her death.

Visions of his mother drifted in his mind. He could see her laying on the massive four-poster canopy bed, ill and dying. The two marble-topped nightstands once held an accoutrement of cups and medicines. The cabinet of polished cherry wood in the corner near the windows was where she had stored her hats, scarves, and books. He pulled out the chintz-covered chair and sat at her baroque style writing desk. He could envision her sitting there, penning a note to a friend.

Regan rose and wandered to the large satinwood wardrobe and swung open its doors. Hanging inside the blue and cream lined interior were his mother's gowns in an array of colors and fabrics.

Her scalloped shaped jewelry box still sat on her dressing table. As a child, it had always enchanted him. Mother of pearl inlaid roses decorated the black enamel sides. Gold paint trimmed its edges. He raised the lid, and the sweet tones of *Für Elise* filled the air; music that always kindled visions of her. Jeweled brooches, bracelets, necklaces, and pearls sparkled within. He closed the lid. The music stopped, and the room fell into an eerie tranquility again. He tucked the jewelry box under his arm to take with him into his room for the time being. One day, he would present it to Amelia.

Regan sat on the bed, almost falling onto it. He stared up at his mother's portrait over the fireplace's mantel. A light coating of dust covered its golden frame. The artist had captured her true essence. She stood before a fireplace decorated with a French vase filled with a colorful array of blooms. Her pale lavender silk gown contrasted with her dark, coiffed hair. Loose curls cascaded over her shoulders. In her hand she held a pink rose.

Her beauty was the first thing anyone noticed. But those who knew her well, understood dark emotions hid behind her innocent expression, anguish clear in the crease of her lovely brow and the down-curve of her full lips. But it was her eyes that affected him the most. They were a deep pool of restless blue, a sea of hopeless grief.

He rose and placed a hand on the painting. "I'm sorry, Mother," he whispered, "for all the terrible things that befell you." He could not help but recall the curse and tragedies that had long plagued the Lockhart family.

He stepped back. For Amelia's sake, he would have it moved to the drawing rooms with the other family portraits. He hoped Clara would have the forethought to replace it with something vibrant that matched the room's décor.

Amelia. How beautiful she had looked on the night of their engagement. Now everything had changed, the wedding postponed for the period of mourning. Already, the fates conspired against him. Yet, he remained determined. Unlike his previous fiancée, this time, this woman would become his wife.

Did she trust him? If so, why didn't she ask him to attend the reading of the will? Before his death, Thomas Belleville had been experiencing financial difficulties. Thomas wanted to transfer the business to him once he and Amelia married. So, he had signed the betrothal contract Thomas had prepared and accepted the dowry offered, and the money had been transferred into his bank account. But Thomas died before the terms outlining their business agreement could be signed. How had things become so damn complicated? No matter. He could achieve his goals despite the lack of documentation.

Regan strode to a smaller, inner door that connected this room to that his father's, which he now occupied. He gave the chamber one last perusal. Yes, this room would suit Amelia very well. Although currently a little stale and dusty, Clara's feminine touch and a good airing would restore it to its former elegance.

With the jewelry box still in hand, he turned back around, swung open the door, and entered his room.

North Chelsea, Massachusetts

UNABLE TO SLEEP, Amelia tossed and turned all night. She had seen the dead before, but only in dreams. Her mother's spirit sometimes came to her this way, as did other long-dead ancestors. Once, even a soldier who had died in the American Revolution appeared to her. But this time was different. Her father's appearance was no dream—she had been awake.

She'd heard talk about people who could see the dead. Was she one such person?

At first, her father seemed joyful and at peace. His expression was distant and empty when he asked her to forgive him. But why? Their last days together had been without conflict. Most puzzling was his warning. *Beware the black petals.* What did it mean?

She lay in bed puzzling over his message until dawn

crept through a gap between her bedroom curtains. Finally, she rose and indulged in a bath before going downstairs.

Amelia spent the morning quietly. She regretted not inviting Regan to the reading of the will. His strength had bolstered her. She could have benefitted from his presence.

William Finnerty arrived promptly at two o'clock. She led him into her father's library, where Mrs. Appleton had set out tea and biscuits.

Amelia fidgeted with her skirt. "Thank you for coming. I thought it best to understand my situation as soon as possible."

"A wise decision." William reached into his portfolio and pulled out the will. "Shall we begin?" He slid on his glasses. "If you don't mind, I'll avoid all the legal jargon and summarize what you need to know."

"I would appreciate that." Amelia closed her eyes and took a deep breath to calm herself.

"As there are no living relatives, Thomas named you sole recipient of all his assets."

This came as no surprise.

William cleared his throat. "Unfortunately, your father's finances have suffered recently. As you know, the Boston Fire destroyed his shipping warehouse and offices on Pearl Street. Although well-insured, when he rebuilt, he expanded. He borrowed against his factory and overextended himself."

"How can that be? The family business has flourished for more than a century. Our wealth has always been stable. Besides, I have been doing the accounting. The various balances and accounts are all in order."

"Not anymore, I'm afraid." He shifted in his chair. "Your father kept a dual set of ledgers. The ones he gave you to update with invoices and receipts were not the official ones."

For her father to do such a thing was so out of character that all she could do was stare at William open mouthed. Her mind formed no thoughts other than to register shock. She closed her mouth, then glanced down at her feet before looking up. "Please continue."

"You must know he did this to protect you. He didn't want you to worry. Of course, I warned him about taking too many risks. But he was certain the business would thrive again with the expansion."

Tentacles of anxiety coiled in her stomach.

"It is difficult to say this, so I will put it as simple as I can. Without a male heir to assume the business, the bank demands immediate repayment. We must sell both the business and your home and the contents to pay off that debt. There can be no delay."

It took a moment for the news to set in, and for her alarm to spread. "My home… it's lost?"

"I'm afraid so."

Myriad questions raced through her panicked mind as she sought to understand. "When I marry Regan, they could consider him a male heir, could he not?" It was a small glimmer of hope.

William stared down at his hands. "A while ago, your father asked Regan to invest in his business, which Regan did." He pulled out a document and slid it across the table to her. "This is the agreement whereby your father promises to repay Regan for the money he invested."

"And did he?" Amelia asked.

"Unfortunately, no. By that time, your father was already in financial difficulty. Unable to repay Regan, your father offered to make him his partner and upon your marriage, he would give Regan the business. They completed negotiating the terms, but your father died before they could sign the paperwork."

"So, if I'm to understand, Regan is a creditor. Had he signed the document, he would have inherited the business and its debts."

"Yes."

To be a burden even before they married was inconceivable. "There is no other money? How will I live? What of Sarah? I can't lose her, and Mr. Seeton and Mrs. Appleton? They have been with my family for decades. How do I pay them?"

"As I've stated, your father already paid the dowry to Regan in exchange for his promise of marriage, and the betrothal agreement is iron clad. It stipulates Sarah is to continue in her role as your personal maid. I will have to find new positions, however, for Margaret Appleton and John Seeton now that the home is to be sold. Your father hoped Regan would one day assume responsibility for his business, but I regret that won't happen now."

"I see," she said, although she did not. It was a man's world, and they clung to information with an iron grip.

William produced a signed copy of the betrothal agreement. "As you can see, the terms are strict and almost impossible to break."

"But matters are different now. I wasn't a pauper when Regan signed it. He might not want to marry me now."

"He might not, but you're both obligated to follow

through with the terms. If he decides not to proceed with the marriage, he must return the dowry in full. But if you were the one to walk away, you would forfeit your dowry."

"My father placed me at a disadvantage. Why would he do such a thing?"

"He wanted you to marry Regan, and was so convinced he was an excellent match, he made the terms highly agreeable, and difficult to disagree with."

"I see," she thought. But in truth, she didn't. "A period of mourning must take place before I can marry. What am I to do until then?" Amelia inhaled a deep calming breath to fight away a growing sense of bitterness.

"There is the matter of where you are to live. It may or may not take time for the house to sell. Do you have a lady friend, a close friend of the family with whom you could live with for six months or a year?"

She shook her head.

"If you wish, I could speak to Regan about this situation. Perhaps we can come up with a solution and convince the bank to give us more time."

Her cheeks heated with humiliation. "No, I prefer not to burden him with my problems."

"But you are to be his wife. He must be told."

"Then I will be the one to tell him and release him from the betrothal if he wishes."

"I doubt that will be the case. Regan seems quite taken with you. I think it's best to talk to him soon. Gossip and rumors already swirl about regarding your father's financial woes, now yours too, and I'm afraid it won't be long before he hears of it all, if he hasn't already." With a deep sigh, his expression became thoughtful. "We must consider your living arrangements immediately."

"Regan and I spoke about that after you left yesterday. He invited me to move to Edenstone, where his elderly aunt and cousin also live."

"An excellent suggestion. The presence of his elderly aunt will prevent scandal of any sort. I recommend you accept Regan's offer. For now, there's no other alternative."

Amelia paused, shocked at the strange, dreamlike lunacy of her situation. "I'll consider it."

"Consider it? Why do you hesitate?"

"Everything is happening so fast. To tell the truth, the thought of moving in with him and his family before our wedding makes me uneasy."

"Whatever you may think about your father's financial problems, I assure you, he was an excellent judge of character. He hoped to see you married to Regan, a good man. But, to reassure you, I'll dig into Regan's finances and reputation. Once I learn something, I'll report back to you. In the meantime, I urge you to accept his offer." He eyed her with sympathy.

She nodded. There was little choice. If William's investigation revealed Regan was not all he appeared to be, the mourning period would give her time to make alternate living arrangements.

"I'm glad. It's the right decision for you."

It was her only option.

He removed his glasses, returned the documents to his portfolio, and rose. "I'll arrange for the sale of your home and furnishings. Take with you any personal possessions and any family heirlooms you wish to keep."

Together, they walked to the entrance hall.

"Take care of yourself, Amelia. Call on me if you need

anything. I'll contact you shortly with the results of my inquiries."

She waited on the porch while he climbed up to the driver's seat in his curricle and drove away.

She stepped back into the house, closed the door, and leaned against it for support. Her legs trembled. She clutched her chest to calm her rapid breaths and fought to keep frantic tears at bay. With every turn, her life was disintegrating. She had lost everything—her family, and the only home she had ever known.

Ahead she faced altered circumstances and uncertainty. She was a young woman with nothing. How could her father have risked everything? Now she understood why he had encouraged her to marry Regan, a man who could provide a secure future. Had he arranged their betrothal because of his financial distress? She had always trusted her father. Did he want her to marry Regan because he was the highest bidder? And what of Regan? How much did he know about her father's financial situation? Would he still want to marry her once she told him she was a pauper?

Amelia pushed herself away from the door and returned to the parlor. Numb, she stood at the window gazing at carriages passing by. The gray tree branches had yet to produce spring's flowers. Yesterday's rain had stopped, but quick moving clouds blocked the sun. Uncertainty, fear, and a thousand other emotions strangled her. She must sort them out, arrange them, impose order somehow, and remain strong in the face of upheaval.

She turned from the window and sat in one of the wing chairs near the fire, staring into the flames. Tormented at first by all the confusion, her thoughts soon took on a startling clarity. Her situation was dire. She had to leave her home.

Before long, she heard Mr. Seeton greet someone at the front door. Amelia knew it was Regan even before she turned around.

He stood as tall and straight as a towering spruce in the doorway. He wore a midnight-blue coat, gray trousers, and a white waistcoat. His deep blue eyes softened as he surveyed her with concern.

"Amelia." His velvet-edged voice broke the silence.

"Regan." She forced herself to smile. "Please come and sit down."

He crossed the room, then halted to caress her hand. "You're pale. Am I intruding? I can return later if you prefer to rest."

"I didn't sleep well last night, but I'm glad you're here."

His mouth curved with tenderness as he sat on the wing chair opposite hers.

Amelia hesitated. If she and Regan were to marry, there should be no secrets between them. So, she told him about the contents of the will, and in the telling, her pain sharpened. She was now a woman reliant on his munificence, his willingness to take her into his home, and to provide for her. The extent and tragedy of loss astounded her. Somehow, she shoved her feelings aside and revealed all to him.

He listened without interruption. His gaze steady upon her the entire time, with no change to his expression.

When Amelia finished, she took a breath. "Now you know everything. I'll understand if you wish to withdraw from the betrothal agreement. It's not fair to hold you to a contract made under different circumstances." Silence befell them.

He leaned forward, rested his elbows on his knees, and clasped his hands. "I didn't know your father was so overextended. But this changes nothing." Compassion laced his deep-toned voice. "I'm a man of my word and intend to honor the agreement. It's what your father wanted for us. Consider Edenstone as your home now. Aunt Beatrice and my cousin Clara are eager to meet you. In fact, they're already preparing for your arrival."

He would adhere to the agreement because her father wanted it. Not because he did. He was a man of business. Was their future marriage just another transaction to him? The very idea stung her to the marrow. "I can't marry until the proper period of mourning is over—one year."

"You're my only concern; not what society dictates is proper."

Perhaps he had some affection for her. She was hesitant but persisted, encouraged by his kind words. "I'm not ready to marry yet, Regan. My spirits are low, and I need more time."

"You can have all the time you need, but at Edenstone where you can be free of all this worry and grief."

"Our wedding would have been next month. I have to cancel all the arrangements."

"I'll take care of everything."

Relief washed through her. She doubted she was up to the ordeal. "May I beg another favor?"

"You only have to ask."

"When we marry, can the ceremony be small and private with family only?" His family, of course, because she had no one.

"Everything will be exactly as you want. Move to Edenstone as soon as you're ready. I'll make sure you have everything you need."

A spark of relief ignited in her breast. A roof over her head, food in her belly, clothes on her back. She need not worry. There was little from her home she could take with her.

Amelia stared into the flames, then gazed at him again. "That's exceedingly kind, but I have a few things to attend to first. I should be ready to leave by late tomorrow afternoon."

She wanted to spend one last night in her home, to bid a last farewell to her old life, to gather strength to embrace a new one. This she kept to herself so he wouldn't think she was too wistful.

"Tomorrow, I'll have my associate, Mr. Henry Townsend, visit you. He'll make a list of items you want to take to Edenstone. His character is impeccable. You can trust him." He stood. Taking her hands in his, he helped her rise from the chair. "I promise all will be well, but now I must leave to deal with an urgent business matter. I look forward to tomorrow when you come home to Edenstone."

Home. The word echoed in her mind. His masculine voice carried depth and authority, so she surrendered to its reassurance. He made her feel safe in a world forever altered. She watched him walk out of the room, his gait confident, and pondered their future together. Recently, she had been certain enough to agree to marry him. But now that she was alone, she must do everything she could to look after herself, to be certain. She hoped the results of Mr. Finnerty's investigation would set her at ease.

Chapter Three

EARLY THE NEXT morning, Regan drove to his carriage factory in Boston. He brought his phaeton to a stop in his usual spot between the blacksmith's forge and barn. Teddy, the young blacksmith's apprentice, came out to unharness the horse and lead it into the barn where fresh water and hay awaited. Regan muttered a word of thanks, then hurried into the main two-story building.

The familiar aroma of sawdust and paint and leather greeted him the moment he stepped inside. In the open space that comprised the main floor, carpenters, painters, and upholsterers were already hard at work, and as he passed, they glanced up to welcome him. He returned each salutation pleasantly and headed up the stairs to the second level where the designers, accountants, and procurers of the materials worked. He bypassed his own corner office and entered the one next to it.

Henry Townsend, his accountant, glanced up from a ledger as Regan plonked himself down on the leather chair opposite the desk. His most trusted employee, and the third generation of Townsends to work at the factory, looked up and smiled. They were the same age, and both similarly dedicated to their work.

"No need to stop what you're doing. I have another job for you."

Henry replaced the lid on his fountain pen and laid it in the book before pushing them to the side. He folded his hands on the desk and cocked his head. "Tell me."

Regan leaned forward and removed a folded note from the inside pocket of his town coat. He slid it across the desk. "I would like you to drive to North Chelsea today and meet with Amelia at her home. That's her address."

Henry took the paper and tucked it into his vest's pocket.

"She'll take you through the house to identify items she wishes to have packed and moved to Edenstone. I would like you to make a list of these items."

"I'd be happy to. Leave it with me and I'll arrange the safe transfer of these items ahead of the wedding."

"Not exactly."

Henry frowned. "What do you mean?"

"You will make the list, of course, but I don't want any of the items taken out of the house. Amelia is never to find out. Make sure she believes you will transfer the items to Edenstone."

"I don't understand. Why?"

"It's better for you not to know."

North Chelsea, Massachusetts

SARAH BEGAN PACKING the contents of Amelia's bedroom early that morning. With much to do, Amelia descended for breakfast, after which she'd face the arduous task of choosing which items to surrender and which to take with her to Edenstone. She stared at her father's empty chair, a grim reminder of her loss. Not long ago, she had been a young girl with loving parents and a promising future. Now with both her mother and father dead and her home lost, sadness hung over her like a black cloud, but she would rise above grief and carry on with life.

Despite having no appetite, she reached for a slice of dry toast, ignoring the butter and jam. She needed her strength to get through the day, so she forced herself to take a nibble. It lodged in her throat. She couldn't swallow it down. Nearly choking, she reached for the teapot and filled her cup. The lukewarm, bitter beverage must have been steeping for a while as it tasted terrible, but it freed the piece of toast in her throat. She pushed the dish away and forwent the meal altogether. Massaging her forehead, she leaned back in the chair and prayed for enough strength to see her through this ordeal. Melancholy pressed like a heavy boulder on her heart at the knowledge this would be a day of many lasts.

Amelia rose and left the dining room. She crossed the hallway and entered her father's library. She sat behind his desk, found paper and pen, and began writing a list of items she wanted to keep.

Mr. Seeton appeared in the doorway. "Pardon me, Miss, but there's a gentleman named Mr. Townsend here to see you. Shall I show him into the parlor?"

The parlor would be the most logical place to start. This was where we kept most of the family heirlooms. "Yes, please. I'll join him in a moment."

Amelia waited for Mr. Seeton to leave, then heaved a sigh. Time to face the inevitable. She could not alter the past but could embrace her future. Gathering her resolve, she left the library.

Outside the parlor door, she straightened her shoulders. With head held high, she breezed in and welcomed the visitor with her most gracious smile. "Mr. Townsend, thank you for coming. I'm Amelia Belleville."

A lanky man greeted her pleasantly. "Ah, Miss Belleville, the pleasure is all mine." He adjusted his cuff, then raised the book in his hand to his chest. In an awkward, reserved voice he said, "Mr. Lockhart tells me I'm to assist you in recording and packing any items you wish moved to Edenstone."

"Yes, but I'm afraid there won't be much. I must sell most of what you see with the house."

He cleared his throat and glanced away. "Whether a little or a lot, I'll make certain everything is transferred safely."

They began at once. As they moved from room to room, he meticulously recorded each item Amelia named and its exact location.

She led him into the dining room and stood in front of the ornate cabinet that held the family Wedgewood dinner service and opened the door. "I'd like to take all of this with me. Please be careful when packing and moving it. It means a great deal to me." Her mother cherished the blue and white patterned dishes with its exquisite Italianate style. Trimmed with flowers and leaves, the set had first belonged to her grandmother. Now they belonged to her; a precious memento of two women whom she had loved dearly. The Wedgewood had decorated the table at all family gatherings. Her mind filled with a vision of her mother's beautiful smile and amiable laughter as she delighted in her guests.

"I will take the utmost care, I assure you." Townsend swallowed as he wrote something in his notebook.

From her father's library, she selected his rarest volumes, the ones he had painstakingly collected over the years, the ones he favored most. He had kept each shelf fastidiously dusted; every book carefully arranged in alphabetical order by author's name. A vision of him sitting in his leather chair reading beside the warm light of the fire in the hearth came to mind. She could not help but smile at the memory.

Mr. Townsend said little and barely looked up from his notebook as he recorded the tomes she pulled from the shelves and stacked on the desk.

Next, they moved to the parlor. "From this room, I'd like the pair of porcelain gilt Limoges vases and that French Aubusson embroidered chair." She ran her hand over the chair's back. "They were favorites of my mother's, both a gift to her from my father." She fondly recalled how enchanted her mother had been when he had brought them home, exclaiming with delight before flinging herself into his loving arms. They'd spent many a day together embroidering in this room, golden sunshine from the large bay windows warming their shoulders.

Mr. Townsend shuffled his feet and chewed nervously on the end of the pen as he waited for her direction.

In the entrance hall, she stopped in front of the two portraits of her parents. "And these, Mr. Townsend, are the most important items of all. Please make sure you do not damage them. They're irreplaceable."

When her eyes met his, he quickly glanced away before writing the information down.

They completed the inventory by midday.

"When will you move the items, Mr. Townsend?"

He swallowed and a long pause ensued. "Uh, um, sometime tomorrow or later this week."

Puzzled by his uncertainty, she asked, "You don't know for certain?"

"Well, no, uh, I mean yes, well, it's up to the movers to give me an exact time. But I can assure you, I will complete all in as timely a manner as possible. I've taken too much of your time already, so with your permission, I'll take my leave and set things in motion. It was a pleasure meeting you, Miss Belleville."

With a nod, his expression relaxed as he grabbed the hat from the hall tree, swung open the front door, and left.

Amelia watched him walk away. Her chest tightened at the realization circumstances had reduced her life to these few items.

She returned to her bedroom to check on Sarah's progress. She had emptied the contents of the wardrobe into two trunks with a third partially filled. Her jewelry box, riding habit, shoes, and toiletries were on the bed, waiting for Sarah to tuck them away.

"I'm nearly finished, Miss."

"Thank you, Sarah. I'll be downstairs. Mr. Lockhart's carriage should arrive soon, but before then, I'd like to walk through my home for one last time." She picked up her embroidered, empty satchel. "Do you need this, Sarah?"

"No, Miss. I was going to pack it into a trunk."

"No need. I can put it to good use. There are some smaller, personal items I wish to take with me."

Sarah's expression softened. "I understand, Miss."

Amelia left Sarah to her work and walked down the hall to her father's bedroom. The room resembled his personality, for it was simple in taste. The neatly made bed held few pillows. No art decorated the walls, and the draperies were a solemn gray. A scattering of small Persian rugs relieved the highly polished wooden floor. And as if the library were not enough, his most cherished books lined a shelf against one wall. The aroma of his favorite cologne, a fragrance reminiscent of a spring morning and orange blossoms lingered in the air. She inhaled to lock the scent into her memory. Amelia picked up the book on his night table beside his gold-rimmed spectacles. It was *Lothair* by Benjamin Disraeli. A silver and ivory bookmark denoted the pages he had last read. She clutched it to her chest. Her throat closed as a hot tear trickled down her cheek. To touch an object which he held so recently tore at her aching heart. She clung to the volume and sat on his bed, rocking back and forth. When her grief settled, she slipped the book into her satchel. He could not finish it, but she would in his honor.

And beneath all the grief lay a pool of anger. Her father had lied to her, kept secrets from her. She wondered if she really and truly knew him. He had kept his losses secret while urging her to marry Regan. Was her betrothal to Regan nothing more than a business transaction to save his business? And she the pawn with which to do it?

Because of his decisions, she was now penniless, her future uncertain, and trapped in a betrothal she had not sought but had too readily accepted because she had trusted him. But that was the past. Now, with no one to rely on but herself, from this day forward, she must keep her eyes wide open. After one last look, she closed the bedroom door and proceeded down to the main floor.

In the kitchen, she recalled the rich aromas of her mother's cakes and biscuits. Inside a cupboard, tucked away on the top shelf, was a journal of favorite recipes. This, too, she took.

In each room, laughter, tears, and memories of the carefree days of her girlhood danced in her thoughts. The nostalgia, a healing balm to her soul. Now, all relics of the past. All these precious remembrances she locked into her heart.

Amelia fought back tears as she said farewell to Mrs. Appleton and Mr. Seeton, who had lovingly cared for her since childhood. The moment Mrs. Appleton drew Amelia to her ample bosom, she wept shamelessly. Her eyes welled with unstoppable tears. Mrs. Appleton traced a comforting hand down her damp cheek. Even Mr. Seeton, always so dignified, pulled her to him in a hearty embrace. When they separated, he asked, "I could not help but notice Mr. Townsend seemed an odd sort. Are you certain Mr. Townsend itemized everything correctly?"

"He seemed very diligent in recording everything in that book of his. I'm sure it will be fine. Otherwise, Regan would not have sent him."

"I suppose," he said reluctantly. "But if all is not right, you know you can count on me."

Her heart warmed at his kindness. He had been like a

second father, always ready with a wise word, always keeping a watchful eye on her whenever her father was away on business.

"Once we know where we will be placed, Mrs. Appleton and I will send you our new addresses. You've only to send word and we will respond should you ever need anything," he said.

Her head rested against his chest and she took comfort in the steady cadence of his heartbeat. "I'll always be grateful for your many kindnesses," she said, pulling away.

As he had done so often in the past, he handed her his own white handkerchief so she could dry her tears.

"Don't you worry about us," Mrs. Appleton said. "Mr. Finnerty has promised to find us placements as close to your new home in Winthrop as possible. You will have Sarah with you at Edenstone, but if you need either of us, as Mr. Seeton just said, you only need to send word." With her hands on either side of Amelia's face, she her wiped tears away with her thumbs. "I'm sure it won't be long before we see each other again."

Head bowed; Mr. Seeton went outside to await the carriage. He had never been one to handle emotional scenes well.

With nothing left to do, Amelia settled on the periwinkle-colored, cushioned bench in the hall near the entrance and stared at the front door. She gripped her skirts, overwhelmed by the desire to stay, to keep all that should have been rightfully hers. She moved to the end of the bench and with a tearful smile, patted it, inviting Mrs. Appleton to sit with her. Mrs. Appleton hesitated at this breach of decorum.

"Please, let's not stand on ceremony today," Amelia insisted and smiled tearfully. "You have been like a mother to me."

When the woman took her seat, she reached for Amelia's hand. The familiarity of her touch, a great comfort, Amelia acknowledged the gesture with a gentle squeeze.

Sarah came into the hall just then. Her mouth fell open at the sight of them holding hands. Then she smiled. "I packed everything." She glanced about. "Are you certain you have forgotten nothing?"

Amelia shook her head. "I have everything I need."

Sarah's look was one of sadness tinged with understanding, having served her for years. Her shoulders relaxed as she accepted the invitation to sit. Gratitude at her father's forethought to keep Sarah swelled in her chest.

Only the tick, tick, tick of the grandfather clock interrupted the silence while they awaited Regan's arrival.

Before long, Mr. Seeton returned. He looked pleased when he saw them crammed together on the bench. "The carriage is here," he announced. "The driver asked me to give this to you."

Amelia took the note into her trembling hand and broke the seal.

> *Amelia,*
> *Please accept my apology for not attending to take you to Edenstone. I am still embroiled in yesterday's urgent business matter. I look forward to greeting you this afternoon.*
>
> *Regan*

A twinge of disappointment pinched her. What could be more important than being here to take her to his home? Regan owned a thriving business. Any manner of problem could arise. She must quell her misgivings. Whatever the urgent business matter, such interruptions were something she must learn to accept.

Ominous grey clouds draped a darkened sky. Dampness hung in the quiet air. The driver handed them into the carriage. Her spirits lifted when she saw the woolen blanket on the opposite seat and the decanter of cherry cordial and glasses tucked neatly into a basket on the floor. How thoughtful of Regan.

Sarah gave her arm a reassuring squeeze.

The driver climbed to his seat at the top of the carriage and urged the horses forward. As they drove away, she turned to look through the small window at the rear of the carriage. One last glance at her home.

Fighting back tears, she straightened and stared ahead. Her future beckoned. She must embrace it with an open heart and mind. A bolt of lightning flashed in the sky. Thunder fractured the silence. It seemed the heavens might split open, as if giving warning of some wrath to come.

Chapter Four

TWO HOURS LATER, the drenching, stormy winds and heavy rain finally stopped. The carriage had arrived at the outskirts of Winthrop, a small town near the entrance of Boston Harbor. As they passed through gates with the Edenstone crest, a shiver crawled down Amelia's spine. An unexplainable sense of foreboding settled into the pit of her stomach. Her chilled hands twisted the reticule on her lap until Sarah reached out to calm her. She gripped it hard to keep her hands still and ground her teeth as she stared out the window to take in the first sight of her new home.

A row of trees lined either side of the road leading to the house, their branches bare and gnarled with a leafless shrubbery at their bases. At the center of a grand driveway that swept in a wide circle in front of the dwelling, sat an ornate fountain, its water overflowing because of the heavy rain.

The driver halted the conveyance in front of a large golden-colored house on acres of green land that gently sloped down to the ocean. Rain sluiced down the roof of the three-story house that boasted many large windows along the first two levels. On the third level, two small round windows sat in gables at either side of a large rectangular window. A double, balustraded stairway joined in the middle to form a balcony at the entrance door. Rain blurred the light shining from the windows.

Amelia gaped at first sight of such a grand home, an impressive mansion. She considered her own home large, but Edenstone dwarfed it. She realized Regan truly had the means to care for her, just as her father wanted.

Marriage to Regan meant it would require her to manage all the responsibilities that came with running such a large home and its servants. Although a bit unsettling, when that day came, she would succeed.

The driver dismounted and swung open the coach door. A stiff wind carried the fragrance of the salty sea, blowing damp air into the carriage. Rain ran down his face as he peered at them from beneath the hood of his drenched black cloak and offered his hand. Amelia raised the hood of her cloak, stepped down, and followed by Sarah, ran up the stairs to the entrance.

The mansion's vast front door swung open. Two women stood in the doorway to let them in. Obviously, Regan had not made it back from the factory yet.

The younger woman, who looked to be in her thirties, stepped forward. Beneath her tightly clutched shawl, she wore a mint green tea dress. The wind loosened tendrils of her neatly coiffured chestnut hair and blew them wildly about her face.

"You must be Amelia," she said. "Welcome to Edenstone. We've been expecting you. Regan sends his regrets because he could not be here to greet you, but he'll be home in time for dinner. I'm Clara Yates, Regan's cousin, and this is my mother, Beatrice Yates." She gestured to the white-haired woman who had hobbled forward with the aid of an ivory-handled cane.

The older woman smiled warmly. "How splendid to meet you, Emily."

"Not Emily, Mother," Clara corrected, "Her name is Amelia."

"Yes, yes, of course. How forgetful of me."

Clara grabbed her mother's arm and tried to pull her back. "The wind is getting in. Let's step away from the door and close it before we all catch a chill."

"Let go of me, Clara." Regan's aunt frowned, yanked her arm from her daughter's grasp, and shooed her away as if she were an annoying fly. "I am not a child who needs coddling." She stepped forward to close the door without aid, then turned around to face everyone. "Well, Clara, where are your manners? Let's get Cornelia and her lady's maid settled."

"Her name is Amelia, Mother, *A-me-li-a*," Clara reiterated with steady patience. She leaned over and whispered in Amelia's ear, "You must be patient with Mother. She's forgetful these days."

"Yes, yes, of course," Aunt Beatrice muttered in an annoyed voice. "Someone, please, take away these poor women's wet clothes."

Two maidservants stepped forward to obey, then quietly left.

Amelia could not help but smile at the lively banter between the two as she ran her hands over her arms to remove the chill.

"Please accept our condolences on the loss of your father," Clara said. "I hope you'll find Edenstone a tranquil place to recover from your grief."

She smiled at the woman's kindness. "Thank you, I'm certain I will. It's a pleasure to meet you both. Regan has told me how fond he is of you and your mother."

"I hope he spoke kindly."

"Of course. And always with a tone of admiration in his voice," Clara added.

Regan's aunt looked pleased. She stepped back and scrutinized Amelia from head to toe. "Regan said you were a beauty. I see he did not exaggerate."

Her cheeks warmed. Kindness lingered beneath the woman's direct words, which she found endearing.

She glanced around the foyer. Regan had told her about Edenstone's splendor, but this exceeded all expectations. Despite the gloomy day, large leaded glass side windows on either side of the front door shed adequate light into the foyer. She stood in a great paneled hall with a black and white tiled floor with an immense grandfather clock glimmering in warm lamplight. Doors on either side led to various rooms. Molded and carved plaster ceilings hovered above exquisite walls of dark oak paneling. A wide central staircase split into two smaller staircases leading off in opposite directions on a half landing.

A fire blazed in a massive carved stone fireplace to her right, casting warmth into the vast entrance. To her left she glimpsed a dining room painted in soft yellow. Many portraits of landscapes hung on its walls. An open door on the opposite side of the hall revealed a library with countless shelves neatly lined with books. From where Amelia stood, she could see a set of glass doors, the vista beyond blurred by the heavy rain and mist. A faint aroma of beeswax and vinegar wafted from the immaculately clean rooms.

She turned her attention to the two staff members who appeared and stood next to each other to greet her.

"This is Edward Simpson, our butler." Clara gestured to a mature man with a full head of thick, white hair. "He has been with the family since Regan was a boy."

Simpson's plain, unadorned appearance projected an air of sensibility and practicality. He gave a stiff, formal smile, but his eyes sparkled with gentleness and good humor. "Welcome to Edenstone, Miss Belleville. I hope you will be comfortable here. We will take your trunks to your room."

Clara nodded to the woman beside him. "And this is Mary Simpson."

"I'm pleased to make your acquaintance," the woman said cordially.

Amelia gestured to Sarah, who stood slightly behind her. "And this is Sarah Banks, my lady's maid."

"Welcome, Sarah," Simpson said.

"If there is anything I can do to help familiarize you with Edenstone, I'll be happy to help," Mary offered.

"I would like that very much." Sarah gave a nod of gratitude.

Regan's aunt waved her cane about impatiently. "Now that we have made the introductions, I insist someone show Sofia to her room so she can warm up and rest before dinner."

Clara's eyes rose in apology to Amelia at her mother's misnomer.

Amelia smiled to reassure Regan's cousin she took no offence.

Clara took her mother's arm. "Let me take you to your

room, Mother. A good afternoon nap is what you need."

"I know better than you what I need, Clara, but yes, I think a nap is in order." She looked at Amelia. "There will be plenty of opportunities for us to get to know each other better, my dear. We dine at eight o'clock. Please be prompt." With that, she allowed her daughter to take her arm and help her up the stairs.

Amelia waited with Mrs. Simpson while Mr. Simpson directed two young men to unload the trunks from the carriage and haul them inside. Once fetched, they followed them up the stairs. At the landing, they selected the staircase to the right. The men carried the trunks into the last room at the far end of a corridor. Simpson was already inside, directing the men where to put them. When they left, Mary invited Amelia to enter. She barely had time to take in the surroundings before Mary spoke. "I'll show Sarah to her room. Then I'll send her back to help you unpack and prepare for supper."

Amelia gave Sarah an encouraging glance before following the Simpsons out the door.

Alone, Amelia studied her surroundings. The men had placed the largest trunk against a wall and the mid-sized one at the foot of a four-poster canopy bed with two nightstands at either side. Decorated in delicate blues and creams, she delighted in the desk—a perfect place to write, as it would catch the morning sun coming from the ocean's horizon. They had put the smallest trunk next to the wardrobe.

Kindling blazed in the fireplace, its snaps, crackles, and warmth soothing. Though impeccably clean and beautifully decorated, beneath all the opulence, she sensed an air of abandonment, of sadness. Unlike the cheerful, simple charm of the sunny yellow bedroom she had left behind in her old home.

She sat at the dressing table and regarded herself in the gilt-framed mirror. Her rosy cheeks had faded. Darkness encircled her eyes, which were now flat, passionless, and reflected an unquenchable grief. Now, with the worst behind her, she could heal and look forward to adjusting to all the changes she faced. Determined to look presentable for dinner, she studied her hair in the mirror. Several golden wisps had loosened from her chignon, so she set about tucking away the wayward strands.

A strong herbal scent suddenly filled the room. From where it came, she could not tell. The aroma reminded her of an earthy scent, like that of roses or lilies. Strange, but not unpleasant.

In the mirror's reflection, something moved swiftly behind her.

Her hand froze at her nape.

A mournful girl stood directly behind her right shoulder. A gentle breeze surrounded her. Long auburn hair and a soft flowing white dress billowed about her. High, freckled cheekbones accentuated desolate, startling eyes—one of ocean blue and the other vibrant green. As if in distress, she beckoned to Amelia with a pale, delicate hand, her fingernails black with grime.

Swiftly, Amelia swung around, but the young woman had vanished.

The hair on the back of her neck rose. A chill ran through her body.

The room was empty.

Chapter Five

AMELIA RAN INTO the corridor, but it too was empty of anyone. She re-entered her bedroom and closed the door, then leaned against it to still her racing heart. How could someone vanish so quickly? Who was the auburn-haired young woman who had seemed so desperate? Without doubt, the apparition, or whatever she was, wanted Amelia to follow. To where and for what purpose? A chill crept through her as she pushed away from the door and flopped on the bed, rubbing her tired eyes. Had she imagined her? Or was she a spirit? If her father's ghost could appear to her, it was possible that another spirit might too. Perhaps the upset of losing her home and possessions had taken its toll. Grief robbed her of a sound sleep. She needed a good night's rest.

Someone rapped on the door and Sarah entered. Her mouth gaped before she spoke. "What's happened? Your face is white as a sheet, Miss," she gasped. "Would you like to rest? I can return later to unpack."

"It'll be time for supper soon. I should change my clothes." Her puzzled thoughts remained with the young woman she saw. "Sarah, when Mrs. Simpson showed you your room, did you encounter an auburn-haired girl in a white gown anywhere?"

"No, Miss. Mrs. Simpson showed me my room, and then we came down the stairs. Why do you ask?"

"She was here, in this room, but disappeared, saying nothing."

"I'm sure we'll encounter her again. Would you like me to search for her? I can ask Mrs. Simpson if there is a servant who fits her description."

"No, that won't be necessary." She doubted the girl was a member of the staff. The garment was as delicate as a shift. And what of the gentle wind that swirled about her? Impossible in a room with a closed window because of inclement weather.

Sarah removed a gown from a trunk and held it up. "Shall I lay this one out for you to wear this evening?"

Amelia considered it. It was one of her favorites, an ivory dress decorated with cerise and jade silk brocade flowers, elegant enough for the family's tastes. "Yes, and my jade necklace will be perfect." Her mother's jewelry, on this first night at Edenstone, would comfort her.

When the supper hour arrived, she made her way down the staircase to the dining hall. The room was a spectacle to behold. Shimmering gold paper covered its walls. An elaborate candelabrum hung from the middle of the ceiling, its crystal pendants reflecting candle flames. At the end of the chamber, floor to ceiling French doors revealed the evening's gloomy skies.

Regan sat at one end of a long, carved oak table with Aunt Beatrice at the other. Bread, pickled vegetables, and sauces bedecked the table. Rich aromas wafted in from the kitchen.

He rose to pull out a chair for her. "My apology for not being here to welcome you earlier today; that business matter is taking up much of my time for now, but I'll have it resolved soon. I trust everything went well and you like your room?" He took his seat.

"Yes. Clara and Aunt Beatrice have been kind when they welcomed me."

Amelia gazed at her betrothed. He looked more handsome than usual tonight. Pomade made his ebony hair glisten in the light. Perfect eyebrows intensified the blue of his eyes.

She reached for her napkin, unfolded it, and spread it over her lap.

"My aunt and cousin are most gracious," he said with a smile. "I've little doubt they made your first day here a pleasant one."

"Of course, we would, Regan," Aunt Beatrice said. "How could it be any other way?" With gnarled fingers, she shifted her wine glass an inch, frowned, then returned it to its original spot.

"I hope you'll like Edenstone," Regan said. "My grandfather finished building it shortly after the Revolution. Although it's nearly a hundred years old, my family has always taken great care to maintain the property and are proud of it."

Mrs. Simpson carried in a tureen and ladled soup rich thick with beef and vegetables.

Amelia sighed. Not even the tempting aroma stirred the appetite sorrow had stolen from her.

After placing the tureen in the center of the table, Mrs. Simpson left the room.

Aunt Beatrice dipped her spoon into her bowl and

tasted the soup. "It's very good, but nothing like the soup my mother made when I was a girl." She turned to Amelia. "What a lovely gown you are wearing, Susanna. The color brings out the pink in your cheeks."

Regan frowned at the blunder, and before Clara could correct the poor woman, Amelia said, "Thank you. It was a gift from my father."

At the mention of him, an awkward silence followed.

"Tell me more about your business, Regan," Amelia said, eager to change the subject. She had known he and his family were affluent, but Edenstone's magnificence proved she under-estimated how much.

He raised an eyebrow. "You're interested?"

"What's important to you is important to me."

His surprised expression turned into a delighted one. "I didn't know matters of business appealed to you."

"My father always kept me informed about his transactions and sales, and I did some of his accounting," she answered. *Everything but his debts, and only with access to a false set of books,* she thought bitterly. "And I was always an eager student."

"Then I'm happy to teach you." He reached for her hand and gave it a squeeze. "There's nothing about me you should not know."

It pleased her he would share his business affairs. She didn't want her future husband to stifle her wish to learn. "My father told me you own a business that makes carriages but said little else about it."

"Yes, it's been in my family for three generations. As a young man in England, my grandfather was a blacksmith. Lured by the many opportunities in the New World, he boarded a ship to Boston and found work at a small carriage shop. Between repairs, and in his spare time, Grandfather designed conveyances and dreamed of building them one day. When the childless owner died, he left my grandfather everything. Bit by bit, his clientele grew, and he manufactured his designs for carriages of the highest quality. The company flourished as the demand for his creations increased. When he died, my father inherited the company, and when my father died, it passed to me. Now, we regularly ship our carriages as far west as California and overseas to England and France, even as far as Italy and Greece."

"Enough about your work, Regan," Clara interrupted, clearly bored. "I'd rather learn more about you, Amelia."

"There is not much to know. After my mother died, my father sent me to a school for girls in England. Father always encouraged my learning, especially because I was his only child. He believed women should be well-educated. I learned Greek and Latin along with literature, politics, mathematics, divinity, and ethics. After completing my studies, I returned home two years ago." She didn't mention the many awards for high marks she had earned for fear of sounding boastful.

"Goodness, my dear," Aunt Beatrice began. "So much learning would make my head spin. I believe a young lady's goal should always be marriage. You know what they say—better any marriage than none. You've made a brilliant choice with Regan." She beamed indulgently at her nephew.

Did Regan wish to marry her because he sought to add her father's business to his already successful one? Ever since she learned about the pending business transfer between Regan and her father, she could not dispel her doubts. Did he want her or the business? Maybe it was because she had only known Regan for a few months and had yet to form a bond of trust with him.

Tray in hand, Mrs. Simpson re-entered to serve meat pie in a standing crust with roasted carrots and turnips. "I hope it is to your liking, Miss," she said as she laid a plate down before her.

"It smells wonderful. I'll do my best to finish it all. I'm afraid I have had little appetite since I lost my father."

Mrs. Simpson's stern expression briefly softened as her lips curved into a tiny, unconscious smile.

Perhaps the woman wasn't as dour as she appeared, Amelia thought.

Aunt Beatrice picked up her dessert spoon and dug into the pie.

"Not that one, Mother." Clara took the spoon from her and handed her a knife and fork. "Here, use this."

"Yes, yes, of course," Aunt Beatrice responded, flustered. "Don't fuss over me. You know I don't like it."

Clara and Regan exchanged a concerned look.

Clearly, Aunt Beatrice's forgetfulness would challenge anyone's patience, but Clara seemed to take it in stride, despite her mother's constant complaints about the aid she received.

While Mary served Clara her pie, Mr. Simpson filled their wineglasses. Amelia took a sip, savoring its fresh mildness.

During a pause in the conversation, Amelia seized the moment. "This afternoon, as I fixed my hair, an auburn-haired girl with the most startling eyes—one blue and one green—came into my room. I saw her reflection in the mirror behind me. She stood so close, I felt I could reach out and touch her. It seemed as if she wanted to tell me something, but when I turned around, she'd disappeared. Can you tell me who she is so I can respond to her?"

The platter Mrs. Simpson held crashed to the floor, spattering meat pies and vegetables in an ugly mess. Her face turned ashen as she raised both hands to her mouth in horror.

Mr. Simpson stopped pouring Regan's wine, set the bottle down in haste, and rushed to comfort his wife, taking her in his arms.

"What is it?" Amelia asked.

Regan stirred uneasily in his chair, a cold expression on his face.

Aunt Beatrice choked, and Clara rushed to pound her back.

"Oh dear, what have I said?" Mortification seized her.

Mrs. Simpson sobbed into her husband's shoulder.

Regan gave him a sympathetic look and with a nod urged him to take her out of the room.

A knot formed in Amelia's stomach. She could not move as she watched the couple leave. Mrs. Simpson's sobs slowly faded as they made their way out of the room. "What's wrong? What have I said?" she asked, her composure a fragile shell.

Aunt Beatrice recovered, so Clara sat down again. Her hands shook as she reached for her napkin. "Are you sure you saw an auburn-haired girl?"

"Yes, I am. She wore a white gown and looked scared, despondent, as if she needed help." Icy tendrils gripped her heart. Obviously, she inadvertently stirred up some painful memory and regretted it.

Clara was about to say something more, but Regan

raised his palm to stop her. "There is no one currently in this house who fits that description."

Currently? She wondered what that meant.

His expression taut and derisive, his clipped voice forbade further questions. "Likely nothing more than a play of light in your bedchamber, built to catch the sunset off the ocean."

Except there was no sunset this evening because of the blackened skies. Rather, he was dismissing her question. Somehow, she touched a nerve or trod upon some forbidden secret. Not for a minute did she believe Regan. They were hiding something from her. Better to say nothing more, but she would seek answers to her questions with Regan later in private. After all, he had assured her there was nothing about him she should not know.

An awkward tension overtook them. Every bite of food tasted like mud in her mouth, so she pushed away her plate, barely touched.

Mr. Simpson returned with the dessert, an apple cobbler. A maid cleared away their plates while another quietly cleaned the mess from the floor.

No one spoke as they ate. Amelia struggled to swallow even one bite.

Having finished, Clara set down her spoon. "Well, it's getting late." She pushed back her chair and went to help Aunt Beatrice. "I think I'll take Mother to her room so we can both retire."

"Yes, my dear, I think it's time." Aunt Beatrice reached for her cane. When Clara tried to take hold of her elbow, she waved her away. "Leave me. I can manage on my own... always buzzing around me like an infuriating bee," she muttered. "The inclement weather these past few days has worsened the pain in my joints."

Her expression one of exasperation, Clara shrugged, then escorted her mother from the room.

Mr. Simpson, having finished serving them, left too.

Alone, Regan and Amelia studied each other across a prolonged, cloying silence.

"I'm afraid I spoiled the evening." Amelia twisted her hands in her lap.

"You could not have known."

His vexed tone puzzled her. "Known what? Please, can you explain it to me?"

"It's nothing more than superstition and lore, and I don't want to encourage it. Pay it no mind. This is a time for you to heal and not burden yourself with such things."

He spoke with a ring of finality. To avoid irritating him, she thought it best not to ask any further questions.

He tossed his napkin on the table and rose. "Come, it's late, and the day has been a long and trying one for you. Let me take you to your room."

They went in silence, side by side. A strange unease seemed to have overtaken him. He walked with her down the vast oaken floored corridor, with its thick dark Oriental carpet, and stopped at her door. He studied her thoughtfully. Taking her hand, he raised it to his lips and kissed it. "All will be well, you'll see." Affectionately, he pushed back a curl from her forehead. "Sleep well."

Amelia watched him stroll slowly away before she went inside. He perplexed her. One moment he appeared affable and considerate, the next secretive and brooding. She didn't know what to make of him. Was he all that he appeared to be? Could she trust such a man?

Sarah greeted her with a smile that swiftly faded. "Are you ill?" She had turned back the bedcovers and laid out her nightgown.

"No, I'm merely a little tired," she said to reassure her, but Sarah knew her too well and it was nearly impossible to sneak something past her.

"What's wrong? Did something happen at supper?"

"Nothing I want to talk about. The day has been long for you, too, Sarah. Help me off with my dress and then you can also get some rest."

Sarah helped remove her gown, then hung it in the armoire. While Amelia brushed her hair, Sarah collected the stockings, stuffed them in the laundry basket, and put the shoes away. When done, she took one candleholder. "Good night, Miss. Rest well. Things will be better in the morning."

"Yes, I'm certain they will." She meant to reassure and bolster them both. "Good night."

After she left, Amelia went to the window and stared into the darkness. Wind blew and rain spattered against the glass. It seemed as if her entire world had turned as dark as the inclement night. Chill seeped in from the window which encouraged her to turn away, climb into bed, and snuff out the candle. Only the firelight lit the room. She shivered beneath the covers and stared up at the ceiling.

Despite the beauty of Edenstone, something dark lingered here and every fiber in her body screamed out in warning. Everyone seemed to know something about the auburn-haired woman. So why didn't anyone offer her an explanation? And what of Regan? Why would he keep such a secret from her? He dismissed her sighting of the girl as nothing more than rumor and innuendo.

But Amelia knew she hadn't imagined the girl. A cold knot of disquiet flourished in her gut. The spirit she saw was real, not some trespasser who escaped through a doorway.

What an unusual family Regan had—an eccentric aunt clearly losing her faculties. And her daughter Clara, upon whom she depended on and who sacrificed her life to care for her.

Amid the sounds of the crackling fire and the creaks of a dormant house, the storm returned. Harsh winds and rain spattered an uneven cadence on the window. Amelia couldn't sleep. Secrets lurked in these walls and it troubled her. Her body shook beneath blankets that failed to keep her warm.

Too many doubts swirled in her mind. She had offered to free Regan from the betrothal contract, yet he said he wanted to proceed with the marriage. Now she feared he was marrying her from a sense of obligation.

An idea came to mind on how she could make certain these were not his intentions.

REGAN ESCORTED AMELIA to her room, then went downstairs. He gathered the servants in the kitchen and questioned them at length about the girl Amelia had glimpsed in the house earlier that evening. Still tearful, Mary Simpson sat in a chair, Edward's hand on her shoulder. No one had seen anyone enter or leave the house, especially during such a stormy night. They never said as much, but he could tell by the fear in their eyes they believed it was a ghost Amelia saw.

He went to his bedroom more frustrated than ever. After pouring himself a brandy from the decanter on his nightstand, he paced the length of the room. How in the blazes could Amelia have known about the girl? She had described her so accurately... auburn hair, with two different colored eyes, a white complexion sprinkled with freckles. It was Annie Simpson, the only person in all of Winthrop who fit that description. Annie, Edward and Mary Simpson's daughter, had gone missing shortly before his mother died. He had gone to considerable effort and cost to search for the girl, but with little result. She had vanished without a trace.

He had done his best to quell the rumors and whispers circulating among Winthrop's townsfolk. And he had deliberately never told Amelia about her. How foolish of him to think it wouldn't reach Amelia's ears, eventually.

He ceased his pacing and quaffed down the entire contents of his glass, letting the burn warm his stomach. Then he poured another. After setting the decanter back down on his nightstand, he ran his fingers through his hair and slumped onto the bed.

Was the girl an imposter someone might have let into the house? Sent here by someone who wanted to play a terrible joke on them all? Or was he being threatened or being sent a message? He could think of no business acquaintances or customers who might commit such an act.

Something was amiss, and he had better do something about it before matters spiraled out of control. He'd have to tell Amelia something.

Chapter Six

MORNING LIGHT GLEAMED through a crack in the bedroom curtains. Peaceful birdsong replaced the thunderous sounds of last night's storm. Amelia sat up in bed. Yesterday's muddled thoughts and uncertainties resurfaced. Before falling asleep, she had reached a decision. Slipping out of bed, she crossed the room to the desk and dipped her pen nib into the inkpot.

> *Dear Mr. Finnerty,*
> *I am writing to ask you to meet with Regan regarding the betrothal agreement with my father. I wish to release him from the contract. Although I have spoken to him about it; he insists on honoring it. Please let him know once more that if he wishes me to, I will release him from any obligation on condition he returns my dowry in full. If he agrees, please prepare the documents. I ask for your help because it is imperative for me to know what his true intentions are. I thank you for your help. Sincerely, Amelia Belleville*

She did not doubt Regan's fondness for her, but obligation should not force him to marry her. It was imperative he wed with an open, willing heart. If he decided not to proceed because of her reduced status, he could return her dowry and free himself, and she would be free to forge a new life for herself. With her education, a post as a governess would be easy to find. Or she could purchase a small boarding house for women alone in the world like she was. Opportunities abounded, but only with the dowry returned to her.

After sealing the letter, she pushed it to the corner of the desk and pulled the bell cord to summon Sarah. Before long, her maid entered carrying a breakfast tray.

"Good morning, Miss. You look well rested."

"I'm much better this morning. I slept through the night."

The aroma of fresh-made bread and hot tea stirred her appetite. For the first time in more than a week, she ate with relish.

Later, with the letter in hand, she went downstairs to search for Simpson. He would know how to post it. She found him in the dining room, sliding a stack of dishes into the sideboard.

He straightened when she entered. "Good morning, Miss Amelia."

He seemed less amiable today, and his greeting carried a slight tension. After her blunder last night, who could blame him?

"And the same to you, Mr. Simpson." She held out the letter. "Can you tell me how to post this?"

"I'll see to it, Miss. I handle all of Edenstone's mail."

She smiled and handed it to him. "Thank you."

Mr. Simpson looked at it. "The address isn't far from here. Our driver leaves for the post office every morning. He hasn't left yet. I'll see he gets it."

"Mr. Simpson," she said, choosing her words carefully, "please know that I sincerely regret what happened last night."

His expression clouded. "You couldn't have known." His voice was calm, his gaze steady.

"I'd like to express my regrets to Mrs. Simpson personally, if I may. Do you know where I may find her?"

"She has gone to market but should be home soon."

"I'd like to reassure her I meant no harm."

"I suspect she already knows, but I'm certain she'll appreciate your personal reassurances."

Amelia left him to his work and ventured into the drawing room. Portraits of Regan's ancestors hung from the walls in gilded frames. At the bottom of each frame, a gilt plaque bore their name. She studied each one as she passed. A collection of people in various outdated fashions. Ringlets and beards, periwigs and mobcaps, satins and velvets, fichus and snuff coats. Their expressions solemn, frozen in time.

She halted to study the painting of Randolph Harrison, Regan's maternal grandfather. He was a distinguished-looking man in elegant attire and a white wig. What struck her most was how sorrowful he looked. His eyes lacked luster, and he appeared dejected. Next to his portrait was one of his wife, Elizabeth. Although pretty, the artist had painted her with cold surly eyes and a severe expression. The couple's misery was clear in every brush stroke. Trapped in a loveless marriage? It reassured her to know she had made the right decision to free Regan from the commitment he made to her father. A life without love was a meaningless one. She longed for the love of a good man. And Regan was such a man. Together, they could build a family, fill this large house with the laughter of children. Once she knew for certain that he willingly and whole-heartedly wished to marry her, and it had nothing to do with benefitting for himself, she could relax. The uncertainties she harbored would disappear. Her heart could fully open to him.

She paused in front of the next set of paintings, those of Regan's parents, Daniel Lockhart and Catherine Harrison. Catherine's portrait made her pause. Regan had never mentioned that Catherine and Beatrice were identical twins. Upon closer inspection, the similarities lessened. Raw pain smoldered in Catherine's expression. But Beatrice sparkled with life and mischief. Even more disconcerting, Regan's mother's eyes uncannily seemed to follow her whenever she shifted or moved. An icy shiver coursed through her.

Regan had inherited his father's ebony hair, stunning blue eyes, and dimpled chin. Handsomeness ran through the men's bloodline.

A slow creak came from behind her. She turned around and recalled she had left the door wide open. Now it was half-closed. The hair on her arms rose.

"Hello," she called out.

No answer.

Had a draft shifted the door and caused it to creak? Or had one of the staff walked past? Whatever caused it, Amelia sensed someone had been observing her. She went to the door and checked the empty hallway.

She crossed into the library. Rays of sunshine beamed

through the glass double doors that opened onto the back garden. Gone was the gloomy weather of the past few days. Eager to rid herself of the sense of unease, she stepped outside and embraced the warmth. Beyond the gardens, white-capped wavelets rippled toward a rocky beach. As she looked up to the azure sky, savoring the warmth and salty breeze against her cheeks, she could not help but wish her life were as soothing as this moment.

Again, she sensed someone behind her. She spun around.

Regan stood in the open doorway studying her.

"How long have you been standing there?" she asked.

"Long enough to appreciate how beautiful you look with the sun on your face."

He moved toward her with stilted, uneasy steps. Evidence that last night's events had affected him, too.

"I thought you would be at work today."

"I wanted to make amends for my absence yesterday, so I stayed at home. Besides, after last night's occurrence, I wanted to make sure you recovered from the shock." He paused. "I thought we might spend the day together." His eyes scrutinized her face as if he wanted to reach into her thoughts.

Did she appear tense? Could he sense her doubts about their future? She maintained a calm expression. Once she received a response from Mr. Finnerty, she'd know Regan's true intentions. For the moment, she swept aside doubts. A day in Regan's company would help her learn more about him, so she nodded and smiled.

His own expression softened. "Would you like to go for a ride?"

Immediately, she thought about her beloved mare,

Cadence, left behind to help settle her father's debts. Her heart ached at the loss. She pushed away the sadness, however, for the day was perfect to indulge her passion for riding. "A wonderful idea, especially now that the weather is so fine."

"Good. I'll wait for you to change into your riding habit and we'll meet back here."

They went inside, separating at the top of the stairs to go to their rooms.

A short time later, dressed in her indigo riding habit, she met him outside the library doors.

His smile put her at ease. "Come, I have a surprise for you."

She followed him into the stable. Saddled, bridled, and cross-haltered between two stalls was her dapple-gray mare, Cadence. Delighted, she ran to the mare and pressed her cheek against the creature's warm neck. Amelia inhaled the familiar earthy scent of horse sweat and sweet hay. In response, Cadence nickered and rubbed her head against her. Amelia's heart swelled with joy as a hot tear trickled down her cheeks. She clasped her hands to her chest. "But how did you acquire her? I thought I'd lost her forever."

"I'm glad you're pleased. I know how much you loved your horse, so when I saw she wasn't included on Townsend's list, I made inquiries. I didn't think it right to leave her behind to sell along with the house and contents. So, I purchased her for you." Pausing, he gazed at her.

"So that was the business matter you've been attending to?"

He grinned roguishly. "One among many other pressing business affairs needing my attention. Are you pleased?"

"Pleased? I'm ecstatic."

Kindness filled his eyes, and it seemed so innocent, so genuine, so endless, and as big as the ocean. It bolstered her spirits, but also made her experience a wave of guilt for doubting his intentions.

He reached out and scratched Cadence's forehead. The mare tossed her head in gratification. "Nothing should come between a lady and her beloved horse, so I couldn't stand by and do nothing. Especially because you've lost so much already."

Amelia glanced away, choked with tears, unable to speak. Amid so much upheaval, she had expected to lose Cadence forever. But Regan bought and returned the horse. That should be proof enough of his true intentions. A wave of gratitude swelled her heart. She grappled to find adequate words to thank him. A small wave of guilt about the letter she wrote to Mr. Finnerty surfaced. Had she acted too hastily? Was she foolish in trying to release him after he had clearly told her he wished to proceed with marriage?

He tilted her chin with his fingertips, inclined his dark head, and kissed her cheek. He stepped back to study her.

"It's the kindest, most generous gift. But I don't want you to feel obligated to come to my aid because of my father's failures."

His shoulders drooped, and he rubbed the back of his neck. "My gift has nothing to do with your father's finances, for which you are blameless. I made a solemn promise to your father to care for you, and intend to keep my word, not because it is my duty, but because I truly care for you, Amelia. This is only the start."

His words seemed genuine, not spoken from any

sense of duty. How could she not believe him?

"You're more than I deserve." Guilt and a longing for love sat like a boulder on her chest.

"Never say that. I am the lucky one."

She swallowed and gave Cadence's neck a pat. "Ready to ride?" she asked, not wishing to further the conversation.

"Yes, please allow me to help you." He reached for a nearby stool, set it in place, and held the sidesaddle immobile while Amelia mounted. He released the cross ties, then mounted his bay gelding.

They rode out of the barn at a walk, taking a path that led away from the fountain. When the countryside stretched ahead, they urged their horses to canter. Dense grass still wet with rain undulated beneath pounding hooves. Warmed by the sun, with the breeze on her face, and surrounded by birdsong, she forgot her troubles. Connected to the land by hoof, indebted to the mare that carried her with loving care, Amelia relinquished herself to the pure pleasure of the ride.

After a while, they slowed their mounts to a walk and entered woods that hummed with life. A gentle flowing brook, poplar trees rustling in the gentle breeze, the tang of moist earth. She gazed up. Sunrays broke through newly sprouted leaves, lighting up the earthen track ahead. The fragrance of wind and nature soothed her. Each breath was like spring water, fresh and cleansing. Wild asters and marigolds and scarlet bergamot adorned either side of the forest path as they rode toward a small clearing.

"Ah, here we are," Regan announced as he leaped off his horse. He helped her down from Cadence and tied the reins to a nearby tree. "Even as a child, I loved this spot. I come here often, especially when I need to forget my worries for a while."

Amelia understood why. "It's lovely."

"I'm glad you like it." Regan reached into his saddlebags and pulled out a blanket. After spreading it over the ground, he removed a small bottle of wine, two pewter cups, a loaf of bread, and cheese before offering his hand to help her sit.

Regan uncorked the bottle and poured wine into the cups. Their fingers touched when he handed her one. In response to the contact, a shiver flowed through her.

"I've been saving it for such an occasion," he said. "The wine, which is from the south of France, has always been my favorite. Let's make a toast."

"What will we toast to?" She smiled.

"To our future, of course."

She faltered at a thought that entered her mind; they might not have a future. She struggled with her conscience but kept her expression blank as she raised her cup to his. She must not succumb to his charm until she knew for certain what his genuine feelings were.

"To a beautiful life together," he said.

Her throat tightened as she took a sip. It was delicate and sweet.

He set his cup down, broke off a piece of bread, and handed it to her. "So far, what do you think of Edenstone? I hope you like it."

Amelia cradled the crusty bread, staring into its soft center and pondered. "It's beautiful." Not a lie, but she kept her misgivings to herself. She changed the topic. "Tell me about your family."

"There's not much to tell. My parents married for

love. My father, Daniel, died of an apoplectic fit and my mother died a year later."

"How sad."

"Yes, and not a day passes when I don't think of them. There's a void in my heart that will never heal because of the loss."

"I feel the same way about my parents." She took another sip of wine. "I didn't know your mother and Beatrice were twins."

"They are. The bond between twins is intense. When Mother died, it seemed as if Aunt Beatrice lost a piece of herself. She's never been the same."

"What of your grandparents? I saw their portraits. They seemed unhappy. Am I right?"

"My mother loved her father, Randolph, but did not get along with her mother, Elizabeth. Theirs was an arranged marriage, forced upon them both by their parents."

So, Regan had some concerns. How could he not? Her father had arranged their betrothal. What had sealed the arrangement? Had she been part of the negotiations, she might not be experiencing doubts about him.

"Let's have some of my favorite cheese," he said. "It's made on a nearby farm."

His change of subject was abrupt. Talk about marriage made her uncomfortable. He had yet to speak of love. No amount of wine would ease her anxiety.

Their talk turned to general matters, for which she was grateful. Like his business. The caw of the occasional bird and the rustling leaves were the only sounds other than their voices.

When they finished eating, they remounted and rode

around the estate's perimeter. It was much larger than she had imagined. As they rode, Regan pointed out landmarks and commented on their surroundings. His affable mood put her at ease. She was glad to head home. It had not been easy to keep the letter she had sent to Mr. Finnerty a secret.

Amelia could not find Sarah when they returned, so she went to her room to change her clothes.

From behind the wall, she heard a thump that sounded like a boot being cast to the floor. She glanced at the door in the wall that connected her room to Regan's. It was then she noticed a small crack between the frame and the door. Blood pulsed in her veins as she rose to peer through it.

Regan stood in the center of his bedchamber. She watched, captivated, as he removed his shirt and tossed it on the bed. He turned a bit and faced the panel behind where she hid. He stood before her in his white linen drawers and naked chest. To see him in such intimate circumstances embarrassed her. It left her ill-at-ease yet enlivened. But she could not turn away from his magnificence. The sunlight streaming in from the windows cast him in a golden light. His chest was bare and firm, his arms muscular, his abdomen lined with supple ridges.

Amelia swallowed; her blood pounding with desire to touch him.

He reached for the pressed white shirt laid out for him on the bed and donned it. With two long strides, he stood before a mirror and ran his hands through his thick dark hair. He appeared pensive, his strong, defined features as firm as granite. Dark eyebrows sloped downwards. His expression serious, his ocean blue eyes intense, Amelia wondered if he was thinking of her.

Embarrassment washed through her for intruding on his privacy. She pushed away a little, and her foot bumped the wall. Terrified that he might discover her peeping at him, she retreated, careful not to make a sound.

How shameful to spy on Regan from the shadows, as if she were a silly schoolgirl. Yet, she could not deny the desire he ignited in her. Desire she must not nurture in case they didn't marry.

After changing into a ruffled lavender skirt with a matching bodice that tied in the front, she went to look for Mrs. Simpson. She found her in a room off the kitchen, sitting at a table, recording receipts into an account book. A shelf behind her held many old ledgers. Mrs. Simpson rose the moment she saw Amelia, hands fidgeting with her apron. "Good morning," she stammered.

Amelia gestured to a vacant chair. "May I sit?"

"Please do," the woman replied.

A brief, uncomfortable silence ensued.

"I wish to apologize for what happened last night. I didn't know my question would stir up such powerful reactions. And for that, I'm sorry."

"You could not have known." Her words faded, as if she embraced a long-lost memory.

"Will you tell me about the auburn-haired girl?" Amelia asked in a soft voice.

Mary hesitated. Her gaze became distant. Then she nodded. "Our daughter, Annie, is auburn-haired. She worked here." She fiddled with her wedding ring.

"May I ask where she is now?"

She turned her gaze downward. "We don't know. Here one day, gone the next."

"Disappeared? Where?"

Mary shook her head and lowered her voice. "No one knows. It appeared as if she vanished into the mists." Her voice cracked with emotion.

Amelia reached across the table and touched Mrs. Simpson's hand. "How painful it must be for you and your husband."

"You cannot know, Miss. It's not like our Annie to leave without telling us." Her posture slumped. "Unless she didn't have the opportunity," she added in a trembling voice.

"Do you mean that something might have happened to her?"

Her eyes filled with tears. "Mr. Lockhart doesn't want anyone to talk about it anymore."

"Please, you can tell me. Perhaps I can be of help."

Uncertainty sharpened her features as if she sought to reassure herself it was safe to tell her. "There are rumors she might be dead. May the Lord help me, but I refuse to believe them. My Annie could not be dead." She broke down sobbing.

Amelia rose, crossed over to where Mrs. Simpson sat, and put her arm around the woman's shoulders.

The memory of the auburn-haired girl's appearance resurfaced in Amelia's mind.

Mrs. Simpson's daughter was dead, and the young lady she had seen was undoubtedly her spirit.

Chapter Seven

IN THE LIBRARY, Amelia stood in front of the bookcases appreciating the magnificence of the collection. Leaves, berries, and birds decorated each tome. One book, bound in peacock blue with gilt decoration, caught her attention: The Scarlet Letter, by Nathaniel Hawthorne, a local author. She had heard much about the novel. Pleased with the discovery, she carried it to a wing chair next to the mullioned window, opened the book, and settled back to read.

Absorbed in the opening chapters and enfolded by the warmth of the sun, she soon lost herself in the tale. It might have been perhaps twenty minutes later when, from the corner of her eye, she noticed a shadow.

"Excuse me, Miss Belleville."

She glanced up at Simpson standing in the doorway.

"My apologies, Miss. I did not mean to alarm you." He held out a letter. "This arrived for you."

Her pulse quickened. The envelope bore William Finnerty's bold script. "Thank you."

With a nod, Simpson left as silently as he had approached. She hesitated, almost afraid to read the response. Had Regan accepted the offer to break the betrothal agreement? Her heart pounded forcefully as she broke open the seal.

> *Dear Amelia,*
>
> *I'm pleased to inform you I've sold your home and its contents. After settling all debts, a small sum remained, which I have placed in an account for you. The amount is not enough to sustain you if you release Mr. Lockhart from the betrothal contract, its terms designed to protect you. If canceled, you would forfeit everything and find yourself in a precarious position. I strongly advise you not to proceed. I have not spoken to Mr. Lockhart as you have asked me to do. To ease your mind, however, I made inquiries about him and am happy to report he has an impeccable past. His businesses thrive, his finances are sound, and he is a well-respected man. I agree you should not rush into marriage, and I recommend you wait a year. If, after that time, you still wish to cancel the contract, I will speak to him and do my best to assist you. Trust in your father's moral judgment. His fondest wish was for you to be happy and cared for.*
>
> *William J. Finnerty*

She sunk deeper into the chair and stared out the window. Mr. Finnerty's words echoed through her mind. She could not discount his wise advice. Why give voice to her doubts? Regan never gave her cause to be wary. Her worries likely arose because her circumstances changed so swiftly, it left her in a constant state of uncertainty. She needed to catch her breath, give herself time to adjust, and stop comparing her past life with the present. Time would provide the clarity she needed. Mr. Finnerty was right. For now, she must resolve to trust him and hope her feelings would align with what her father wanted for her.

She tucked the letter into the book and leaned her head against the back of the chair. Regan was never far from her thoughts. In the short time she had known him, he had become her anchor, her one point of stability in a world filled with chaos, and she desperately needed that in her life. She cared for him too, but was it love? Of that, she was not yet certain. Was she afraid of love, or losing love that she most feared? How long does it take to fall in love? A moment? A year? All she knew was that he never spoke an unkind word or treated her callously. He was strong, but so was she. He had stood with her through the darkest of days and comforted her when she needed it the most. In his letter, Mr. Finnerty re-assured her Regan was a good man. From all that she had seen, he had the heart of a lion and the soul of an angel. Best to set her worries aside and yield her heart to him. Maybe Regan's obligation to her was enough.

A peace settled over her then. She opened the book and focused on Hester Prynne's difficulties, rather than her own.

LATER THAT AFTERNOON, Regan invited her to see the sights. He assisted her into a black cabriolet upholstered with lush blue velvet and drawn by a stunning bay mare. The day was pleasant enough, despite a vigorous breeze and a slightly cloudy sky. With a gentle snap of the reins and a click of his tongue, Regan urged the horse into a walk.

They drove eastward, following the shoreline. At a spot where the land rose to form cliffs overlooking the waters of Winthrop Bay, he reined in. Regan helped her alight and led her to the edge of a short cliff overlooking the ocean. She closed her eyes to the serenade of the crashing waves and breathed in deeply to savor the salty air.

When she reopened them, he was looking at her, a smile on his boldly handsome face. The wind whipped his hair about, fully exposing his rugged features.

Below the cliff, foamy crests of indigo waves crashed onto a rocky beach. He pointed to a small, nearby island. "That is the notorious Deer Island with its sordid past."

"I've known about it but have never seen it from this close." Deer Island's dark history was always a keen topic of discussion among Bostonians.

"But did you know that about a hundred years ago they used to house a rebellious group of Indians there?"

"No, I've never heard that. Why? What happened to them?"

"The natives launched an armed resistance against the English settlers. They lost. In the aftermath, the English rounded up five hundred or more, removed them from their homes and villages, and sent them to Deer Island. They did not provide adequate food. Poor shelters exposed them to the harsh winter weather, and many died. Some escaped, but not for long. The English recaptured them and brought them back to the island."

"How cruel. I was only aware of the Irish who fled the potato famine and landed on Deer Island, poverty-stricken and sick, then treated at the hospital there before being allowed to proceed to Boston's port. Now it's an almshouse for paupers." She gazed at the four-story structure, with its wings and turrets, that loomed from the center of the island. Shivering, I clutched her wrap tighter around herself. If not for the betrothal agreement, it could have been her housed in that forsaken building.

The warmth of Regan's hand as he took hers was almost unbearably tender, his touch and nearness, reassuring.

"Come with me," he said as he turned and led her down a path to the shore and to a rocky outcrop that jutted into the bay. With an effortless move, he leaped up onto a large boulder and offered her his hand. Then, with one easy pull of his muscular arm, she stood beside him on the rocks. To her surprise, he kept hold of her hand. Her frigid fingers gloried in the contact's warmth. He guided her over the uneven rocks until they reached the largest one at the end. There, they sat side by side and gazed at the vista that spread out before them, to where the grey clouds met the blue horizon. The ocean always conjured comforting thoughts in her mind. With Regan at her side, she felt at ease.

"When I was a boy, my mother's father often brought me here. He came to this very spot whenever he needed to think or find some peace." With a tip of his head, he motioned toward Deer Island.

As he gazed out over the water, she admired the inherent strength in his face and was acutely conscious of his tall, athletic physique.

"He donated considerable amounts of food and money to the poor who lived there. After my grandfather died, my father took up the cause on his behalf. He had always admired his father-in-law, and they had become close over the years. Besides, the gesture pleased my mother and helped ease her grief over his loss. Now that they are all gone, I continue the donations in their memory."

"Your grandfather must have been a good man."

"One of the best. Everyone who knew him felt the same way. Except his own wife, Elizabeth." He gazed at the horizon as if lost in memories. "My grandmother was a miserable woman, never truly happy, and marriage and children brought out the worst in her. She took most of her misery out on my mother and grandfather, but never Aunt Beatrice, whom she favored. My poor mother. Aunt Beatrice could do no wrong, while she was shunned and maltreated. My grandfather dealt with the unhappiness in his marriage with an immense outpouring of love for my mother and me. He gave me all his attention, shared his most private thoughts, and spent as much time with me as possible. Our bond was unbreakable. I sorely miss him." He seemed wistful, and his voice trembled from emotion as he spoke.

"Knowing there was so much vitriol in your family could not have been easy for you."

"My father told me all about the loveless marriage of my mother's parents, and how they tried to shield me from my grandmother's animosity."

"A blessing."

"I daresay you're right. But my parents had a fortunate marriage, and they truly and deeply loved each other. Most of my recollections are of a happy, loving couple affectionate with each other who both doted on me. My father loved his work designing carriages. It kept him away from home a lot, but my mother never complained. Some say over-work killed him."

She placed her hand on his arm as a token of sympathy, sensing his pain, perceiving he had much more to tell. "I'm very sorry for your losses." She longed to reciprocate the warmth, consistent care, and patience he had shown her.

"We've both lost our parents, but I've learned to appreciate the many blessings in my life; Edenstone, Aunt Beatrice, and Clara." He studied me for a moment. "And now, you."

Those sweet words of possession reassured her. A happy quiver shook her. She'd had enough grief and longed to relegate it to the past. No longer would she wallow in its depths or allow it to swallow her.

He put his arm around her waist and pulled her close. She sank into the embrace, enjoying the feel of his strong, protective, brawny arms. His nearness comforted her, and she lost herself in a world where only she and Regan existed. They sat huddled in silence for quite some time, immersed in mutual affection.

She glanced up at the sky. Ominous clouds had gathered; dark and unyielding, oppressive. The salty breeze gathered strength and gave life to a wave vehement enough to strike the boulder on which they sat. The spray dampened the rock and their clothes. In the distance, thunder crackled.

Regan swiftly stood and offered her his hand. "It was foolish to come out to the rocks. I think we had better leave," he said, his tone urgent, his expression grim. "These storms come up fast."

As he pulled her up, a gigantic wave rolled in, stronger and more powerful than the last. It bashed against the rock with such force, her foot slipped on the slick stone and she lost her balance. Regan's grip tightened on her wet hand but slipped. The strong wind and a high wave sucked her into the water as it receded.

She sank like a rock. The cold icy water smothered her breath and stung her eyes, weighted by her clothes. Cold, wet darkness swallowed her deeper into its depths as the water closed in around her. Terror and a deep dread took hold. Dear God, she could not swim. She thrashed and flailed. Her lungs screamed for air. The strong, turbulent waves held her in its clutches, threatening to draw her into the seaweeds and murky depths.

Instinct forced her to find something to push against, anything at all. Only water surrounded her—water that prevented her from breathing in precious air. Silent panic gripped her. Heart racing and lungs on fire, she wanted to scream but could not. Frightened, she clawed and whirled in the sea, kicking her legs, but her boots and heavy skirts dragged her downward. Anguish, more profound than pain, ruled her heart.

Enormous strain crushed her chest. Her lungs burned, heart pulsating. Fiery agony seared her throat as a pounding in her head hammered. She could not stop herself, gave into the desperate need to breathe, and inhaled. Icy cold water gushed into her nostrils and cascaded into the back of her throat. Pain shot through her lungs as seawater filled them.

Then slowly, the tumult of the sea faded, muting into

an eerie silence. Darkness became more profound. She stopped thrashing and let herself float. Her vision and consciousness faded. Her body became numb. An explosion of bubbles burst from her lips as she waited for death.

Chapter Eight

DARK SKIES PREVAILED when Regan felt Amelia's hand slip from his tight grip. Crushing waves swallowed her into caliginous waters. Her head bobbed once and then disappeared into the churning sea.

He dove. Darkness enveloped him as he swam to where he had last seen her. His arms searching, reaching. The water closed in around him, filling him with dread. Not again, he thought, not again. Not with Amelia. He needed her. With arms and legs, he thrashed about, hoping to feel a limb, her gown, anything. Dark, indigo water swirled about him as he searched. His lungs throbbed as if they were on fire. He pushed upwards through the water, breathed in deeply, then dove again.

He spun and whirled about, fighting the powerful current, his resolve absolute. Then he brushed against her body. He wrapped his arm around her chest. She was not moving. With powerful thrusts of his legs, he heaved her limp body to the surface.

THE WATER SHIFTED. A brawny arm yanked Amelia up. Wrenched upwards from the cold dark depths, she gasped in precious air, filling her lungs. With his arm tightly clutched around her chest, Regan swam toward shore. The moment his feet touched rocks and sand, he lifted Amelia into his powerful arms as if she were light as a rag-doll and waded to shore. When he set her down, her fingers dug into the sand as she gulped air in noisy rasps. Amelia rolled onto her side, coughing.

Wet and dripping, Regan's chest heaved from exertion. He knelt next to her, rubbing her back as she sputtered out the dregs of water trapped in her chest, throat, and nose. It seemed like an eternity before she could take a normal breath.

He let out an enormous sigh of relief. "Thank God you aren't hurt."

"I can't swim," Amelia uttered between coughs.

He sat frozen. From alarm or confusion, she couldn't tell.

"Thank you," Amelia said in barely more than a whisper.

"For what?" His voice was low and husky, his face chalk-white with fear. She could see he tried to hide his alarm, but the slight tremor in his voice told her he was shaken.

"You saved me." Amelia's voice wavered. Her body still trembled with a terrible combination of cold and fear. "And you did it without hesitation."

"I don't deserve your thanks. I should never have put you at risk. What I need more than anything is your forgiveness." He turned to her with tortured eyes, pain burning in their depths.

Regan stood and pulled her up into his arms. She rested her head against him and took comfort from the steady cadence of his beating heart. Amelia splayed her hand against his chest, intending to push him away, but left it there, too exhausted, too chilled. He nuzzled her neck with delicate kisses, as faint as snowflakes against her skin. Her limp body shook uncontrollably, and her thoughts were barren of everything except for a longing to be safe. "Please take me home."

He lifted her into his arms once more.

"You don't have to carry me. I can walk."

"No," he said in an anguished voice. "I need to keep you safe." He conveyed her effortlessly back up the path to the waiting cabriolet.

The wind had become colder still. Amelia couldn't stop her teeth from chattering, her body from shaking against the chill that settled in her bones. He set her down on the velvet cushions, reached for the neatly folded blanket beneath the seat, and wrapped it around her. With a snap of the reins, they sped off.

The daylight dwindled as he rushed Amelia home. A heavy silence lingered between them. A vision of her near drowning replayed in her mind—the enormous wave that struck them, his firm grip that had failed to hold her steady and allowed her to fall. Now, the first doubts came to life. Had he let her go on purpose? Amelia's mouth went dry, and her stomach churned. She turned to look at him.

His expression was a tense mask, intent on the road before him as he drove the horses harder.

Amelia tried to battle a growing sense of suspicions and unease. The chill in her body was shutting down her ability to think logically. Of course, he had tried to stop her from falling. The wave had been so powerful; it had pulled her in, nothing more. It caught them both unaware. Their hands were wet, and that was why he had lost his grip. Besides, he had immediately jumped into the stormy waters after her and pulled her to safety. If he had wanted to harm her, he would have let her drown.

The moment they arrived at Edenstone, Regan jumped down from the cabriolet, swept her into his arms, and raced up the stairs to the entrance. Unable to use his hands to knock, he kicked the front door furiously. It seemed an eternity before Simpson opened it. The man's eyes widened at the sight of them, both wet and dripping.

"Have a hot bath drawn immediately," Regan ordered as he rushed past him to get inside. "Miss Amelia fell into the ocean and she's chilled."

Simpson immediately turned and, running off to the kitchen, shouted urgent demands to servants who gaped at the sight of Regan carrying her up the stairs. In her room, he set her down on the bed and buried her beneath several blankets. Sarah lit a fire in the grate and pulled dry, warm clothes out of the wardrobe.

Servants soon hurried in with a large tub and returned several times to fill it with buckets filled with steaming water.

"Sarah and I'll see to Miss Amelia, now," Mrs. Simpson said to Regan—an acceptable way to tell him to leave so they could begin stripping her of the wet clothes.

"Yes, yes, of course." After giving her one last troubled glance, he left, shoulders drooping, head hung low.

Aunt Beatrice and Clara came running into the room. Their mouths fell open at the sight of Amelia's state. "We heard all the commotion. What happened?" Clara asked.

Through chattering teeth, Amelia said, "We were on the rocks when an enormous wave crashed over us. I fell in and nearly drowned. Regan saved me."

"Just like before," Aunt Beatrice tutted.

Amelia froze, confused as to her meaning.

Clara cast her mother a worried glance. "Come, let me take you to your room. Amelia is ready for her bath. We can talk to her and find out what happened later."

She led Aunt Beatrice out into the hallway, closing the door behind them.

WARMED BY THE bath water, exhaustion set in. Amelia forewent dinner and fell asleep. A deep, restful slumber ensued, and she slept soundly through the night.

In the morning, she awoke when Sarah entered the room with a breakfast tray. She set it on the writing table near the window and swept open the curtains. Sunlight shone through the glass and danced on the polished wooden floor like sweet honey.

"Mr. Lockhart wanted me to check on you, to see if he needed to summon a doctor if you are unwell."

"As you can see, I'm well and that won't be necessary."

"It will reassure Regan to know that. You had us all worried, especially him. Are you hungry?"

"Famished," Amelia answered.

Sarah propped and fluffed the pillows so Amelia could sit up, then set the tray down over her lap. The aroma of poached eggs with bacon and toast roused her hunger pangs as she grabbed a piece of bacon and bit into it heartily.

Sarah sighed, like a gentle spring breeze. "I'm glad you didn't catch fever."

Amelia gave her a smile. "I've been strong and healthy all my life. It will take more than a spill into the ocean to make me fall ill."

Sarah giggled. "I'll let you eat, but I'll be back soon to help you dress."

Blanketed by warm rays of sunlight, Amelia enjoyed every morsel of her breakfast. As she swallowed the last bite, someone knocked on the door.

"Enter," Amelia called out.

Clara stepped in and peered cautiously at her. "Amelia. Good morning. You're looking much better than yesterday. Regan asked me to check on you. How are you feeling?"

That was two people Regan had sent in to check on her. She needed to get dressed soon and let him see for himself that she was well.

Amelia waved Clara in and motioned to the chair near the bed. "Come and sit with me. I'm well, as you can see. I've recovered from my ordeal, but it will be awhile before I'll want to visit the shore again, at least until the weather is warmer."

Clara smiled at her attempt at humor. "I don't doubt that. Will you be dressing and going down today, or do you need more rest? Regan is sick with worry."

Amelia nodded. "I know. I'd better dress immediately and seek him out."

"I'm glad. He spent the entire night in his library. I did my best to persuade him to go to bed, but he preferred to stay there, with only a bottle of cognac for company."

Dismay swept through her at the knowledge that Regan had taken what happened so hard. "But I don't understand. As you can see, I came to no harm. When he brought me home, I was merely wet and chilled. Nothing more."

Clara rose. Hands clasped behind her, she strolled to the window. A moment or two passed before she turned to face me. "Regan had a young lady friend before you. Although there was no official talk of marriage, Regan seemed as fond of her as she was of him. One day, they took a boat out. A sudden squall overtook them, tossing their small boat about. A powerful wave capsized it. Regan tried to save her, but an undercurrent swept her away. We never found her. The loss devastated him. I think it explains why he spent the entire night pacing and not sleeping."

Amelia raised a hand to her throat. "I did not know."

"It's a painful memory for Regan, so we never speak of it. Of course, there was a brief inquiry into the accident, but I believe Regan never stopped blaming himself. And when you fell into the water yesterday, I'm sure it brought up long-buried emotions."

Amelia couldn't help but wonder why Mr. Finnerty hadn't discovered this information and relayed it to her.

"I must speak to him." Poor Regan. Amelia pulled the bell rope to summon Sarah, threw off her covers, swung her legs over the bed, and slid her feet into slippers.

Clara sat on the bed next to her. "I completely agree. Speaking with him will put his mind at ease. He'll appreciate it, poor man." She took Amelia's hand. "You're good for him, and I'm glad you'll marry Regan one day. I hope we can be friends and that you'll be happy here. I know Aunt Beatrice is already very fond of you, even though she struggles to remember your name."

Amelia smiled. "Not nearly as fond as I am of her. And forgetting my name doesn't bother me in the least. It only adds to her charm. I, too, am glad to have you as a friend." She paused. Now that she was alone with Clara, she wanted to bring up the matter of the auburn-haired girl in the hopes Clara could shed some light on her disappearance.

"I regret what happened at dinner that other night, about Annie. Believe me, had I known my question would be so upsetting to Mr. and Mrs. Simpson, I would never have asked it. Is there anything more you can tell me about their missing daughter?"

Clara shook her head and stared down at her hands. "Her parents raised Annie in this house, and most recently, the young woman worked here as a maid. She was a shy girl who attended to her tasks so quietly we hardly knew when she was in the room—obedient, hardworking, and never a problem. Then one day, she disappeared. No one knows why she left or where she went. She didn't leave a note and didn't tell anyone she was going out. Regan organized several search parties to comb the area to look for her, but after a few weeks of exhaustive searching, no one found any sign of her."

"How terrible."

"It was so painful, so devastating. No one speaks about it any longer. To make matters worse, there has been much speculation by the townsfolk she is dead, and that her ghost now haunts Edenstone. Over the years, many declined invitations to visit, which resulted in our isolation.

Regan is of the belief that if no one speaks about her, all conjecture will die."

"May I ask you a question?"

"Of course," Clara said warmly.

"Do you believe in ghosts?"

She raised her eyebrows in interest. "Do you?"

"Yes, I believe it is possible to see the dead."

"Some say it's nothing more than vivid imagination or rampant superstition."

"I assure you it is not. I have seen the dead before. My father appeared to me shortly after his death. Would you believe me if I told you I think it was Annie's ghost I saw on my first night here?"

Her expression tightened and her posture grew rigid. "I hope not, because then it would confirm she truly is dead." She rose and faced her. "Everyone has always harbored the hope that she came to no harm and is alive somewhere."

Sarah's appearance in the doorway caught their attention and ended any further talk.

Clara stood up and made her way to the door. With one last glance at Amelia from over her shoulder, she said, "Oh, I almost forgot. Mother and I have invited Phillip Wakefield and his sister, Hannah to dine with us tomorrow tonight. They are long-standing close friends of the family and live nearby. As children, we spent all our time together. They are excited to meet you. I hope you enjoy their company as much as we do."

REGAN STOOD WITH his back to the door, staring out

the window clutching a half-filled glass of amber liquid. What had he been thinking to take her to the outcrop of rocks on a day that threatened inclement weather? He almost lost her. Haunting memories of the past swirled in his mind.

"Regan." He heard Amelia's soft whisper behind him and swung swiftly around. Through bleary, tired eyes, he took in the sight of her. She stood in the doorway, cheeks flushed, brows clumped together. Was it concern he saw in her expression or apprehension? He could not be sure. Setting his glass down on the desk, he ran a hand over his unshaven face then went to her. He placed his hands on her upper arms and studied her. She looked hale, with no signs of fever or lingering after-effects. His breathing softened as his anguish melted away. The worry he noticed in the depths of her gaze touched him. It seemed she was as worried about him as he had been about her. "You look well."

"I am well," Amelia responded. "A hot bath and a good night's rest helped. I'm fully restored." Amelia twirled around to prove it.

A twinge of guilt at what she had suffered twisted in his belly. He had not slept the entire night. Did she blame him for what happened? Did she suspect him of something nefarious or doubt his intentions toward her? He would not blame her if she did. He took her hand and raised it to his mouth and kissed it. "Please forgive me."

"Forgive you for saving my life? Surely you're not serious."

"I shouldn't have taken you out to the rocks. I should have known they would become slick with a gale in the offing."

"You couldn't have known. No one could. The weather was bright when we left."

"I promise it won't happen again. The next time, we'll go on a warm, windless day and spread a blanket over the sand."

Amelia let out a small laugh. "I won't argue with that." She took a step back and placed both hands on her hips. "Now, I think you need more sleep. Clara told me we're having Phillip and Hannah Wakefield as guests for dinner tomorrow evening. I think it might be wise for you to get some rest before then."

Relief arose from deep inside his chest. "Careful, my dear, you already sound like a wife."

Chapter Nine

THE NEXT EVENING, Amelia stood next to Regan in the foyer, waiting to greet the guests. During the afternoon, dark clouds formed to extinguish the brightness of day. Overcast skies and a cool breeze carried the threat of rain.

"I know you'll like our guests, especially Hannah," Regan said as they watched an elegant carriage come down the drive and enter the circle. "Phillip has been quietly in love with Clara for many years, but every effort to pry her away from Aunt Beatrice always fails. Because Clara is Aunt Beatrice's only child, she feels responsible for her mother, rarely leaving her side. After her husband died, I invited them both to live at Edenstone. I thought it would be good to reunite Aunt Beatrice with her sister… the bond between twins, and all."

"That was thoughtful of you."

"Family is the most important thing in my life. It worked out well for the sisters, and for my cousin Clara and me, too, as we are both only children."

The elegant carriage came to a stop in front of the house. Amelia watched a handsome young man and beautiful woman of slight build step down. Both were well-dressed with golden colored hair. He followed her up the steps and into the house.

Regan greeted his friend with a warm smile. "Phillip, you rogue!"

They embraced and patted each other's backs so hard, it made Amelia wince.

"It's about time you came for a visit. I thought you'd left the country." Regan turned to the young woman. "Hannah, you look more beautiful each time I see you."

She beamed at him and blushed. Clearly, Phillip and Hannah were as fond of Regan as he was of them.

"And who have we here?" Phillip swept off his top hat and took Amelia's hand. Hannah stood beside him and smiled. They scrutinized her from the top of her peacock-blue satin gown to the beaded blue slippers on her feet.

"Could this be the lovely Amelia I have heard so much about?" Phillip asked.

Amelia's cheeks grew warm. "It's a pleasure to meet you both."

"Amelia," Regan said, "May I introduce you to Hannah and Phillip Wakefield? Our families have been close for decades, as far back as our grandfathers, Randolph Lockhart and Robert Wakefield, who were old school chums. As children, we often played together."

"And you, dear Amelia, shall be a wonderful addition to our little group," Phillip said with a wink.

Hannah slid her arm through Amelia's. "Finally, Clara and I have a confidante against these two scoundrels. I know we shall be the best of friends."

Her heart bounced at the instant rapport she experienced.

Regan peered up at the sky, then gestured to the front door. "Come, we'd best get inside. It looks like it's going to rain."

Clara and Aunt Beatrice were already in the drawing room when they entered. They all chatted pleasantly, savored their wine, and enjoyed appetizers of bread, pickled vegetables, and various cheeses.

Amid all the pleasant conversations, Amelia noticed how affectionate Phillip and Clara were. Their gazes met often, and Clara's cheeks blushed with each compliment he gave her.

When Simpson announced dinner was ready, they strolled into the dining room.

Outside, a steady rain had begun, but inside, amid the candlelight and the warmth from the crackling fire, warmth and good cheer abounded.

As they enjoyed a meal of soup, fried haddock, Anadama bread, and vegetables, the banter was jovial. Phillip was so attentive to Clara, he could barely look away, but whenever he did, he turned his attentions to Aunt Beatrice. He complimented her flamboyantly, and with such sincerity, it touched Amelia's heart. The dear old woman blushed and fluttered her lashes at each compliment, as if she were a young lady once more enjoying the praises of her suitors.

It was endearing to watch Philip and Clara together, and Amelia wished to encourage the lovebirds.

"I hope the rain doesn't last too long. Shall we all go riding on the next sunny day?" Phillip asked with a hopeful look at Clara. "We'll make the best of the pleasant spring weather."

Clara stared silently down at her plate.

"I'd like that very much," Amelia interjected, hopeful that Clara would follow her lead. Besides, Cadence could use a good run. So much inclement weather over the past few days had kept everyone inside, including the horses.

"What a wonderful idea," Hannah added.

"I will be happy to join you if I can take the day off work," Regan said. "Sometimes my business does not allow it. If there are too many urgent repairs or orders, or if there's a shipment ready to go out or arrive, it won't be possible, but regardless of whether I can join you, Amelia should go."

Phillip raised his wineglass. "Hear, hear. I agree." He turned to Clara. "What do you say, my dear?"

Clara shook her head. "I would love to, but I can't leave Mother, especially now that there's a terrible ague making its rounds."

"Nonsense," Regan objected. "A pleasant ride will do wonders for your health, and it will raise your spirits. Being indoors for too long is not good for anyone. Fresh air and sunshine is what we all need."

"I would love to go for a ride, too," Aunt Beatrice announced with a clap of her hands.

"I'm sure you would, but you've never ridden, Mother," Clara said.

"Well, it's never too late to learn, is it?" Aunt Beatrice harrumphed.

In the shocked silence that followed, no one either encouraged or discouraged the poor woman.

"Please reconsider, Clara," Amelia said, eager to distract them from an argument breaking out between mother and daughter. "Besides, Mrs. Simpson is here. I'm sure she wouldn't mind keeping Aunt Beatrice occupied for a few hours."

"And who is this woman, Mrs. Simpson?" Aunt Beatrice asked, her expression confused.

Clara gave us all a pointed look. "I'm very sorry, I appreciate the invitation, but as you can see, it's best if I stay with Mother."

Phillip stared into his glass, his expression glum.

Amelia pitied him. Judging by the many tender looks he gave Clara; it was clear he was hopelessly in love with her. It made her even more determined to find some way for them to be together. She would invite Hannah and Phillip to afternoon tea. While she and Hannah kept Aunt Beatrice occupied, the pair could steal a few minutes alone. When it came to Aunt Beatrice, it would take some time for Amelia to earn Clara's trust, but her future happiness depended on it.

After they had finished a dessert of cake, they returned to the drawing room.

The curtains at the large windows were open, and there, too, a fire blazed in the hearth. Outside, the wind became stronger. It swirled and blew and bent branches of surrounding shrubs.

A Chickering rosewood pianoforte in the room's corner next to the large windows drew Amelia's attention. A sorrow tugged at her heart for having had to sell her own pianoforte with her home. Now that she was living at Edenstone, she could not help but notice the beautiful instrument each time she entered this room.

Regan caught her looking at it. "You play, don't you, Amelia?"

"I do, but I haven't for a while."

"How delightful," Hannah exclaimed. "Won't you play

for us?"

"I couldn't. I'm out of practice."

"Oh, please do, dear Julia," Aunt Beatrice encouraged. "A nice little ditty would be a wonderful end to our evening."

At the inaccurate name, Clara closed her eyes and shook her head in dismay. Phillip gave Clara an indulgent smile. Hannah cast Amelia an apologetic look, while Regan, who knew Amelia was already well-accustomed to Aunt Beatrice's forgetfulness, winked at her.

After further words of assurance and encouragement, she sat on the embroidered stool, raised the lid, and rested her fingers on the cool keys. She played 'Love and Duty' - a romantic lament about a woman whose family disapproved of the poor shop owner she loved. It was one of the slower, easier songs in her repertoire, one she had played often, and with less potential for errors.

Outside the storm worsened, but inside, surrounded by the warmth of the fire, new friends, and seated in front of the lovely Boston-made pianoforte, Amelia played.

Immersed in the beautiful melody, her surroundings faded away. Nothing existed but the music as her fingers danced across the keyboard. The sweet vibrations melded with the beat of her heart. Sweet music filled the air without effort, like waves ebbing and flowing on the shore, the rich sound immersing every person in the room with its magic.

Then a sudden, hard thud resounded.

Glass shattered.

Something black and bloody fell onto the piano keys.

Blood seeped onto her fingers.

A dead raven, its neck at an impossible angle, lay

sprawled on the piano keys.

Chapter Ten

AMELIA'S SCREAM TORE through the room. She thrust herself away from the pianoforte. The piano stool crashed to the floor behind her. Shattered glass littered the floor and piano top. The raven twitched as its life ebbed away and its eyes glazed over in death. A rivulet of blood seeped from its beak. Wind and rain blew through the smashed window.

Her fingers trembled as if in spasm and her legs became weak. Regan rushed to her side, pulled her into his arms, and guided her to the settee.

Aunt Beatrice, her face tense and drained of all color, clutched her chair's armrests. "A terrible omen," she murmured. "Oh, dear, I feel faint. Clara, please take me to my room."

"Of course, Mother." Clara helped Aunt Beatrice to her feet. "Please excuse us." With an arm around her waist, Clara guided her parent to the door.

The distraught women nearly collided with Simpson, who had heard the commotion. He let the women pass before entering. His eyes widened when he saw the shattered window and the dead bird.

"Simpson, I'll take everyone into the library while you fetch someone to clean up this mess," Regan said.

Amid the overpowering tension in the room, Phillip took Hannah's hand. "The storm's getting worse." He helped her stand. "I see you're upset. Let me take you home. We should leave right away. The heavy rain will soon make the roads muddy and unpassable." He turned to Regan. "Please accept our apologies, I hope you can understand."

"Of course," Regan responded. "It's best not to get caught on these roads in terrible weather."

Amelia stood too. "I'm so sorry this spoiled our evening."

"There's nothing for you to be sorry about, Amelia," Hannah placed her hand on Amelia's arm. "No one could have foreseen this incident, but I agree with Phillip. It's best if we go, now. We live close by, so I'm sure there'll be plenty of opportunity for us to meet soon."

"It would set my mind at ease if you would both stay here for the night," Regan said.

Phillip nodded, but Hannah shook her head. "I'm afraid that's not possible. I have an early appointment in the morning with the dressmaker."

Phillip shrugged and gave in to his sister's wishes.

Regan and Amelia showed them to the front door. Mrs. Simpson appeared with an umbrella to use while they ran to the waiting carriage, the driver huddled beneath a caped raincoat, his hat pulled low.

Phillip helped Hannah inside, folded the umbrella, then climbed in. Before he shut the door, he called out, "Don't forget my promise to go riding on the first sunny day. I'm looking forward to it."

Regan and Amelia stood in the doorway, the wind driving swirling rain all around them, and watched them drive away until the light from the vehicle's lanterns faded into the dark.

"I'm sorry, Amelia," Regan said. "Such a horrible thing to have happened."

"I can't get the sight of that poor bird out of my head. Your aunt's right about its portent."

"Try not to let it worry you. Let me take you to your room. I'll ask Mrs. Simpson to bring up chamomile tea to help you sleep."

But worried she was. Dead blackbirds were symbolic of many things; an unresolved tension, messengers between the dead or living, or warnings of death.

A blast of thunder shook the house. She froze.

"Don't be frightened." Regan took her into the safety of his arms. When they pulled apart, he grasped her fingers, raised them to his lips, and kissed them. With her hand in his, they climbed the stairs together.

At her bedroom door, he scrutinized her face as if to assure himself she was fine. He frowned. "You look tired. Is there anything else I can do for you?"

Amelia shook her head. "All I need is a good night's sleep."

"It's your strength, your resilience that I admire most. I promise there'll be many more evenings with Phillip and Hannah. I could tell you liked them."

"Yes, very much."

"They're excellent friends of mine. Get some rest. I'll see you in the morning. By that time, I'll have everything restored."

In the hallway's candlelight, he raised her chin and

pressed his mouth to hers. The world around her fell away as a reassuring warmth spread through her body. Nothing existed but the touch of his lips against hers. A kiss so slow and soft, it comforted her in ways words could not. His finger caressed her cheek as their breaths mingled.

Slowly, it seemed, and to her regret, he pulled away, his eyes aglow with tenderness. "When I'm with you like this, you make me want to hold you forever. I hope you know there's nothing I wouldn't do to protect you."

Amelia caressed his cheek. "Yes, I'm coming to that realization." She took a step back and turned toward the bedroom.

He reached behind her for the knob and swung open the door.

"Thank you, Regan. Will I see you in the morning?"

He nodded. "You can count on it. If only to ensure all the women in my life are unscathed by tonight's disaster."

She gave him a smile, then stepped inside her room.

When the door closed, she leaned back against it until her heartbeat slowed. A fire burned in the hearth, and its warm glow lit the room. Sarah had already laid her nightgown on the bed. Humming the tune, *Love and Duty,* she had played earlier; she prepared for bed.

After a knock on the door, Mrs. Simpson entered with a cup of tea. "I hope this helps you sleep, Miss. It was a terrible thing that happened tonight." She handed it to Amelia.

"How thoughtful. Chamomile is exactly what I need right now."

Despite the shock Mrs. Simpson experienced when Amelia had inadvertently blurted out how she had seen the young lady in her mirror's reflection, a mutual bond was developing between them. "If you need anything more, pull the bell cord." Mrs. Simpson left, the door clicking shut behind her.

Tucked beneath the covers, Amelia sipped her beverage and listened to the abating storm, the wind fading away and the rain cascading mildly now. Weather that would wash everything anew. Exhaustion soon set in, and she struggled to keep her eyes open. After snuffing out the light, she plumped the pillow and pulled the covers up to her ears.

Memories of the evening's calamity faded at the sound of the rain pattering against the window. Fire in the grate crackled and popped. Tranquility spread through her, and she drifted into the void that existed between wakefulness and sleep.

From somewhere in the recesses of her mind came the sound of a woman weeping, and it wrenched her from deepening slumber. This was no dream. Could Clara or Aunt Beatrice be in distress? She sat up and lit the candle. Donning robe and slippers, and with candleholder in hand, she hurried into the dark, vacant hallway as the crying intensified.

Amelia paused in front of Aunt Beatrice's door and rested her ear against it, but heard only silence. She rushed to Clara's door, but again encountered only silence.

The weeping became more mournful, desperate, and quite upsetting. It seemed to come from the floor above. She made her way to the stairs at the end of the hallway which led to the uppermost level. At the top, she halted. The weeping, stronger now, seemed to come from a door at the end of the hallway that was partially open. A soft light shone from within. Cautiously, she crept forward.

As soon as Amelia touched the door, it slammed shut with a firm click of a lock. The weeping continued. Icy fear gripped her as she knocked, then jiggled the doorknob. "Please, let me in. I want to help."

The keening stopped. The door remained locked.

ICY DISCOMFORT PRESSED down on Amelia's chest and made it difficult for her to fall into slumber. She spent the rest of the night gazing up at the ceiling, her thoughts clouded by what she had heard. Her confused mind churned in the darkness, time trickling by; the hours marked only by the faint chimes of the grandfather clock in the entrance hall. Who could have been weeping behind that locked door? And why?

When she rose and went downstairs, the first thing Amelia did was search for Mrs. Simpson. She found her in the parlor, dust cloth in hand, staring out a window.

Amelia cleared her throat.

Mrs. Simpson turned swiftly around. "I didn't hear you, Miss. Is there anything I can do for you?"

"I hope you can. I've been familiarizing myself with the house and have encountered some locked doors. Is there a set of keys you could lend me?"

"As the future lady of the house, it makes sense for you to have your own. I have several spare ones. I'll bring a set up to your room right away."

"There's no need to rush."

Mrs. Simpson twisted the cloth in her hands. "May I ask you something, Miss?"

"Of course."

"Did you truly see my daughter on your first night here?" Her voice cracked and her shoulders drooped. "You're certain it wasn't a dream?"

"In hindsight, I cannot be sure. In the mirror's reflection, the young lady with red hair seemed so real. Common sense tells me it might have been my imagination, brought on by fatigue, but in my heart, I believe the young woman I saw was genuine; it was her spirit. After he died, my father appeared to me, too. And ever since, I have not been sleeping well."

Mrs. Simpson hesitated, her body stiff, and her expression anguished. She opened her mouth as if to say something but stopped herself.

Amelia gestured to a nearby settee. "Let's sit together, Mrs. Simpson. Tell me what is bothering you."

After they were both seated, Mrs. Simpson clasped her hands in her lap. "Ever since your vision of the auburn-haired girl, I've desperately wanted to know for certain if it was my Annie you saw. I want to believe she's alive and well, but a mother's heart knows the truth… I'm afraid I'll never see her again. I'm convinced my Annie is dead." The suffering in her expression severe, she bit her quivering lip, and blinked to keep her tears at bay.

Amelia reached out to take her hand, not knowing what to say.

"Oh, Miss, I know it was her ghost you saw. She's not at rest. I sense her presence in this house, in its hallways and rooms. I have never seen her, but you have. Am I right? There are people who can see the dead. Are you one of them?"

"I don't know if I could be such a person… but when my father came to me on the night he died, I was fully awake. He appeared to me only briefly and said little." She stared into the fire, the memory of that night gradually returning with sharp clarity.

She faced Mrs. Simpson again. "The young woman I saw in the reflection had waist-length, auburn hair as wild and free as the wind. Her striking eyes, one green and one blue, appeared deeply troubled and mysterious. There were delicate freckles on her up-turned nose. She had a haunted look about her."

"It's my Annie, I'm certain of it now." With a trembling hand, Mrs. Simpson reached beneath her collar and pulled out a silver chain with an oval locket, its front engraved with flowers. "Inside is a likeness of her and a lock of hair taken from her when she was a child. Perhaps if you carry it with you, it will draw her out and she'll come to you again." She unclasped the chain from around her neck and dropped it into Amelia's palm.

Slowly, Amelia opened the locket. On the left side was a lock of hair, deep auburn, glossy and bound by a small white ribbon. But the likeness on the right made Amelia catch her breath.

Mrs. Simpson crumpled as tears filled her eyes. "The look on your face tells me it *was* Annie you saw. You described her perfectly." She wept. "Oh, my Annie, what happened to you?"

Amelia handed her the handkerchief from her pocket.

"How foolish of me to have hoped she was still alive. Of course, she is dead," Mrs. Simpson continued, distressed. "Her spirit came to you. Surely, you understand she seeks your help. She wants to tell someone what happened to her, and she chose you, Miss Amelia, she chose you because she knows you will help us learn the truth."

Amelia reached for her hand to comfort her again, uncertain how to proceed now that the poor woman finally believed her daughter was dead. "I'm not sure of anything, Mrs. Simpson. What can I do that hasn't been done already? Regan told me he arranged many searches to find her, but all his efforts revealed nothing."

"My Annie was headstrong and determined. I know she'll appear to you again. I'm certain of it. She was always an excellent judge of character and had a good head on her shoulders. My daughter would have liked you, trusted you. If she comes to you again, heed what she tells you. It will be important."

"The girl I saw didn't speak. She only beckoned to me."

"Then you must follow her. Promise me you will."

Amelia admired this dignified woman who had shared her most intimate hopes. How could she disappoint a mother who bore such pain? "You have my promise. If she returns, I'll do all I can to learn what she wants to tell me."

Mrs. Simpson expelled a long breath, then leaned forward and gripped Amelia's hand. "Thank you, but you must take care. Something terrible happened to her, I'm sure of it. I've sensed it ever since my Annie went missing. Please do all you can. My husband and I will never find peace until we know what became of our poor girl."

"I give you my word that I'll do my very best."

"Be careful. If something bad happened to her, it, or they might still be about."

Amelia swallowed despite the knot forming in her throat. So many warnings, so few explanations.

LATER THAT DAY, Amelia found the key ring on her nightstand. At least two dozen polished brass skeleton keys, carefully labeled, and each with a unique design dangled from a silver ring held closed by a lobster claw clasp. Mrs. Simpson had wasted no time. Amelia knew she had found an ally and intended to help her in any way she could.

Amelia explored the attic. Although there was plenty of daylight, there were very few windows on the uppermost level, and she knew the attic would be dark. She lit the candle in the holder and carried it with her up to the third floor.

Dim light streamed in from the only window at the end of the corridor. Amelia stopped in front of the door from where the weeping had come from the night before. By daylight, she noticed scratches on the door, brown varnish chipped and worn, and the doorknob and brass lock dull with age.

She held out the key ring, located the right key, and slid it into the lock. The levers and tumblers clicked, and the knob turned. Amelia pushed open the creaky door and entered a small anteroom void of furniture. She crossed the room to the velvet blue curtains. Dust clouded the air as she drew them open. Opposite her, a narrow set of wooden stairs led upward. The candle lit her way as she ascended.

She found herself in a vast garret lit only by a thick-paned window obscured with cobwebs. Heavy timber lined the walls and floor. An eerie silence lingered in the musty air.

Dusty furniture and old possessions cluttered the space. A stack of mildewed patchwork quilts lay on the mattress of a massive four-poster canopy bed in the center of the room. Inverted wooden chairs sat on an oak dining table. An old broken dress form lay toppled in one corner. She passed a row of empty bookcases and opened the door of an old wardrobe, empty except for a pair of embroidered slippers. The space was a graveyard for discarded belongings whose value had waned long ago.

Scattered amid the hoard of antiquated items, Amelia noticed several enormous trunks. She approached an ornate one that caught her interest and admired the hand-carved ornamental flowers and flourishes on the top and sides. Amelia ran her hands across the engraved initials on the top—CHL—Catherine Harrison Lockhart. Regan's mother.

Carefully, she raised the dust encrusted lid. The faint smell of mothballs wafted out. On top of an array of colorful gowns lay a small, thick journal bound in red leather with gilt designs on the cover. The volume was beautiful. She knew there was something special about it from the moment she picked it up. Lovely to hold, and no larger than her hand, she flipped it open, and turned the pages to a random entry. Pressed in thin, almost transparent parchment, she saw a black flower.

Amelia's heart raced so fast it felt as if it would explode. *Beware of black petals,* her father had warned. She unfolded the parchment to study the fragile bloom and avoided touching it lest it crumble. She had seen nothing like it before. The flower reminded her of a simple rose, but it had flat, leathery petals on a short stem. She carefully refolded the paper and tucked it back into the book.

Delicate, neat handwriting filled each page. She turned a few more pages and stopped somewhere near the center of the book.

> *My mother, Elizabeth Harrison, was a genuine beauty in her time. I am told both me and my twin look like her, but beauty brings its own perils. As an only child, my mother was to inherit her family's home and fortune. Long-standing friends with the Lockhart family, the Harrisons arranged a marriage between their children, Elizabeth and Randolph; a marriage of convenience to join their family fortunes. But my mother had always been in love with another man, Robert Wakefield, and marriage to my father did not quell her undying love for him. And so, she became bitter and melancholic and resented the marriage she had been forced into. She once confessed to me that when she was expecting my sister and I, she threw herself down the stairs hoping to kill herself. If she could not have Robert Wakefield, she preferred to die. Obviously, the attempt failed. And from the day I was born, she hated me. But not Beatrice. Beatrice, she tolerated. It was me whom she cursed.*

Amelia sucked in a breath. Regan had once mentioned the intricate connection between the Wakefield and Lockhart families. Did he know about his grandmother's unrequited love for Robert Wakefield, Phillip and

Hannah's grandfather? Regan's mother, Catherine, had been keenly aware of it and had written about it in her diary. Had she told her son about it? Her heart broke for Regan's mother. She struggled to comprehend how Elizabeth could reject Catherine so vehemently. In her mind she visualized a young Catherine growing up shunned, ignored, dejected, and found it impossible to fathom. Was it Catherine's spirit she had heard weeping? Or was it Annie's? Disturbed by all she had read, and unable to read any more, she tucked the diary into her pocket, closed the trunk, and returned to her room to prepare for dinner.

Chapter Eleven

IT RAINED FOR three days. On the fourth, Amelia woke early, pulled back the curtains, and gazed out at dawn breaking with hues of lavender, rose, and amber.

Later Sarah brought her breakfast tray and handed her a note. Phillip and Hannah would arrive at one o'clock to take her riding.

Amelia sweetened her hot porridge with honey and added a touch of cream, relishing each spoonful. Regan was an early riser and likely already at work. She hoped he might return early to join them for their ride. The thought caught her by surprise, and she realized how much she relied on him and his reassuring presence.

After Sarah took the tray away, Amelia was free for several hours before the ride. She retrieved Catherine's diary from the nightstand and flipped through its pages. One page caught her attention:

> *Hours after Regan was born, Mother arrived at Edenstone. Upon entering my room, she dismissed the nursemaid, strode to the cradle where my son slept, and stared down at him. I*

invited her to pick him up, hoping she would react with a semblance of warmth. Her upper lip rose in a sneer, and she told me she had no desire to familiarize herself with any spawn of mine. It pained me to see her eyes void of any tenderness. Why did it surprise me? Why had I allowed myself to hope things might be different between us? I asked her why she came if she had no interest in her grandchild. Wounding me, she revealed it was only to keep up appearances, for she did not wish to give either my servants, or hers, any reason to gossip.

I could barely speak, but somehow asked her why she hated me so much? Why did she think I merited such animosity and cruelty when I had always been a dutiful daughter? Why couldn't she return it with a little kindness of her own?

She did not answer.

I asked her why she could not show any love for her new, innocent grandson, Regan, her own flesh and blood.

Her eyes narrowed. I can still hear the horrible words she uttered. "Sons are acceptable. Daughters are an affliction. I curse any girl born in this house with death and madness."

Mother's cruelty shattered my heart. Anguish whirled around me, stifling my breath. A whirlpool of despair swallowed me. I turned away so she would not see my tears. Without another word, she strode out of the room.

Amelia shuddered as a chill ran along her spine at the

merciless callousness of Catherine's mother, and it broke her heart. Every word in the diary reflected her sadness. She recalled the sound of weeping that led her to the attic. Was it linked to Catherine's unhappiness? She would find out.

The clock in the hall struck noon. Hannah and Phillip would arrive in an hour to take her riding. She donned her light gray riding habit and matching top hat.

When she went downstairs, Phillip and Hannah were waiting for her in the parlor. Aunt Beatrice chattered away to them about the coming winter while Clara, blushing at something Phillip must have said to her, served tea and biscuits.

Phillip stood when she entered. "Amelia, I'm glad to see you looking so well. Judging by your smile and rosy cheeks, you've recovered from the shock of that last night when we all supped together."

"I have, though I admit I was a little frightened when the storm flung that poor creature through the glass."

"It disconcerted everyone," Hannah said.

Amelia smiled in appreciation of her support and sat on the sofa opposite them.

"Take care, all of you," Aunt Beatrice said. "A dead raven is a horrible omen, a clear sign of death." Her teacup clattered on the saucer.

"Such nonsense, Mother," Clara said. "Try not to think about it. It was a storm, nothing more. It could as easily have been a sea gull or pigeon or hawk that hurtled through that glass. Let's put it out of our minds." Clara then turned to Amelia, her look of exasperation fading. "Would you like some tea?"

"No, thank you. I'll wait until we have returned from

our ride."

"Will Regan be joining us?" Phillip asked.

"I'm afraid not," Clara replied. "Simpson told me Regan rushed out of the house early this morning. Apparently, there was an urgent matter at his factory that required his attention."

Philip leaned forward and in a soft voice said, "Are you certain you wouldn't like to ride with us, Clara? It'll be more enjoyable if we make it a foursome."

Clara hesitated, but then shook her head. "I wish I could, I truly do, but I have to take mother to the dressmaker in town. Her new gown is ready for a last fitting. Perhaps next time."

Phillip's disappointment was apparent in his slumped posture as he stared down at his hands. "I'll hold you to that."

"Thank you for your understanding, Philip." Her tone rang with disappointment.

Clearly the two were fond of each other. Amelia resolved that one day, she would find opportunities to bring them together. She commended Clara's dedication to her mother, but it was a bar to her own happiness. She needed a life of her own, lest she waste away into spinsterhood. Aunt Beatrice could benefit from a hired companion or nurse, which would free Clara. She would broach the subject with Regan.

After tea, they went to the stables, where their saddled horses waited in the sunshine. Cadence nickered when Amelia patted his neck.

Lush countryside stretched before them as they set off at a trot. The earth smelled fragrant after the rains. Occasionally, they rode past a wooded area or farmhouse which separated the fields. Rambling through pastures, Amelia reveled in the pleasure of riding in the countryside on a sunny day.

They had been riding for more than an hour when they came upon a dashing brook with a small cascade. They dismounted to water the horses.

Phillip pulled a blanket from his saddlebags, whipped it into the air, and let it settle on the grassy bank. He removed pewter cups, a small flask, bread, and some cheese.

The fresh air stirred Amelia's appetite, and she appreciated his forethought.

Hannah tucked back an unruly lock of hair from her forehead. "Such a pity Regan and Clara couldn't join us today."

"Regan is overly dedicated to his work, I'm afraid, but manages to get away when he can. Pity today wasn't such a time." Phillip tore his chunk of bread in half. "Clara is much more difficult to convince to abandon her mother for even a short time."

"I see you care for her very much," Amelia said.

One of Phillip's eyebrows rose. "It's that apparent?"

Hannah poured lemonade into their cups. "My brother has been in love with Clara for as long as I can remember. He's even proposed marriage."

About to nibble a piece of cheese, Amelia paused. "That's wonderful news, Phillip. I'm happy for you and Clara."

Phillip tensed. "She hasn't given me an answer. Clara feels responsible for her mother and refuses to leave her. I've even suggested Beatrice should live with us if we married, but Clara believes changing her mother's residence would add to the poor woman's confusion."

"What about you, Amelia?" Hannah asked. "Have you settled into Edenstone?"

"I'm doing my best."

Phillip perked up his head. "What do you mean?"

Amelia immediately regretted not giving a more affirmative answer. "Oh, everything at Edenstone is lovely…"

"But?" Phillip asked, cocking his head in expectation.

"So many things… I'm not quite comfortable yet."

"Oh, you must mean the incident with the raven," Hannah said as she reached for a piece of cheese. "We shouldn't have reacted so strongly. We meant no harm."

"No, I don't mean the raven."

"Is there something else that is bothering you?"

Amelia struggled with an answer. How much could she tell them? "I'm still getting to know the house and the family history."

"Such as?" Phillip asked.

She suspected they might know something about Edenstone's secrets, so she confided in them. "One night, in the reflection of my mirror, a young auburn-haired woman beckoned me. When I turned around, there was no one there."

Hannah gasped as her hand flew to her chest. "Annie's ghost."

Phillip swallowed and exchanged a nervous glance with Hannah. "How much have you heard about this auburn-haired girl?"

"I know she's the daughter of Edward and Mary Simpson, who both work at Edenstone, and that she went missing one day."

"Yes, Annie is, was, the Simpson's daughter. Most people believe she is dead, and it's her ghost seen walking the halls of Edenstone," Phillip said, "but Regan and I believe it's more superstition than truth. Are you certain you saw her?"

"She seemed real, and then there was…" Amelia turned the cup in her hands.

"There is more?" Phillip asked, one eyebrow raised.

"One night I heard a woman crying. I traced the weeping to the attic door, but it slammed shut when I tried to enter. Then the sound halted. I have yet to find the source."

"Perhaps it is a ghost." Hannah spoke in a voice tense with fright. "Who else could it be other than Mary's daughter, Annie?"

"Nonsense." Phillip rose abruptly. "We've finished eating. I'll pack things up." He gathered the leftover food and other items, then went to his horse to tuck them back in his saddlebags.

With her brother out of earshot, Hannah leaned closer. "What does Regan have to say about it?"

"Much the same as Phillip. He doesn't believe the rumors. He knows about the sighting, but not about the woman I heard weeping. I haven't told him about that yet."

Hannah's hand rose to her mouth and her eyes widened. "You're afraid he won't believe you?"

Amelia nodded.

Hannah took hold of both her hands. "Although I haven't seen her with my own eyes, I believe it when others tell me that there's been some strange occurrences at Edenstone. What happened the other night with the raven is such an example. You should tell Regan. He's a good man, but he's had some misfortune." She glanced over her shoulder at Phillip, who was busy tightening cinch straps. "I've seen some things too whenever I visit. Something breaking without apparent cause or sounds I can't explain. Are you aware of what you are getting into by marrying Regan?"

Amelia frowned. "What do you mean?"

"Unhappiness and tragedy have plagued every generation of that family. There's talk of a family curse."

"Were you aware that Regan nearly married someone?"

"Yes. I heard she drowned in a boating accident, and poor Regan was grief stricken at her loss."

"Ladies, the horses are ready," Phillip called out. "There is much more I want to show you."

As they rose, Hannah gripped her arm. "Take care. I can't exactly explain it, and we can't speak of it now, but there's something evil at Edenstone, and much more you should know."

Chapter Twelve

SUNLIGHT STREAMED THROUGH the space between the curtains when Amelia awoke. Soft rays danced on the floor as she stretched, then turned onto her side. An exquisite plum riding habit with matching leather gauntlets and round topper hung on the inside of the wardrobe's open door. On the floor below it sat a pair of black patent leather riding boots and a delicately twined whip. The elegance of the garment took her breath away. She flung back the covers and plucked off the note pinned to the habit.

> *My dear Amelia,*
> *Please accept this gift as an apology for missing yesterday's outing with Phillip and Hannah Wakefield. I hope the new habit will persuade you to ride with me today. Sarah helped me to ensure a perfect fit.*
>
> *Regan*

She ran her hand down the sleeve of the jacket, relishing the touch of the soft silk beneath her palm. A pair of breeches matched the velveteen safety skirt. The exquisite habit looked as if it cost a small fortune; Regan's thoughtful generosity filled her heart.

She washed and dressed, eager to try out the habit. When finished, she stood in front of the mirror. From the comfortable white chemisette beneath the jacket, to the thick skirt that covered the breeches and shining boots, everything fit perfectly. Even the topper with its beautiful, sweeping white feather and gauze veil suited her.

As she placed her hand on the doorknob, she stopped, recalling Hannah's disturbing warning about Edenstone. Ever since she met him, Regan rarely spoke about himself or his family. Now that she was here and about to marry him, she wanted to learn as much as she could about his family's history. So many niggling doubts urged her to dig deeper so she could feel at ease in this house. A ride together gave her the perfect opportunity.

When she entered the dining room, Regan broke into a wide grin. He stood and pulled out a chair for her. "I knew the color would suit you."

"The habit is lovely, Regan. It's one of my favorite colors and fits perfectly." To emphasize her point, she did a spin.

"I confess. Were it not for Sarah, and left to my own resources, I doubt my choice would have been so successful."

"I must thank her for helping you. And she never said a word about it."

He chuckled heartily. "I told her to keep it a secret."

"And that she did, although how she kept it from me is a mystery. But she is a romantic at heart. And a gift like this would impress her. It's no wonder she praises you at every turn."

"And I thought I was losing my charm with the ladies," he said, hand over his heart, feigning relief.

Their good-humored chatter continued as they ate. Between nibbles of toast and eggs, Amelia scrutinized him, searching for sincerity, honesty, integrity, trustworthiness, all qualities she sought in a husband. They seemed to be all there and more. It encouraged her to pose more personal questions later, which she hoped he would answer honestly.

Upon going outdoors, they found their horses waiting, already saddled.

Together they trotted around the perimeter of the estate, enjoying the sunny day and the gentle breeze, that aroma of damp loam and the saltiness of the sea.

After a while, they slowed their mounts to a walk. Tucked away in a corner, behind a leafless row of bushes, Amelia noticed a gray stone wall that surrounded a small graveyard. Intrigued, she halted Cadence in front of the wrought-iron gate. Beyond it lay two tidy rows of graves bathed in sunlight. Centuries of weather discolored the older tombstones, while others were of newer marble. From where they sat, she couldn't read any of the epitaphs. She shivered in response to the aura of sadness echoed from the lonely graves.

"Your family?"

Regan nodded. "Unfortunately, we've had more than our fair share of death in our family." He stared distantly at the graveyard. "That day when you fell into the ocean brought back a terrible memory. Thank God I didn't lose you too."

"Will you tell me about it?"

He leaned forward in his saddle. "I had just asked Nellie to marry me and invited her to sail with me on my boat." He paused and swallowed hard.

"I know this must be difficult."

He inhaled a deep breath, and his fingers gripped the reins. "The weather suddenly turned nasty, and before I could turn back to shore, a colossal wave struck, overturning the vessel. Turbulent waters swallowed us and pulled us down." His clenched jaw twitched as he faltered. "Rough water made it a struggle to swim, but I surfaced. I looked for her, screaming her name, but the storm smothered my voice. Despite the waves tossing me about, seized by terror, I dove again and again, desperate to find her. My strength waned, but I hoped to swim to shore for help or risk drowning myself. I reached shore and summoned help, but the water was too dangerous to send out any men in boats. When the storm lessened, boatmen went out to sea, but they all came back without her." His voice wavered as he continued. "Her body washed up on shore near Winthrop. I blamed myself. Had I not brought her out on the water, she would be alive today. I live with that awful truth every day of my life."

Amelia placed her hand on his arm. "And the day I fell into the water, you relived that nightmare."

He swallowed and nodded.

"Is she buried here?" Amelia asked, her voice reflecting the compassion she bore in her heart for what he had endured.

He shook his head. "Her family took her back home to Philadelphia and buried her in the family plot there."

This was a man haunted by such a horrendous memory, and her heart broke for him. A feeling of remorse stung her for suspecting he had intentionally let go of her hand when she had clearly and accidentally fallen into the water. Such a thing was not within his character.

"I should have been the one to drown, not her."

"Don't blame yourself. You couldn't have known the weather would turn so suddenly. No one can predict what fate has planned for us."

"And that's why graveyards like this are so meaningful. To lose someone you love feels akin to having a limb torn from your body. When you visit their grave, you can feel close to them once more."

"It certainly does," she agreed.

Above, a sea gull winged and squawked. A gentle breeze blew through the tree, making newly sprung leaves tremble. A dead branch, a remnant from winter, rolled between the graves. Amelia could see the pain on Regan's face. It was in the faraway look in his eyes, the stillness of his body, the tension in his hands. She longed to do or say something to comfort him.

"Should we go in and pay our respects?" she asked.

He shook his head. "Maybe one day, but not now. I've spoiled this beautiful day with talk of so much sadness."

Amelia understood. With a tap of her heels, she reined Cadence into a turn. Regan followed.

Hidden secrets called out to her from that graveyard, capturing her interest. She would explore it another day.

They rode for another hour; their only conversation about less important matters—when he showed her the tree he had climbed as a child or the field where he once fell asleep.

"Let's canter home," he suggested, after a while.

Conversation after leaving the graveyard had been

awkward, forced, meaningless chatter. It came as a relief to head back home. She set Cadence in a canter, reveling in the sound of pounding hooves and the freedom of riding fast and free through the rolling field.

Breathless, but invigorated, they arrived at the stable. Two stable lads hurried forth to tend to the horses. Regan directed Amelia to a nearby bench where they gazed out over the land they had just ridden through. He stared down at his hands, then turned to her. "I enjoyed spending time with you, Amelia. I hope you haven't changed your mind about marrying me." Suddenly, he seemed innocent, almost fearful, like a small boy desperate for friendship.

Her heart lurched. Had she revealed her inner doubts about him through word or action? "There's a betrothal agreement between us, Regan, and you've been good to me, kind and patient. I care deeply for you." He was all she had now, but could he love her?

He pulled her close to him. His lips grazed her cheek. "That's not enough. I want you to love me. There's plenty of gossip about Edenstone and this family, but I don't want you to believe any of it. If ever you need to know something about me or my family, you need only to ask. I want to be the one to tell you whatever you wish to know." He held her hand. "I'm falling in love with you, Amelia. I know it's too soon to expect you to return my feelings, but with time, I hope you'll be able to say that you love me too."

Speechless, her heart overflowed with joy and tears brimmed in her eyes. These were the words she had dreamed of her entire life. Then why did she still have so many small misgivings?

"I promise to be a good husband but want you to

come freely into marriage with an open heart. Not because of the betrothal contract that binds us. Your financial situation after your father's death has put you in a vulnerable position. Your father paid me the dowry he promised, but I don't need the money. I'd rather you keep it. So, I've returned it to you in full. It sits in an account in your name at the bank in Winthrop. I never want to see you unhappy, but if a life with me is not what you want, then you're free to choose a different future. I release you from the contract to marry."

In a single swoop, Amelia's misgivings vanished. Happiness flowed through her, as warm as the rays of an early summer sun. She felt herself break out into a grand smile. "I don't know what to say."

"Tell me you think you might one day love me too, that you will stay here at Edenstone. That will be enough, for now. I ask nothing more from you."

"I'm falling in love with you, too. And of course, I am staying. You mean so much to me. You're a good man, your family is my family now. I couldn't be any happier."

"I intend to make you even happier. I want you to feel as if Edenstone is your home. Ever since my parents died, I've neglected the house. If there are any improvements or changes you wish to make, please tell me."

Tears of relief and joy rained down her cheeks. How could she have doubted this good-hearted man?

Regan placed his hands on either side of her face and wiped away the tears with his thumbs. He leaned forward, his forehead against hers.

"I thank you with all my heart," she said, too emotional to speak in more than a whisper.

His lips touched hers, then he pulled away. "Amelia, I

live for the day you will become my wife," he whispered slowly, prolonging each word as if he wanted her to sear them into her heart.

The warmth of his cheek against hers reassured her. She was no longer alone in the world. Her heart fluttered as he pulled her into a fiery and passionate kiss that made the world fall away.

Chapter Thirteen

THE NEXT MORNING, after donning a sun hat, Amelia set off for a walk. Wildflowers rose in a riot of color, a feast for bee and butterfly. The early sunlight was soft and diffused. Dew evaporated in the burgeoning warmth. The aroma of newly sprouted blooms enhanced the fresh morning air. Now that she no longer doubted Regan's intentions, she viewed him with fresh eyes. She wanted to learn everything about him and his family and soon found herself at the little graveyard's gates.

Amelia passed between the unlocked gates and walked along a gravel-laden path. Short rows of tombstones stood erect. Some headstones had crumbled with the weathering of decades. Others were of newer stone with clear black writing on them. She strolled past the tombs of Regan's great-grandparents, then paused before those of his mother, Catherine, and his father, Daniel.

What she saw next to them made the hairs on her neck rise. She raised her hand to her open mouth to stifle a gasp.

Three tiny graves lay next to each other, a winged angel carved on each headstone—Cecilia Lockhart 1851-

1851, Annabelle Lockhart 1853-1855, and Isabelle Lockhart 1856-1857. Engraved beneath each name were the words Beloved Daughter. Regan's younger sisters. Had the curse Elizabeth uttered to Catherine been so powerful, so real, that all her female children perished? It was not unheard of for young children to die from illness or accident, but to lose all her daughters while her only son thrived was beyond Amelia's comprehension. Was it coincidence or the curse? She hoped Catherine's diary might contain the answers.

Sadness sat heavy on her chest, extinguishing her spirit, dulling all other emotions. A black mist seemed to settle over her, refusing to shift, despite the bright sunlight.

Shaken by her discovery, Amelia gathered wildflowers to place on their graves. She wanted to do more, but for now, this would have to do. After resting her hand on the top of each tombstone in farewell, she left the dead to their rest.

Amelia headed back toward the house. Instead of finding answers, many more questions raced through her mind. How did Catherine's losses affect Regan; a boy too young to understand death? How had his parents coped? Once more, she prayed Catherine's diary would reveal the answers.

AMELIA ENCOUNTERED CLARA coming out of Aunt Beatrice's room. She raised a finger to her lips. "Mother has just gone down for a nap. Join me in the parlor for some tea?"

Amelia nodded and followed her downstairs. They sat

in chairs next to the tall windows where sunlight shed warmth. Mrs. Simpson entered with a tray of tea and molasses biscuits.

"You've been outdoors. Your cheeks are bright pink. Getting to know more of Edenstone?" Clara asked as she added sugar to her tea and stirred it.

"I wanted to take advantage of the pleasant weather, so I walked to the graveyard."

Clara sipped her tea. She tilted her head to the side and raised her eyebrows. "Did you now?" She placed her cup on the saucer and set it down. "I haven't been there for a while, what with Mother taking up most of my time these days."

"My heart broke at the sight of the three little graves." Her appetite stirred by fresh air, she reached for a biscuit. "How tragic for the family to lose so many children."

Clara gazed into the garden, her eyes sad and distant. "I'll never forget that terrible time. Sickly and weak at birth, Cecilia, the eldest of the girls born after Regan, the poor soul, only lived for five days. Two years after that, my Aunt Catherine gave birth to another girl they named Annabelle. When she was two years of age, on a sunny summer day, while everyone was busy, she found the front door open, went outside, climbed into the water fountain, and drowned. And then there was little Isabelle. Hale and hearty at birth, she breathed her last when she caught influenza at little more than a year old."

"I can't imagine how devastating it must have been for the family, especially for Catherine."

"She barely survived the loss of Cecilia, but when she lost Annabelle, well, she fell into a deep melancholy. Then, after Isabelle died, she became even more despondent and refused to leave her room. To his credit, her husband, my uncle Daniel, doted on her. He loved her very much, but no amount of coaxing on his part raised her spirits. Her depressed state of mind continued for many years until Regan had grown into a young man. But when my uncle died, it seemed all the light inside Catherine died along with him. Death is never kind. It doesn't care who to take or when to snatch someone away, taking people who are far too young, far too good. So many deaths in so short a time finally broke her. She fell into a deeper gloom than ever before. Her face became sunken and haunted, her mind cold and empty. I knew she longed for death to take her."

Having lost her appetite, Amelia set her saucer and biscuit on the tea table between them. "What about the curse?"

Clara's brows rose. "You know about that?"

"Yes."

"Well, I suppose you would eventually have heard of it. There is always gossip in Winthrop. My grandmother, Elizabeth, was a cold, heartless woman, hated by most everyone who knew her, including her own husband. She cursed Catherine, her own daughter. She proclaimed that if Catherine birthed any girls, none would survive, or some such nonsense, which proved true. Too bad the old woman didn't suffer the curse herself. That woman deserved to suffer as much as the rest of us." Clara nibbled a molasses biscuit, then put it down on her saucer. "But, enough of such dreary talk. The dressmaker is coming tomorrow to fit Mother and me with some new day gowns. I'm sure she'll have time to take your measurements. The woman is talented with a needle and thread. Why don't you join us?"

"I would like that very much."

Their talk then turned to lighter matters. The clock struck three o'clock. "I think I'll retire to my room to do a little mending." Amelia was keen to return to her room to read more of Catherine's diary.

She rose, but Clara stopped her with a wave of her hand.

"Stay with me a while longer. With Mother napping, it's nice to have a little company. I'll ask her to bring more tea."

Amelia heaved a sigh. The diary would have to wait a little longer.

AFTER DINNER, TUCKED neatly in bed, and with the entire house silent, Amelia leaned back into her pillows. By the light of the solitary candle next to her on the nightstand, she opened Catherine's diary and flipped to the page where she last finished reading.

> *Weakness took my beloved Cecilia from my arms. My grief is vast as the ocean. A fathomless despair overwhelms me. I yearn for death so I can be with my baby. My mind thinks of ways to end my life, but I lack the courage and strength of mind. Even that is too much of an effort. Darkness strangles me. I am lost, blinded by my tears. I cannot rise to greet the day. The pain is too much to bear.*
>
> *Daniel rarely leaves me, his grief as great as*

mine. He coaxes me to eat, to drink, to dress. Numbly, I try, but my attempts are feeble. Time is lost to me as the days pass in swelling pain. Daniel brings Regan to me each day. A son needs his mother, Daniel whispers as I hold my beloved son in my arms. A glimmer of love rises to overpower my grief. For my son, I must live.

Amelia read on until her eyes grew weary. After snuffing the flame, she curled up beneath the covers, her mind plagued with sadness for Catherine. When she finally fell asleep, she dreamed about a tall, ornate mirror in the center of the room. Its silvery surface reflected a strange, unnatural glow awash with sunset's gold and cerise colors. Beautiful to behold, it beckoned her closer until she stood before it. The surface rippled, its exquisite colors blurring. When the waves settled, she no longer saw her reflection. Instead, lush trees, thousands of flowers in bloom, and a sparkling blue pond appeared.

Her father walked down a small slope toward her, the flush of youth on his face. He came to a stop within arm's reach and gazed at her with eyes brimming with love. Slowly, he held out his hand. Amelia reached out to touch him but could not.

"Be careful, my daughter," he warned.

It seemed forever since she last saw and talked with him. She wanted to throw herself into his arms so everything could be the same as before his death, without worry or haunting thoughts. She yearned to take his hand and to hear his laughter.

His hands shook as his expression became ominous. "Beware of black flowers and their petals, my child. They grow where you will walk." His voice quivered like grass in the wind.

"Father. Tell me more," she begged.

The reflection in the oval mirror shimmered and broke into ripples again. "No, don't go. Please come back," she screamed.

By the time the waves ceased undulating, he had vanished, and nature's beauty went with him. The mirror turned black and she could no longer see her reflection on the silvery glass. Panic-stricken; her chest heaved.

She opened her eyes. As she stared up at the ceiling, her pulse slowly returned to normal. Deep melancholy pressed down on her chest. The dream seemed so real. Amelia wept, not only because she missed her father but also because she did not understand his dire warning. How could she protect herself from black flowers and petals when she was aware no such plant existed?

Chapter Fourteen

HER FATHER'S SECOND warning about the black flowers weighed heavily on Amelia's mind. Did they exist, and if so, why did he persist in alerting her about them? She headed to the small conservatory at the rear of the house, hoping that might yield some information.

Warm, humid air carrying the cloying scent of soil and peat assailed her when she entered. Potted plants lined each wall. Aunt Beatrice stood at a table in the center of the floor, repotting plants, humming, deeply engrossed in the task at hand. To avoid startling her, Amelia called out in a soft voice. "Aunt Beatrice?"

The woman glanced up from her work; her look blank before recognition brightened her eyes. "Oh, it's you, Audrey, how nice to see you."

Accepting of her forgetfulness and of the many names she called her, Amelia stood by her side. "It looks as if you're busy."

Aunt Beatrice upended a small pot to remove a plant and placed it into a larger pot. "I've always been fond of gardening. The touch of earth between my fingers brings me a sense of calm amid all the turmoil that life throws in our path." She grabbed a handful of dirt and packed it around the plant.

"If there has been turmoil here, you've survived it well." Amelia hoped to encourage her into a more profound conversation.

"Oh, life is full of woe sometimes, but you've brought a great deal of light and joy into this house." A heartfelt smile extended to her eyes.

"That's kind of you to say, especially since the circumstances of my arrival at Edenstone weren't ideal." Amelia swallowed to avoid the twinge of sadness and grief coming to life inside of her again.

"Regan seems happier with you here. He's very taken with you, my girl. Has he asked you to marry him yet?"

Amelia gave her a smile, happy to remind her of what she had forgotten. "Yes, he has."

Her eyes filled with tears. "I'm so happy for you, Flora. This house has seen far too much sadness, and we're all eager to put it behind us." Aunt Beatrice resumed her work, and as she did, her tears dried, and she hummed a tune in forgetfulness.

After a few moments, Amelia said, "You seem well-informed about plants. Perhaps you can answer a question for me."

"Well, I've always been passionate about gardening, but I think I've forgotten more than I remember."

"Someone mentioned black flowers to me recently. Do you know where they grow or if there are any nearby?"

Aunt Beatrice wiped her forehead with the back of her gloved hand. "Hmm, black flowers... I've seen dark purple ones which look almost black."

Amelia's heart skipped a beat. "Here at Edenstone?"

She shook her head. "Oh dear, I don't know. I hope not. I can't remember. They are evil. If you come across one, stay away."

"Evil? I don't understand."

Animation left Aunt Beatrice's face. "I must stay away from there. They are poisonous, extremely dangerous." Her hands shook and her voice quivered. "I must not grow them. Let me see, where did I see them last? I can't remember. Oh dear, I can't recall anymore."

"Please don't fret, Aunt Beatrice. I didn't mean to upset you. Please forget I mentioned them. It's not important."

But Aunt Beatrice's face had lost all color, and her breathing became more frantic. Fearing she might faint, Amelia fetched a chair from the other side of the table and helped her sit.

"What's going on here?" Clara stood in the doorway, her tone wary, eyes wide with alarm.

Before Amelia could respond, Clara hurried over to where Aunt Beatrice now sat and shoved Amelia aside. "It's all right, Mother. Calm yourself. I'm here now." Clara riveted her glare on Amelia. "What did you say to distress her?"

"We were merely talking about flowers, dark-colored ones, and that's when she became upset. I would not hurt her."

Clara's nostrils flared. "You should know by now that Mother gets confused easily." She waved Amelia away as she helped her mother stand.

Amelia reached for the cane and handed it to Clara, who whisked it out of her hand. "Let's go to your room, Mother. First, I'll help you get cleaned up, then I'll have some chamomile tea sent up. You'll feel much better after your nap."

Before they passed through the doorway, Clara glanced back over her shoulder. Something flashed beneath the surface of her hardened expression. Then she led her mother away.

Amelia flopped down onto the chair and took a deep breath to quell her frustration. Despite her failure at acquiring the information she needed, she had found out Aunt Beatrice knew something about poisonous black flowers. But why did she become so distraught? Even more curious was Clara's vehement reaction. Was it over concern for her mother or because of the black flowers? Clearly, she had touched upon something very sensitive, but what exactly? What did it all mean?

DURING DINNER, CLARA engaged freely with Regan or Aunt Beatrice, but whenever Amelia posed a question, she received the briefest of answers or no response at all. Yet, it seemed no one else noticed Clara's aloofness toward her.

As for Aunt Beatrice, she seemed to have completely forgotten what happened in the conservatory. With color in her cheeks, she seemed well and joined in each discussion.

In good spirits, Regan told them about the latest carriage orders he received.

When the meal ended, Clara made her excuses and hurried her mother away to retire for the night.

Now that they were alone, Regan smiled at Amelia

from across the table. "It seems we have the rest of the evening to ourselves." He pushed back his chair, came to her side, and held out his arm.

In the drawing room, she sat with him before a crackling fire in the hearth. Simpson interrupted their solitude when he entered to serve them with two snifters of brandy, and then he left.

Conversation flowed freely. She listened as he told her stories about his antics as a boy and some of his more interesting carriage orders. He answered all her queries and treated her comments with respect. Amelia appreciated how he spoke to her as an equal and welcomed his encouragement when she presented a different opinion. Her heart swelled with affection. He listened as if her words were golden, like an elixir he had been longing for.

Time flew by too quickly. The clock struck eleven, past the time for her to retire, yet she was loath to end their time together.

"Amelia," he said tenderly. "I enjoy every minute we spend together. I'm glad you're here at Edenstone."

"The move was a little daunting. Change is hard, but I'm feeling more at ease here now that I'm getting to know you and your family better."

"I've said it before and don't mind saying it again. Whatever you want to know, you only need to ask." He took her hand and kissed it. "I'm in love with you." He turned to face her and stroked her cheek. "I want you, Amelia. I've never desired a woman more." He took her chin between his thumb and forefinger and brought her to meet his steady gaze. "And I know you want me, too."

Amelia trembled as his lips descended toward hers. The world fell away. The kiss was slow and soft, comforting, laced with the taste of brandy. His hand rested below her ear, his thumb caressing her cheek as their breaths mingled. She knew she should pull away before she lost herself, but could not.

When he drew back, she took shaky, shallow breaths, unprepared for the pleasure his kiss had ignited.

He rested his forehead against hers, then pressed her head to his chest. His warm breath stirred in her hair. Of course, they should stop, but couldn't she ask him to? Hesitating, she looked into his eyes. Swirls of desire lit them. Before she could think, or answer, he swept her to him and covered her mouth with a hungry kiss. Magic that made her feel as if she were walking on air. His mouth was so fiery, the caress of his lips so silky, she melted and let out a low moan.

When he stopped, he whispered, "I have to stop, Amelia." His tone was husky, his eyes filled with longing.

Her limbs quaked and her pulse raced. She slid her hands around his shoulders and kissed him.

This time, he parted her lips, and his tongue explored her mouth. She welcomed the invasion and returned some pressure of her own, the taste of his lips as rich as the brandy he had sipped.

When they separated, he tightened his hold around her. "Damn. When you kiss me like that, it takes every shred of will for me to restrain myself."

Her pulse slowed as she laid her cheek against the warmth of his dinner jacket. His heart pounded, and she gloried in the feel of his chin and lips against her hair.

"You must think I'm brazen," she said.

"I think you're magnificent." Honesty rang so deep in his voice that the words caught her by surprise, and she didn't know what to say.

In his protective embrace, seduced by his touch and kisses, Amelia clung to him. It was easy to let herself topple into the tempting abyss of affection. It was only a kiss, she told herself. Nothing more.

His lips touched her cheek and roamed to the edge of her mouth. She kissed him with so much intensity he moaned. He returned her kiss hungrily and laid her down on the sofa.

That set her body aflame.

His searing tongue compelled her lips to part, and God help her, she surrendered. Her body became an untamed instrument, jolted by so many wild, new sensations. She marveled at his fiery magnificence as her hands rejoiced at the feel of his well-muscled shoulders and forearms. With reckless abandon, she returned his kisses. It fueled his desire, and she basked in the closeness and the feeling of power it gave her.

The kiss seemed to last an eternity. When they came apart, she ached to experience it again. He leaned over her with eyes aflame and ran his fingers over her lips. His chest pressed against hers, she felt every one of his throbbing heartbeats. His tense expression and ruddy cheeks revealed his struggle to control his passion.

She lowered her gaze to his sensuous lips.

"Don't look at me like that," he cautioned in a distressed voice. "You tempt me beyond reason."

"I can't seem to help myself," she admitted, knowing she should put a stop to this. But an unleashed mystery aroused her curiosity. So, this was what intimacy felt like.

She caressed his neck and shoulders. He sighed before crushing her to him. This time his kiss was more feral, more potent. But he caught himself and wrenched his lips away. "Amelia, I have to stop."

She didn't know what to say. Guilt warred with the new sensations she experienced. Yet she kissed him again, anyway.

It released the passion he had been fighting to keep in check.

Their deep kiss pushed her into a sensuous dance that set her heart racing. She knew she must stop but didn't know how. His hand roved down to her breast, and it made her tense.

How had she led him to this? Such yearning in his voice stunned her as she searched his face, trying to understand how she allowed this to happen.

He looked down her gown's bodice to her breasts that rose and fell beneath his hand. His tense expression warned her he fought an inner battle to stop or succumb.

Motionless beneath the muscular hand against her, Amelia gazed into his eyes, unafraid to let him see her desire. A moment passed. Then she pressed her hands against the nape of his neck and turned her body willingly into his.

He reacted as if she set him on fire and kept his gaze steady on hers.

She held her breath and didn't move, but her hesitation vanished as Regan kissed her into a stupor. She buried her fingers in his hair.

Then he stopped, pulled his hand off her chest, and took a slow, agonized breath. "No Amelia, I need to stop."

All her passion vanished. In its place came shame. How could she, an unmarried Christian woman, have allowed this? "I should go," she muttered as she pushed herself up from the settee.

Her body quivered as she turned to rush to the door, but he seized her arm and stopped her.

"Don't be upset. We're going to marry soon…"

Shame and distress exploded inside her. She pulled free from his clasp and spun around to face him. "I'm at fault too." How could she have been so weak? Regret like slow waves on a beach washed over her. She should never have let this happen. She wasn't ready, but there was no way back.

"We should wait until we're married." His tone echoed with regret.

"Yes, we should. I'm sorry." Amelia turned away and left him.

After preparing herself for bed, to distract her thoughts from the intimacy that just happened between her and Regan, she read more of Catherine's diary.

> *No one recovers from the loss of a beloved child. I am no exception. Afraid my mother's curse had come true, I could not gather the strength needed to live again. Were it not for Daniel's love and patience, I doubt I would have survived. But in time, my despair lifted. My spirit, long buried in grief, slowly healed, and I felt restored once more.*
>
> *Then great joy followed. I was with child again. With a hopeful heart, I nurtured the forthcoming baby with nutritious food and sleep. As the months passed and my belly grew, I discovered a semblance of peace.*
>
> *On a cool, rainy day, a messenger arrived*

with a note from my father. My mother lay dying and wanted to speak with me. If I could, I should come immediately.

I could. But did I want to? What did she want to say to me from her deathbed? A small glimmer of hope arose inside me. Perhaps she wanted to clear her conscience and ask for my forgiveness. Of course, she did, for the dying sought peace. I paced in the hallway, unsure of what to do. It was morning and Daniel was at work. My first instinct was to refuse. Why should I give her the peace she had denied me? And what of my own fragile serenity? Only her words could grant me the ability to put our animosity behind me. My charitable and dutiful heart convinced me to go. I ordered my maid to prepare a small trunk and pack enough for me to be away for several days, then ordered the carriage brought around. By mid-afternoon, I arrived at my familial home.

I hurried up the staircase and down the hall to my mother's bedroom. I stopped and stood silently by the open door, peering inside. My mother lay on pillows of silk and lace, her hair in two long braids over her chest. Her eyes were closed, and her breaths shallow. My father sat in a chair at the side of the bed with Julia, my mother's maid, at the other.

Sensing my presence, my father looked up and saw me, his expression half-relieved, half-pleased. He beckoned me to enter. I stopped at the foot of Mother's bed and looked down at her.

"The doctor...?" I asked.

My father shook his head. "He has been and gone. There is nothing more he can do for her. When she heard the news, she asked me to send for you."

Our voices must have roused her, for she opened her eyes.

"Mother, I came as soon as I heard."

Her eyes narrowed as she studied me, then her glance shifted to my growing belly.

"Mother, despite our differences, I love you. Let there not be bad feelings between us."

"You are with child again," she rasped after a hard breath.

"Yes, God willing. The child will be here by the end of summer."

She coughed harshly. Julia put a cup to her mouth to help her drink. When Mother settled back against the pillows, she heaved a sigh and stared at me. "All the days of my life, I resented you. You and your father stripped me of happiness."

My legs weakened but, but I stood straight in response as she spewed her vitriol. In my peripheral view, I saw my father stand. He came to my side, placed his arm around my shoulders, and tried to turn me toward the door.

But my mother's hatred seemed to have revived her. "I cursed you once and I'll curse you again. You don't deserve to have children. Look at what you did to me, to my life. You ruined it. You will have another daughter, and I hope she *will not live. And may you suffer for it."*

A sob escaped me as my father pulled me from the room. With his heel, he kicked the bedroom door shut, wrapped me firmly in his arms, and held me to his chest as I sobbed.

Chapter Fifteen

THE INTIMACY BETWEEN her and Regan replayed itself in her mind. How easily her body had betrayed her. Yet she couldn't deny she welcomed his touches. One moment she felt as if she was falling in love with him, and at other times, she was guarded. It was all so confusing.

Unable to sleep, she propped herself up on the pillows to read more of Catherine's diary. She opened the journal and flipped to the page last read. But after reading a paragraph, she found she couldn't concentrate. Regan remained fixed in her thoughts. She closed the diary and held it to her chest for a moment. Heaving a sigh, she set the book on the night table, snuffed out the candle, and plumped up her pillows.

She lay on her back and stared up at the ceiling. It was clear Regan had loved his mother very much, as she had loved him. To protect her son from his grandmother's cruelty, Catherine would have avoided contact with her mother. Amelia suspected that was why he rarely mentioned his grandparents—he barely knew them.

Her thoughts shifted to Regan's past, to the fiancée he had lost at sea. To have fallen in love and proposed marriage, only to watch her die in such a tragic manner, must also have left deep scars.

And then there was the Simpson's missing daughter, Annie. As master of Edenstone, Regan was responsible for his family and servants. All his efforts to find her failed. And the mystery cast a lingering pall over Edenstone—a house of secrets smothered with the stench of tragedy. No wonder few people came to visit. For Regan's sake, Amelia wanted to uncover the truth about what happened. Regan had offered her so much. He had been a stalwart support in her darkest days, and she wanted to do something for him in return.

Gradually, she fell into a restless sleep, tormented by one nightmare after another. In disturbing flashes, she heard woeful cries from the little girls from their graves, her father's warnings of black petals, and the auburn-haired girl weeping at her feet. Visions of drowning in a field of black flowers and voices that beckoned her to unknown places plagued her until they merged into one horrible reverie. Images so upsetting, so chilling, Amelia jerked awake in a cold sweat.

Her racing heart pounded as she shifted from one side of the bed to the other, the sheets tumbled around her in an untidy tangle. What did all the horrible images mean?

Unable to fall back asleep, Amelia lit the solitary candle in its brass holder, slid her feet into slippers, and her arms into her robe. With candle holder in hand, she made her way quietly down the stairs to the library.

The door creaked when she pushed it open and entered the room. She raised the candle to shed light on each shelf so she could read the spines. On a lower shelf, she noticed a book entitled *Species Plantarum* by Carl

Linnaeus, and pulled it out, hoping the large, heavy volume might contain at least a mention of black flowers. She set it on the reading table, then finished searching the remaining shelves. Finding no other book related to horticulture, she hefted the tome and carried it back to her room, intent on reading it in the morning.

Her restlessness continued until dawn's first rays broke through a gap between her bedroom curtains. She finally gave up trying to sleep and waited for Sarah to arrive and help her dress.

Afterwards, she went downstairs for breakfast, carrying the volume in her arms. The aroma of freshly toasted bread and ham filled the hall as she made her way to the dining room. She paused in the doorway. It was too early for Aunt Beatrice or Clara to be awake, but Regan, always an early riser up at dawn, sat at the table, his breakfast of eggs, ham, and toast nearly finished.

Amelia hesitated. She could not help but admire his interesting presence, the confident set of his shoulders, totally engrossed by whatever he was reading in the newspaper next to his plate. Light streaming in from the windows behind him brought out the shine of his ebony hair. He sighed at something he read, flipped the page, and then raised a cup to his mouth and sipped. Only when he glanced away from the paper to replace the cup on its saucer, did he notice her.

Heat burned Amelia's cheeks at the memory of the intimacy between them last night. What had possessed her to let him touch and kiss her so freely? When it came to men, she admitted she was naïve, unused to such closeness, but she could not say the same about Regan. He had kissed and touched her with easy confidence. He had drawn her into a height of passion she had never experienced before, and she eagerly returned his affection without restraint.

Regan riveted his gaze on her face before letting it roam over her body. He seemed unabashed and unaffected and gave her an irresistible, devastating smile. He rose to pull out her chair as if there was nothing to feel awkward about.

"Good morning. What a pleasant surprise. I didn't expect to see you this early." He sat down. "I'm glad you're here." He looked at Amelia with interest, without hesitation or worry, while she felt herself blushing like a young girl instead.

She set down the book and rested her hands on her lap. "To tell you the truth, I didn't sleep very well last night."

The smile on his lips faded and the intensity of his gaze held her still. "About last night, if I caused—"

Amelia stopped him with her raised hand. A suffocating tension lodged in her throat. "No, please, it's not that. I enjoyed your company." Instantly, she regretted her choice of words. Had she just inadvertently admitted that she had enjoyed last night's intimacy? Of course, she had. Now he must think her utterly shameless. A woman too eager for the fire he had ignited within her. "No, that's not what I meant to say. What I mean is that we should wait until we marry."

He tilted his head and said, "I agree and regret if my advances offended you. I know better and should have shown more restraint. From now on, I promise to keep a respectful distance." A muscle quivered at his jaw as his face turned a little too serious. "Besides, what would the servants think if they had walked in on us?"

The thought shattered her, leaving her incapable of uttering a word.

And then his lips curved into a slow, charismatic smile and his eyes glimmered with a teasing merriment. He placed his hand over his heart, then tossed back his head and let out a peal of laughter.

Amelia couldn't help herself and broke out into a laugh of her own. Their mirth exploded, blissful and whole-hearted. Any tension between them vanished.

"You're far too serious sometimes, Amelia. But I understand and swear on my honor to be good from now on. A gentleman, I assure you."

She reached for the teapot and filled her cup, doing her best to avoid the steady heat of his scrutiny.

Regan passed her the milk and sugar.

"Thank you, but I think I'll take my tea black this morning." She sipped, then set her cup down.

"And I thought you liked your tea sweet, just like I am." His eyes twinkled in merriment as he brought his own cup to his lips to drink. When he set it back down, he said, "I look forward to learning more of these lovely little details about you." A muscle twitched involuntarily at the corner of his lips.

Amelia tried to adopt a serious air. She hoped he couldn't hear her pounding heart.

His gaze darted to the book she had set down next to her plate. "I didn't know you are interested in horticulture."

"There's much you don't know about me," Amelia replied, relieved to talk about something other than last night.

He smiled as he reached for another slice of toast. "I'm very intrigued. Please, tell me more."

She tried to look serious, but her smile refused to comply. She fully enjoyed this new joviality between them.

Several moments of silence passed as she nibbled her toast. Her lack of sleep brought on a yawn and she politely raised her hand to her mouth to suppress it.

"So, it *is* true. You *are* tired."

"Yes, I already admitted I didn't sleep at all last night."

"Were you not feeling well? Is it your room or your bed? I can have them changed today if need be."

"My sleeplessness wasn't because of ill health or discomfort. Terrible dreams kept me up and I can't make any sense of them."

He leaned forward. "Talking about them might help." He covered her hand with his. "I've been told I'm good at listening and there's plenty of time before I have to leave for work."

Amelia rested her back against the chair and sighed. Would he think her foolish? Even more worrisome, would he believe her when she told him she had seen her dead father and Annie? She chanced it.

He listened intently as she told him about the dreams of her father and his warnings about black flowers, of the weeping that came from the attic that led to the discovery of his mother's diary, and his grandmother's curse. The only thing she didn't bring up was any mention of the auburn-haired girl because things hadn't gone well when she had commented on it the first time.

He listened carefully to it all, without interruption. When she mentioned the curse, his expression didn't change. This confirmed he was aware of it.

153

His gaze darted to the book. "Black flowers, you say? How odd. I've never heard of them before. So that's why you're carrying around that heavy book."

"I hope it will list a few such species. There must be some reason Father keeps warning me about black petals."

"If they exist, I'm sure you'll find them in that book. It's one of the most comprehensive ever written. I am intrigued. Let's leaf through it together."

He moved to the chair next to her and they studied each page. Written in 1753, the book was old, its pages stiff and dusty.

Time became lost to them as they thumbed past each page. About two-thirds of the way through, they stopped at a drawing of a black flower.

"I think this might be it, Regan." She read the caption below it. "Helleborus. It says the plant bears black to black-purple flowers that bloom in early spring and last for six weeks. Its seeds grow in pods that appear once the blossoms are spent."

Regan marked the page with his finger and flipped through to the end. "It's the only reference to a black flower in the entire book." He put it down, keeping it open at the page. "What I can't understand, is why your father is warning you about them. They look harmless enough to me."

"I wish I knew. It makes no sense."

"This book only gives us the most basic information about this plant. We need to learn more." He scratched his head. "I'll make some inquiries in town."

"So, you believe me when I say my father's spirit came to me?"

"There's much in the world that is unexplainable. Who

am I to judge? If you say your father appeared to you, then yes, I believe it."

Surprised, Amelia sagged in her chair. He believed her. That's all that mattered. She could face anything knowing she had his support. Amelia leaned over to embrace him.

His response was immediate. He wrapped his arms around her and kissed her lips. In the light of day, his touch lacked the fiery passion of last night, but it was warm and loving and reassured her. She could feel her heart opening even more to this intriguing man.

FROM THE BALCONY, Amelia watched Regan leave the house and walk down the front stairs. He paused outside his carriage to look up at her. With a grin and a tip of his hat, he climbed inside. The driver snapped the reins. The carriage drove down the stretch of road towards the gates.

Amelia yawned again. The morning sun shone brightly, illuminating the dew glistening on the grass. The estate looked majestic, alluring. A long morning walk followed by an afternoon nap would invigorate her.

She went back inside, fetched her shawl, then set out. The sound of her shoes crunching over the gravel on the path soothed her, and she delighted in the fresh morning fragrance of wildflowers and damp soil. She listened to a bird trill from a nearby tree. As she resumed her walk, a white-winged butterfly flitted past. With a pleasurable sigh and a smile, Amelia followed her intuition and headed for the graveyard, a place of tranquility where she could reflect on her dreams and what they meant.

The iron gates squealed when she pushed them open. She strolled over to a stone bench that sat between two large trees near the stone wall. Rows of tombstones stood erect. What truths lay buried with them? She contemplated the meaning of life and the permanence of death. Those souls lay dead in their graves while her feet rested on green wands of grass. She could not help but feel grateful at the promise of the rich life ahead of her.

Amelia closed her eyes and inhaled deeply. She found peace sitting alone in the graveyard. Perhaps the tranquility here could help her solve the puzzles of Edenstone.

A strong wind arose, rustling the leaves and causing the long grass at her feet to undulate. At first, there was nothing more than a chill in the air. Then a glittering mist formed into a pearly-white translucence that transformed into the shape of a woman. Her breath hitched in her throat.

The auburn-haired girl stood before her dressed in a white, flowing gown. Her hair and dress swirled and danced about in the wind. She stood so close Amelia could touch her.

"Annie," Amelia whispered.

The girl's haunted eyes blinked in acknowledgement. Her expressionless face saddened, and she wept. "Help me," she moaned in a rasping voice. Her soulless eyes overflowed with tears. She reached out her hand and beckoned to Amelia before she turned and hastened away. Her gown billowed behind her as she ran between the rows of graves towards a portion of wall covered with brambles. There she came to a stop.

Amelia hesitated, unsure of what to do. There was nothing there other than bushes. She waited, but the girl stood utterly still. Amelia took a tentative step forward. The girl beckoned her closer.

With long, bony white fingers, the girl pointed at the overgrowth, which revealed a small door in the wall. Then she turned to face Amelia. Slowly, her mouth opened in a soundless, petrifying scream. A white mist swirled and surrounded her. It spun around her form until it stopped, and she vanished.

"Wait. Annie. Don't go," Amelia called out, her body trembling.

A long, drawn out silence ensued. When her heart stopped pounding, Amelia took a cautious step forward to look through the arched wooden door. On the other side, she spotted an old well. Worn and crumbling, its decay a marker of time long ago. At its foot grew a small patch of dark flowers. Amelia passed through the doorway and went to the well. She studied the black flowers—all nearly depleted of life. They resembled the ones in the book, innocuous, and oddly pretty. A few spent blooms revealed seedpods. Most of the petals had shriveled, but the ones that clung to life looked supple. Her father's warning had been clear that the flowers were black, but these weren't. Clearly, they were an inky purple. She doubted these were the ones he warned her about.

As she kneeled for a closer look, her heel caught in the hem of her gown and she lost her balance. She fell forward, her face and hands striking the flowers. An herbal scent with faint rose and peony overtones filled her nostrils. A pod toppled onto her, and seeds and sap spilled onto her skin. Her fingers tingled and the skin on her face burned. The world spun as she struggled to stand. Numbing sensations spread to her wrists. Horrified, she watched as her flesh turned red, then purple, then throbbed and itched. The burning was unbearable. Nausea threatened as she struggled for breath. Her heart raced and vision blurred. Terrified, she rose and stumbled back through the door and into the graveyard.

Her legs could barely carry her, but she ran gasping and moaning toward the house. When she reached the foot of the stairs at the front entrance, she tried to scream but could not gather enough breath. Staggering towards the first few steps, Amelia fell to the ground. The world spiraled around her, and then it turned black.

Chapter Sixteen

BURNING PAIN AND an unappeasable itch drew Amelia out of unconsciousness. Gradually, the familiarity of her bedroom came into focus.

A silver-haired man peered down at her. Although he smiled, she saw the concern on his puckered brow and in his troubled eyes. "It's good you've come to. I'm Doctor Morris. You gave us quite a scare, young lady." His rich baritone voice sounded confident, practiced.

Behind him, Amelia noticed Regan pacing like a caged animal. When he noticed she was awake, he turned and studied her before coming to her bedside with a strained expression, hands clutched at his sides.

A fiery burn ran from Amelia's wrists to her fingers. "My hands." She grimaced at the sight of her inflamed digits, but failed to lift them.

"They found you unconscious at the bottom of the stairs leading to the house. Can you tell us what happened?" Dr. Morris dipped a cloth into a basin of water and gently applied it to her irritated cheek. She winced at the sudden sting.

Her gaze flitted from the doctor to Regan and back

again. "I found a patch of dark purple flowers growing next to an abandoned well behind a door in the graveyard wall."

"Dark purple or black?" Regan asked.

"From a distance, they looked black, but when I came closer, they were an inky purple." She struggled to speak through her muddled thoughts.

"You touched them?" the doctor asked.

"Yes, I picked a bloom to examine it, inhale its fragrance to see if it was like the one listed in the botanical book. I would not have done that had they been purely black. These looked harmless, half dead…" She had made a mistake and should not have touched them at all. Her father had warned her in her dreams.

The doctor stroked his chin. "The flower might have caused your rashes, but I would need to see one to be certain."

"I'll send someone to fetch one." Regan stepped into the hallway and called out for Simpson, who responded from the bottom of the stairs. He gave his order, then came back into the room. "Simpson has agreed to go, and I've warned him to wear gloves. It shouldn't take long."

The doctor reached into his satchel and removed a yellow tin jar with red lettering on it. He unscrewed the lid, dipped his finger into the white salve, and held his hand above Amelia's cheek. "Allow me to spread some of this over your face and hands. It'll soothe and should relieve much of the discomfort you're experiencing."

Grateful, she nodded.

He dabbed some gently onto her skin. She grimaced at first, but soon the balm calmed the irritation. The aroma was pleasant, a combination of beeswax, olive oil, and sassafras. When he finished applying it to her face, he rubbed some onto her hands and wrists before wrapping them with linen strips. He worked efficiently while Regan watched in silence. When finished, the doctor appraised his handiwork with a look of satisfaction.

"Will I have scars?" Amelia asked.

"You need not worry. All should return to normal as the inflammation heals."

Simpson appeared in the doorway, holding a folded burlap cloth in his gloved hands. "Here's the flower you asked me to find. It was exactly where you said it would be."

The doctor stood. "I have no gloves with me. Would you mind laying it out on the desk and removing it from the cloth for me to examine?"

Simpson carefully unfolded the wrapping while Regan and the doctor watched, their heads and necks craned over the table for a close look.

The physician gingerly raised a corner of the cloth, tilting the flower for Amelia to see. "Is this the flower, Miss Belleville?" the physician asked.

No longer in bright sunlight, the flower now appeared blacker, its purple hues hard to discern. "Yes... that's it."

Dr. Morris reached into his satchel once more and retrieved an enormous set of tweezers with which he picked up the flower and held it up for closer scrutiny. "I'm not familiar with this plant, but with your permission, I'll take the sample with me for research."

"It's called Helleborus. At least that's how the botanical book labeled them."

"We appreciate anything you can tell us, Dr. Morris," Regan said.

"In the meantime, I recommend you seal the cemetery door or get rid of the flowers, throw them in the fire pit to keep anyone else from coming into contact with them; at least until we understand what we are facing." With great care, the doctor folded the cloth around flower and tucked it into his satchel. He pulled out a small dark glass bottle and set it on the nightstand. "I'll leave you with a little laudanum to help ease any discomfort and to help you sleep, but only take a teaspoon if you truly think you need it."

"I understand, thank you," Amelia said, fully aware of the addicting qualities of the mixture.

"When I return to check on you, I hope to have something to report to shed some light on this mystery." With a tip of the brim of his black bowler hat, the doctor left the room.

Regan stroked his chin, his pensive eyes never leaving hers as he took the seat next to her bed. From the hallway downstairs, the grandfather clock chimed time. Outside, seagulls cried as they winged past the house.

He leaned forward and rested his elbows on his knees, the fingers of both hands entwined. His crumpled brow and tense, tight lips exposed his concern. "When I left for work this morning, you were a vision on the balcony, waving to me as I rode away, sunlight playing on your hair, your dress fluttering around you. Only an hour later, Simpson found you unconscious on the ground outside the front door. What happened? How did you discover the door in the graveyard? I've lived here my entire life and was unaware of its existence."

She glanced behind him at the window where white clouds floated against a light blue sky. Would he trust her if she told him it was Annie's ghost who showed her the hidden door? He had assured her this morning he did not discount the possibility of such things.

Amelia swallowed and returned his gaze. "I walked to the graveyard. While I sat on the bench against the wall near the entrance, a gust of wind rose and the auburn-haired girl, Annie, appeared."

He remained expressionless, intent on her every word.

"She led me to a spot in the wall and shoved aside some overgrown brambles and bushes. Behind them was an old, rickety door. Then she vanished as quickly and as silently as she appeared."

Regan looked down at his hands and cracked his knuckles.

Disappointment clogged her throat. "You don't believe me."

"I didn't say that, but you must admit, it's hard to accept ghosts as true, especially when we have no proof Annie is dead."

Amelia tensed. "I am certain she is dead. It was Annie... or Annie's spirit. Then she disappeared. I looked around, but there was no trace of her."

"What did you do next?"

"I opened the door and saw an old stone well surrounded by trees and bushes. A patch of dark purple and black flowers grew between the stones at its base. Like the ones Father warned me about. So, I picked one and raised it to my nose. I became so ill; I was convinced I was going to die." Her voice trembled.

Regan reached out to stroke her hair. "Hush, Amelia, don't fret. It terrified me we were going to lose you, but the doctor assures me you'll make a full recovery. Promise me you'll touch no unfamiliar plants again."

She nodded.

"And if you ever decide to go exploring again, take someone with you."

"I promise." In response to his kind words, and still overwhelmed by her trial, a tear slid from her eye. Another followed, and then another, until a steady stream of tears ran down her cheeks. Regan had become the light from the sun, his eyes and arms and heart open to her. His presence gave her a sense of safeness.

As if he read her thoughts, he leaned down and carefully kissed her forehead. "You need to rest. Try to nap. It will do you good."

As he was about to stand, Amelia raised a hand to stop him. "Please don't leave me."

He smiled warmly. "I'll be here when you wake up. Would you like a drink of water?"

"Yes, please."

He reached for the glass of water on the nightstand and helped her take a sip. He drew the curtains and leaned back in the chair.

She needed strong, steady Regan to hold on to. Her only thoughts were about him as she drifted off to sleep.

AMELIA'S ARMS THROBBED. The pain dominated her unconscious thoughts and pulled her from blessed sleep. For a few seconds, she remained confused, unsure of why her face and hands hurt so much. Then she remembered, and her eyes sprang open.

The sun's rays lay long across the floral handwoven

wool rug in the room.

Regan was still at her bedside, watching her from the wing chair he sat in. With a frown, he leaned forward. "How do you feel?"

"So much pain… thirsty." Her parched throat made talking an effort.

He reached for the cup of water on the nightstand and placed it to her lips. Savoring each drop, she drained the glass.

"What time is it?" she asked as he returned the glass to the nightstand.

He pulled out his gold watch and stared at it. "It's almost two o'clock. Are you hungry? Mrs. Simpson has been in the kitchen all morning cooking for you."

Amelia raised her bandaged hands. "She shouldn't bother. I doubt I can hold a spoon."

"Food is her way of solving the world's problems. You gave her a scare. It's how she copes."

"Then I promise to do my best to eat. She is a kind woman. You are lucky to have her working for you."

A sound caught their attention. Clara and Aunt Beatrice stood in the doorway. They must have overheard them speaking because Aunt Beatrice said, "There will be no shortage of people in this house who will help you eat, my dear Alma." She then swept into the room with a rustle of her gray cotton and lace overskirt.

"Her name is Amelia," Clara corrected as she followed her mother inside.

Aunt Beatrice frowned. With a wave of her hand, she hushed Clara.

Regan gave up his seat to his aunt who sat then smoothed a crease in her gown before looking Amelia over. "Oh dear, what a terrible rash. Is it painful?"

"Yes, very."

From her pocket Aunt Beatrice removed a small jar and set it on the nightstand. "Some aloe juice for you, Alicia. Rub a little on your wounds to encourage healing."

"How kind of you," Amelia said.

Aunt Beatrice leaned back in her chair, looking pleased.

Simpson appeared in the doorway and announced Dr. Morris, who stepped into the room, bowler hat in one hand, satchel in the other. He put them on the writing table next to the window before shaking Regan's hand and greeting Clara and Aunt Beatrice.

"How is my patient?" He smiled as he made his way to Amelia's bedside.

"A little better, but my skin still burns."

"I'm not surprised. It will take a few days, but you'll find those nasty symptoms will gradually fade and you'll feel better soon."

"Have you learned anything about the flower?" Regan asked.

Dr. Morris inhaled a deep breath as he laid his hand lightly on Amelia's shoulder. "The news isn't good. The flower you touched is Helleborus Niger. That's its Latin name. It's more commonly called Black Hellebore. The plant is very poisonous."

Amelia's breath hitched in her throat.

Aunt Beatrice gasped.

Clara raised her hand to her mouth and shifted uncomfortably where she stood.

"Poisonous." Regan repeated the word as if he doubted its veracity and needed to be certain.

"Yes. The ancients used black hellebore to treat many illnesses including insanity, melancholy, gout, and epilepsy. They also used it to kill. But my news is far worse. The flower I had tested is a rare hybrid of some sort, specifically bred to be more lethal than the normal species. You may thank God that you merely touched the plant and didn't ingest it. Had you done so, even a small amount would have resulted in a stupor, difficulty breathing, a swelling of the tongue and throat. Your heart would have slowed until it stopped altogether."

She might have died. At the knowledge, a rush of blood pumped through her body. A ringing scream vibrated in her ears and her heart thumped against her chest.

Aunt Beatrice moaned. Her breaths became rapid and shallow, her eyes distant. She stood and fanned her face with her hand. "Oh, dear, no. It can't be. Not again."

"What do you mean, Aunt Beatrice? Are you aware of these flowers? Was someone else harmed by them?" Amelia asked.

Clara swept to her mother's side and placed an arm around her. "Hush, Mother, please, calm yourself. There is nothing for you to worry about. Amelia will recover, won't she, Dr. Morris?"

"I assure you that Miss Belleville will make a full recovery."

"See, Mother, there is nothing for you to worry about. Let me take you back to your room." Clara led Aunt Beatrice out, the poor woman muttering and shaking, clutching her chest as she went.

The doctor cleared his throat. "Black hellebore is not native to North America and does not grow wild. It is also difficult to grow because it thrives in rich, moist soil and does not like the full sun. Someone must have deliberately planted them there, and they thrived because of the shade from the well and the surrounding dampness."

Complete silence followed.

Regan stared out the window. Then he swung swiftly about. "Someone planted the poisonous flowers in that obscure, damp spot at the foot of an old well. And whoever the culprit is, planned to put the plant's nefarious properties to use. What I wish to comprehend is why."

"Yes, that is it exactly," Dr. Morris replied.

Fear engulfed her mind, knocking all other thoughts aside. Who was diabolic enough to do such a thing, and for what purpose? The only answer caused her to break into a sweat—to kill someone. How many years had the flowers been there?

Regan stroked his chin. "For what purpose?"

Amelia's own thoughts raced. Why had Annie led her to them? What did she want her to understand? Even more concerning was that Aunt Beatrice seemed aware of the flowers too.

Chapter Seventeen

LONG AFTER EVERYONE retired for the night, Amelia lay awake, unable to sleep. Dr. Morris's sinister revelations about the black flowers haunted her thoughts. Her hands and cheeks continued to burn and itch. The balm reduced the discomfort, but she didn't want to take any more laudanum. Although it would help her sleep, she couldn't risk becoming dependent on it. Besides, she needed all her wits about her to decipher all the mysteries surrounding Annie's appearances.

By the light of the solitary candle, she pulled open the top drawer of her night table and retrieved Catherine's diary hidden at the back. With the heels of her bandaged hands, she opened the book to the page she had last read.

The Lord saw fit to give me another child, an angelic daughter we named Isabelle. Where there was sorrow, she brought joy. In her, I placed all my hopes and dreams. Out of fear, like a lioness protecting her cub, I watched my child, never letting her out of my sight. In the dead of night, when she woke, I fed and rocked her, soothing her with lullabies while I stroked her tiny back and soft hair. Wherever I went, she came with me. Into her ears I whispered the sweetest words. Onto her cheeks I placed my gentlest kisses. My love for Isabelle was mightier than the wind. My arms grew strong because I carried her everywhere. Each night I slept on a small bed next to her cot. It was the only way to keep my baby safe.

But it was not to be. Influenza spread through the world, leaving no country or city untouched, striking down the old, the infirm, and the very young. Under a light cotton sheet, Isabelle radiated heat like a brick from the fire. So diminished was her appetite, when coaxed, she only accepted a spoonful of milk or soup. Despite the constant fire burning in the hearth, her cough worsened, and she barked and wheezed with nearly every breath she took. I yearned for her to get well, to get up and play, but she did not improve.

The doctor came. He examined her and said he could do nothing more for her. God held her life in His hands.

Dark shadows stalked my family again—the angel of death was near. I watched helplessly as the illness progressed, a gruesome countdown drawing death ever closer, something I could not stop. The chill of its icy breath raised the hairs on the back of my neck.

Isabelle died in my arms as dawn heralded a new day. An infinite darkness swallowed me, robbing me of my senses, paralyzing me. It was a choking, smothering darkness that left me bereft, hollow, and wanting. The blackness strangled and squeezed the life from me and tormented my memories. Why did God persist in taking my children? In the aftermath of Isabelle's death, my life lost all purpose. Deep, penetrating blackness pierced my soul. My only wish was for God to take me too.

As the days passed, strange voices stole into my mind, offering me perilous notions and suggestions I once would have considered bizarre. But now they gave me hope. Ideas took root that I was helpless to control. The voices smothered who I once was until I become lost and unrecognizable, even to myself.

Guided only by the voices, I lived in a new reality, in an inescapable maze, a prison without walls. The voices compelled me to believe the evil that lurked in my mother's soul, and if I wanted a child who would not die, I must end the evil curse she had placed on me.

"To end the curse, you must take a life," the voices whispered, haunting me. No matter how hard I fought to ignore their wickedness, the voices proved too strong to overcome.

"A poisonous flower you must find," they urged.

On a gray blustery morning, I took the carriage into the city and entered the Boston Horticultural Hall on Tremont Street. I walked past the shops on the first floor and took the stairs to the second-floor library, which held the most comprehensive collection of horticultural works in the country. I pulled five books about poisonous plants from the shelves and spent the afternoon thumbing through the pages, reading.

Whenever I came to a certain page such as foxglove or hemlock, the voices disapproved and urged me to read on. Only when I came upon the page featuring black hellebore, were they satisfied. But it was not available in Boston, and I would have to order it through the mail from England. The librarian was suspicious, but I eased her mind by telling her I needed the Helleborus to show as a sample to my Ladies' Gardening Group. Guided by the librarian and various seed catalogues, I ordered a packet of seeds from an obscure vendor.

For a while, the voices grew silent, as if I had appeased them somehow.

The seeds arrived two months later. I planted them at the bottom of an abandoned well in a clearing a respectful distance from the house. All the while I waited for the black hellebore to grow, the voices in my mind continued relentlessly. They grew ever more insistent that I should find someone to poison. But who?

And then one night, Annie Simpson came to my bedchamber carrying a load of freshly laundered clothes. The voices told me this was the person whose life I must take.

The diary abruptly ended there. Heaving a frustrated sigh, Amelia closed the book and clutched it to her chest. Questions reeled through her mind. Did Catherine's story continue in another journal hidden somewhere? In her desperation to end the jinx, did she obey the taunting voices and kill young, naïve Annie? The thought was inconceivable, shocking even, and it sent Amelia's mind into a riotous tumult. She failed to comprehend or process the terrible images it invoked.

Her thoughts churned, filled with consoling words for Catherine who had endured such inconceivable loss. And, for her own father, who loved her so much that he came to her in death to warn her about the deadly black petals. Amelia's head swam at the assumption that madness forced Catherine to commit murder to end her torment. Her heart felt as if it pumped tar instead of blood. Catherine's melancholy hung over her like a black cloud.

She had touched the poisonous flowers, breathed them in, and it might have killed her.

A sudden chill raised the hair on her arms. An unexplainable dread spread throughout her body. She sensed a presence, as if someone were watching her, and glanced at the bedroom door. It was slightly ajar, yet she distinctly recalled that Sarah had shut it when she left the room earlier. In the opening, she saw a flash of movement followed by a shadow on the hallway carpet. And then it vanished. Amelia flung back the covers, ran to the door, and swung it open. The corridor stood empty, void of anyone or any sound.

Yet, she was certain someone had been watching her. Amelia secured the door, returned to bed, snuffed out the candle, and settled beneath the blankets. Blood pumped through her body. Her heart raced so fast she feared it might explode. She stared at the ceiling and let her thoughts wander. Who had been watching her, and why? Whoever it was had seen her reading the diary. But from the doorway, it would be impossible to know the diary belonged to Catherine.

She pondered the voices that drove Catherine to murder Annie. A more sinister concept entered her mind. What if there was another death imminent in the family? Or if the curse would follow to harm subsequent generations? She refused to accept this as a possibility. The knowledge that the curse might affect any daughters born to her and Regan was too terrible to contemplate.

Regan needed to know the truth, all of it, but first, she must find irrevocable proof. It would break his heart when he learned his mother was a murderess, so she must be certain of everything before she told him. To do that, she must search the attic once more because if another diary existed, it would likely be hidden there. But first, she'd have to wait for her hands to heal.

EACH MORNING AND night, Mrs. Simpson changed Amelia's bandages. The skin on her fingers had turned almost black. Hard and chitinous, they burned painfully. With each passing day, the dead skin peeled away to reveal fresh growth. Finally, to Amelia's relief, the day came when her hands no longer required bandages and they were removed for the last time.

Dr. Morris's salve proved true, and she healed. While incapacitated, she never stopped pondering Catherine and the voices. Her need to unravel the secret that dwelled in this house compelled her to keep diligent and search for answers.

Eager to leave her room, she donned gloves to protect her skin, then climbed the stairs to the attic. She searched Catherine's trunk, removing gowns, fans, books, shoes, and more until it was empty. She searched the sides and bottom for a hidden compartment but didn't find one. After repacking all the items, she repeated her task with the other trunks, wardrobes, drawers, and crates without success.

Fists on her hips, Amelia glanced around. If she were Catherine, where would she hide a diary possibly full of incrimination? The answer came to her easily—in her bedroom, of course. It made sense. If a diary existed, it would surely be there. With the ring of household keys in hand, she left the attic and its anteroom, then made her way back down to her own bedchamber that had once belonged to Catherine.

A swarm of reasons not to proceed flooded her mind, but her desire to learn the truth overpowered her misgivings. She stepped inside. Sarah had already made the bed. She began with the night tables and pulled out all the drawers. Tucked in the back of the bottom drawer of the first night table, the one she rarely used, she discovered a Bible and an exquisite silver chatelaine with a whistle, a folding buttonhook, coin purse, combination vinaigrette and perfume bottle, and a thimble. The bottom drawer in the other nightstand held only a white nightcap.

She fumbled through the entire wardrobe, the rear of the uppermost shelf, on the shoe rack, in the drawers below. She shoved aside the gowns to press her hand against the rear partition, hoping to find a secret compartment. Nothing. She ransacked the writing desk, pulling out drawers and reaching behind them. No diary or journal was found anywhere in the room.

She glanced around the room, hoping to find an area she might have missed. The portrait of Regan's mother hanging over the mantle beckoned to her. Regan had mentioned that he wanted the portrait moved prior to her arrival at Edenstone, and had asked Clara to replace it, but she had forgotten. Amelia had assured him she was fond of the painting and wanted it to remain. And he had consented to her wish. Now she studied this portrait with a more critical eye. Catherine wore a dark purple gown and appeared much older in this depiction than the one hanging in the drawing room. The artist had captured her expression of grief. Her feral, sharp eyes seemed touched with madness. A tremor ran up and down Amelia's spine.

She touched the hem of the painted gown and whispered, "What happened to you, Catherine? How far did you tumble into madness? Why didn't anyone notice your descent into darkness?"

Chapter Eighteen

AMELIA GAVE THE room one final regard, then huffed and flopped into a chair. There must be a second diary. Where would Catherine hide something that held her deepest secrets? She glanced at the floor. Of course. She had searched everywhere except beneath the floorboards. Might there be a hollow space beneath a loose wooden strip?

Beside the bed lay an Aubusson carpet with a floral pattern on a light blue background. She jumped out of her chair and took hold of one corner, then dragged it aside. None of the floorboards beneath it looked loose. She kneeled to scrutinize the floor beneath the bed, but all looked normal. Rising, she shoved aside furniture, tapping the wooden slats beneath each item with her foot, but all her efforts yielded nothing.

She wiped sweat from her forehead. If a second diary existed, it certainly was not in this room. Her need to learn the truth about Catherine and Annie Simpson gnawed at her. Convinced Annie had appeared to her because she wanted to tell her something, likely to name her murderer, compelled Amelia to uncover the truth.

Her only recourse was to speak with those who might know something—Regan, Aunt Beatrice, Clara. But she needed to be patient, seizing on perfect moments to speak to each of them and broach the subject carefully, otherwise they might feel threatened and wouldn't be forthcoming. Someone had to know something. She shuddered at the thought that someone in this house might be a killer.

On her way downstairs, she passed Aunt Beatrice's room. The sound of muffled, angry voices and sobbing brought her to a sudden stop. She stepped closer and craned her neck toward the door. It sounded as if Clara was arguing and Aunt Beatrice was crying. What in God's name was going on? Amelia raised her hand to knock, but the sound of a sharp slap stopped her.

"Stop it, Mother," Clara rasped.

Amelia tried the handle, but found the door locked. She knocked on the door. "Aunt Beatrice. Is everything all right? May I come in?"

Amelia heard Clara hush her mother, but after the briefest pause, the sobbing continued.

"My mother is fine," Clara responded in a false, buttery sweet voice. "She's having one of her spells. I'm merely trying to calm her."

"Then let me in. Perhaps I can be of help."

"There's nothing for you to worry about, Amelia," Clara said. "All is well here. Please leave us."

Clearly it was not. Amelia placed her ear against the door. It was no simple task to care for someone so elderly and with a demented mind. The poor old woman was clearly distraught about something. She needed to ensure Aunt Beatrice wasn't being maltreated. But how could she if Clara refused to let her enter? Mrs. Simpson had given her the keys to the house. If ever there was a time to use them, it was now. She didn't care if Clara became upset if she entered uninvited.

"Very well," Amelia said. "I'll be in my room. Let me know if you change your mind."

With deliberate, heavy footsteps, Amelia walked back to her room. Then with keys in hand, she tiptoed back and placed her ear against the door once more.

"I'm so afraid," Aunt Beatrice said. "Blood stains my hands. It's that red-haired girl. She's here. I can feel her. She's watching me, following me, and won't let me rest."

It sounded as if Aunt Beatrice had stopped weeping, yet she still carried plenty of distress in her voice.

"Hush, Mother. The red-haired girl is not here. It's your forgetful mind playing tricks on you."

"You don't understand. I can feel her everywhere I go in this house. She's here, I say. Why won't you believe me? You're heartless. Please, make her go away, Clara. Make her stop."

"I told you to stop thinking about her. Forget the past. You must never speak of it again, to anyone. Do you hear me?" Clara raised her voice even louder. "Stop crying. It's nothing more than your forgetfulness that makes you believe such nonsense."

Aunt Beatrice wailed.

"I said stop," Clara shouted. "I've had enough of your caterwauling, Mother. Do you hear me?"

Amelia envisioned Clara shaking Aunt Beatrice. Shocked by Clara's callousness, Amelia's heart broke for the dear old woman. She refused to stand idly by, and with hands shaking with outrage, she fumbled for the key to Aunt Beatrice's door and inserted it. As she was about to turn it, she heard Clara's voice soften and paused.

"You're over tired, that's all, Mother. Let me make you an herbal tea to help you sleep. Lay down. I'll be back shortly."

Fearing Clara would swing open the door and find her standing there, Amelia yanked out the key, lifted her skirts, and ran back to her room. There, hidden behind the door, she listened and waited for Clara's footsteps to fade as she descended the stairs. She rushed back to Aunt Beatrice's room and tried the door. It was open. She peered into the room. The drawn curtains kept the room dim. Nothing seemed disturbed or out of place. Aunt Beatrice lay in bed beneath the covers, her eyes closed, her breaths slowing to normalcy. To talk to her now would only upset her. The poor woman had suffered enough today. Besides, Clara might return any moment now, and Amelia didn't want to be caught in her mother's room after being told to leave them. It would do no good to make an enemy of Clara. She needed to keep the channels of communication open if she wanted to learn anything from her or uncover any family secrets. So, she quietly backed out and closed the door, and returned to her room.

Deep concern filled her mind, and it left her disturbed and even angry. Aunt Beatrice's words echoed in her mind. "Blood stains my hands. It's that red-haired girl. She's here. I can feel her. She's watching me, following me, and won't let me rest." It was a confession. Clouded by a demented mind, had Aunt Beatrice killed Annie, purposefully or by accident? She tried to dispel the preposterous thought but could not deny it was possible. Then an even more diabolical thought entered her mind. What if Clara had killed Annie, and then to keep from getting caught, had convinced Aunt Beatrice she had done it?

Aunt Beatrice's dementia was worse than anyone imagined. Clearly, it was more than Clara could handle. Her patience had worn thin with her mother's diminishing mind, and she was likely exhausted. That would explain why Clara had treated her mother so angrily and why Aunt Beatrice became so upset and confused. Clara was not the patient, loving person she appeared to be. Perhaps because tending to her mother's mental and physical deterioration overwhelmed her.

And how much did Regan know? An iciness settled in her stomach at the thought that he might very well be aware of all of it and was keeping silent to protect his family from suffering the consequences if the killer was discovered.

WHEN AMELIA ENTERED the dining room for dinner, she found Regan sitting in his place at the table alone. The corners of his mouth lifted into a smile that created slight dimples on his cheeks. He wore a burgundy jacket over a white shirt. Candlelight added sheen to his ebony hair.

When he rose to pull out her chair and she took her seat, she noticed only their two places had been set. Reaching for her napkin, she draped it over her lap. "Clara and Aunt Beatrice won't be joining us?"

"Unfortunately, not." Regan reached for the red wine and filled their glasses. "Apparently, Aunt Beatrice had some kind of fit earlier, so Clara decided it was best for them to dine alone upstairs."

To hide her suspicious expression, Amelia raised the wine glass to her lips and sipped the smooth, sweet liquid. She must choose her words carefully. "Do you know what upset her?"

"Not exactly, but I suspect it is her confusion over something or other. What else could it be? I fear that her disorientation and muddled thoughts are worsening with each passing day." Regan reached for the breadbasket and offered it to her.

She took a dinner roll and put it on her plate.

"The more her mind deteriorates, the more she becomes bewildered over everyday tasks." He sliced open his roll and spread butter on it. "Sometimes the smallest things set her off. Her decline has been difficult to watch. In her younger days, her mind was sharp, and she was full of humor and mischief. But ever since my mother died, her faculties are failing."

"It's to be expected, I suppose. They were twins after all, and twins have the strongest of bonds, so it must have been devastating for Aunt Beatrice." Devastating enough to lose her mind and commit murder? The idea warred with her observations about the sweet, old woman who had never exhibited even a shred of ill-temper or malice.

He offered her the butter, which she turned down with a slight shake of her head.

Mrs. Simpson entered with a soup tureen and set it on the table. When she lifted the lid, it released a rich aroma that stirred her appetite.

Amelia watched as she ladled the jade-colored soup into their bowls. "Thank you, Mrs. Simpson. It smells divine. Split pea soup is one of my favorites."

Mrs. Simpson puffed out her chest. "My mother's own recipe. If you don't mind me saying, I have yet to find another to compete with it."

"I can attest to that." Regan dipped a spoon into his bowl.

Her back and shoulders straight and head a little higher than when she entered the dining room, Mrs. Simpson left them to enjoy the meal.

Amelia didn't want to abandon their conversation about Aunt Beatrice. "This afternoon, when I walked past Aunt Beatrice's room, I heard her crying. Clara was scolding her. I heard a slap. When I tried to open the door, it was locked. I begged Clara to let me in to help, but she refused."

Regan's brows puckered. "You're certain it was a slap you heard?"

"Clear as a bell. It couldn't have been anything else." So, he was not aware of any troubles between the two.

Regan set down his spoon and frowned. "That worries me. Are you convinced it was Clara who slapped Aunt Beatrice and not the other way around? I've seen my aunt strike out at Clara before when she becomes overly frustrated."

"That's certainly a possibility, and I can't say for certain, but I am convinced that Clara was the one raising her voice and Aunt Beatrice was the one crying." She glanced out the window to the serenity of the grounds and then turned back to look at him. "Do you think it might be wise to hire some help? A nurse to help Clara care for her mother; to bathe and dress her?"

"I've made that same offer several times, but Clara always refuses. She loves her mother very much and does her best to take good care of her. I suspect her pride keeps her from accepting any outside help."

Amelia frowned. "Then I'll do my best to help whenever I can. I've become very fond of your aunt." Despite her earlier suspicions, Amelia experienced a strong feeling of protectiveness over Regan's aunt, born from her respect for the vulnerable and elderly. Any misgivings about Clara, she kept to herself.

A break in conversation followed and as they finished their soup, Mrs. Simpson returned to serve the main course, roast beef, peas, diced carrots, and potatoes. Amelia poured thick rich gravy onto her food.

"If the weather is good tomorrow, would you like to ride with me?" she asked as she picked up her knife.

Regan shook his head. "I'd love to, but I have to go into Boston tomorrow to place an ad in the Boston Post for a new bookkeeper. My current man, Percival Cawley, is frail and ill. He wishes to retire. My father employed him decades ago, and during all those years, he never missed a day of work. I'm sad to see him go. It won't be easy to replace someone who has such high standards of honesty and integrity."

Amelia put down her cutlery and leaned forward, her interest piqued. "Would you consider letting me help with the books? At least until you find a replacement."

He cocked his head and looked at her with interest.

"Because my father had no male heir," she continued, "he put all his hopes and aspirations into me. He spent years teaching me how to manage every aspect of his shoe factory; everything from purchasing the finest leathers to hiring the most talented cobblers. I also learned how to keep the books. To be honest, I loved it. I have a good head for numbers. It would please me if you let me manage the books until you hire someone." A vision of them working side by side flashed through her mind with great appeal.

He leaned back in his chair and stroked his chin. All the while, his contemplative gaze never left her. A slow grin spread over his face. "Amelia Belleville, you never cease to amaze me."

"I'll take that as a yes, and a compliment," she said as they raised their wine glasses and clinked them.

They shared a hearty laugh.

After dessert, Regan invited her to enjoy a brandy with him in the parlor. She sat on the settee before a blazing fire and watched him pour the drinks. He handed her one and then took his place beside her. She watched him take a long, slow sip while he gazed into the fire.

Firelight danced on his dark hair, while she admired his attractive profile with its well-defined chin and nose. *I want to love him, but every time my heart opens, something makes me doubt him.* She allowed these sentiments to rule her mind, fighting her desire to believe in him fully.

He turned an unwavering gaze to her. His eyes expressed wonder, curious, deep longing. He took a deep breath, rose to his feet, and pulled something out of his pocket, which he hid in his palm.

"I meant to do this on the night of our engagement party, but your father's death and the fates conspired against me. Since then, I've waited for the right moment to give it to you. Now is as good a time as any." He knelt before her. "Amelia Belleville. I love you as I've loved no other. You mean more to me than the sunshine and the air I breathe. I'm yours in mind, body, and soul and promise to protect you with my life, to comfort you in difficult and painful times, and dance and celebrate with you when times are good. I will never betray you, never give up on you." He took her hand and placed the item on her palm, closing her fingers around it.

Her heart swelled at the sweet words, yet a tiny voice in the back of her mind warned her to be cautious, preventing her from fully trusting what he said.

She opened her hand and stared at an exquisite sterling silver repousse box engraved with lovers on the lid, and its legs shaped like roses on leaves. She turned it over in her hands, letting her eyes roam freely over every elegant feature, stunned by its beauty.

"Go ahead, open it." He kept an expectant gaze on her.

With shaking hands, she raised the lid. On a bed of black velvet lay a magnificent sapphire ring set in white gold. Numerous diamonds surrounded the large stone at its center. The sight of the magnificent gem which sparkled in firelight, left her speechless, awestruck by its beauty.

He pressed his lips together as he continued to study her reaction. "Well? Do you like it?"

"Oh, Regan, of course I do. It's beautiful."

"It was my mother's ring. She once told me that sapphires are stones of wisdom and prophecy, said to protect and bring good fortune. They symbolize power and strength, but also kindness and wise judgment. She believed those were the qualities I should look for in a future wife." He reached over to remove the ring from the box and slid it onto her finger. "And I have found them in you."

His compelling eyes glowed with so much affection, tears welled up in hers. Every ounce of breath lay trapped in her lungs. It was as if the world stopped, leaving just the two of them wrapped in this precious moment. This was genuine love; a story she never wanted to end. For so long she had dreamed of it, and now it had come to her. She yearned to believe in him with an open heart, and must stop doubting him one minute, then succumbing to his affections the next.

He took her hand and raised her from the settee.

She allowed him to embrace her, and her tears dampened the shoulder of his dinner jacket.

"Am I correct in assuming you are happy?" He wiped away a tear and gazed down at her with smoldering eyes that glinted with delight.

"Your love has been kind in deeds and thoughtful actions. How could I not be happy to have found so good a man?" Guilt sat heavy on her chest, cutting deep, for every time she doubted him, his kind, loving actions dispelled those qualms. She needed to stop her foolish nonsense and believe in him and his intentions. Her father would not have betrothed her to him if it were otherwise.

He sat down next to her and they gazed at each other with longing; not a word spoken by either of them. Amelia lost herself in the warmth of his loving eyes. His lips touched hers, not innocently but full of heat and fire, passionate and demanding. They tasted like brandy as the world fell away. Time, wind, sun, and rain no longer existed.

His kiss deepened; slow and passionate, comforting in ways that words would never be. She ran her fingers down his spine, pulling him closer until there was no space left between her and his beating heart. With his body against hers, he kissed her neck, which made her legs so weak that she feared she might fall. She clung to him and he strengthened his hold. She wanted to pull away before she lost control, but couldn't do so.

"Amelia," he whispered slowly. "Not here, not like this. The time has to be right… a night in each other's arms neither of us will forget."

Her heart fluttered. He was right. She needed more time to build up her trust so that she would never again waver in her faith for him.

Chapter Nineteen

THE NEXT DAY, during lunch, Amelia kept glancing out of the dining-room windows at the darkening skies, hoping it wouldn't rain. Regan had coaxed Clara to go riding with Phillip Wakefield, so Amelia was free to question Aunt Beatrice.

Today was Saturday, so Regan didn't have to work. On such days, he spent his time in the stables mending harnesses, tending to the horses, even cleaning tack. She prayed the rain would hold off, but it looked as if the weather deteriorated. The ocean beyond looked rough with powerful waves crashing against the shore. A blustering wind blew through the trees, shaking branches and fluttering leaves. To keep the house warm, wood-fires blazed in all the principal rooms.

Finally, Regan pushed back his chair and stood. "Now that I've eaten, I hope you ladies won't mind if I leave to check on the horses," he said and bowed slightly.

"Oh, Regan, do you really have to go?" Aunt Beatrice pouted. "I've enjoyed having you and Camilla all to myself. You two never make a fuss over me like Clara does."

Regan came around the table to peck his aunt's lined

cheek. "Clara and I are going for a ride with friends, but I know you and *Amelia* will have much to talk about." He winked at Amelia as he emphasized her name. "After all, there is a wedding to plan."

"We'll have a lovely time, won't we, Aunt Beatrice?"

Regan kissed Amelia's cheek, smiled roguishly, and left.

"I hope so, my dear. With any luck, Clara won't return early and interrupt us. I've wanted to get to know you better, just you and I…" She clapped her wrinkled hands. "And now we finally have that opportunity." She leaned closer to Amelia. "Did I hear correctly? Did Regan mention a wedding? Oh, dear, I wonder who he could be marrying. Has he told you who the fortunate woman is?"

Amelia smiled and raised her left hand. "He has proposed to me, and I have accepted." Despite the dull day, the ring glittered and shone.

"Oh, my dear, that was my mother's ring. I always admired it, but when she died, it went to Catherine because she was first out of the womb. How did you come by it? I haven't seen it for a very long time."

"Regan gave it to me when he proposed marriage, and I'm very honored to wear it. I hope you approve."

She patted Amelia's ringed hand. "Of course, I approve." She glanced around the room. "Now, shall we find somewhere more comfortable to sit?"

Amelia helped her out of her chair, and, arm-in-arm, led her into the drawing room where the floor to ceiling windows let in more light. She settled Aunt Beatrice on the settee, sat next to her, and gazed into the crackling fire, enjoying the comforting aroma of the burning logs. A warm ambience settled over them. "I hope you're feeling much better."

Aunt Beatrice wrinkled her nose. "Better? I've not been ill. Whatever do you mean?"

"I heard you crying the other day, and it worried me a great deal. But Clara was with you and she assured me all was well."

The old lady dismissed her comment with a flick of her hand. "Nonsense, I haven't cried for years."

Amelia let out a small breath of exasperation. Questioning her and receiving proper answers from such a confused mind would not be easy.

Just then, Mrs. Simpson entered the room and rolled a tea cart to a stop in front of them. "I know you didn't ask for tea, but I just pulled these biscuits out of the oven and couldn't resist bringing you some while they're still warm." She smiled at Aunt Beatrice as she picked up the plate and offered it to them. "My sister gave me the recipe. She swears it is the original lost recipe from Black Joe's Tavern in Marblehead. Have you heard of it?"

Amelia shook her head and pushed aside a growing twinge of impatience. She had waited so long to question Aunt Beatrice; she wanted to make good use of their limited time together. But Mrs. Simpson's thoughtfulness deserved her gratitude, so she yielded graciously to the act of kindness.

"The tavern was near a frog pond. The biscuits became so popular; they became known as Joe Froggers."

Amelia took up a biscuit and examined it. "Such a strange name for them."

"Have a taste and tell me what you think," Mrs. Simpson urged.

Aunt Beatrice took a healthy bite while Amelia nibbled

at an edge. Almost instantly, rich flavors of butter, rum, ginger, and nutmeg tantalized her tastebuds. Firm on the outside with a soft chewy center, she could understand why these biscuits, if indeed made from the original recipe, were so popular.

"Delicious. These are truly the best Froggers you've ever made," Aunt Beatrice said as she and Mrs. Simpson both turned to Amelia, awaiting her verdict.

"I couldn't agree more."

Mrs. Simpson beamed. "I'm so pleased you like them. There's plenty more where these come from. Send for me if you want more. Enjoy your tea, I have another batch to put in the oven." With her head held high and a rustle of her skirts, she left the room.

Eager to begin their conversation and ask the many questions racing through her thoughts, Amelia said, "It's wonderful to see Mrs. Simpson in such good spirits. How tragic for her only daughter to have mysteriously disappeared."

Aunt Beatrice set down her biscuit, clasped her hands on her lap, and stared at them in silence.

"My greatest wish would be to find out exactly what happened to Annie so I can put her parent's minds at ease. I can't imagine how worried they must be."

Again, silence followed.

Eager to draw her answers out, Amelia asked, "Were you here the day she went missing? Do you remember anything that happened?"

"Annie Simpson is dead."

She sucked in a breath at hearing confirmation of what she had long suspected. "How do you know?"

"Because I see her. She comes to me in my dreams.

Sometimes at night, I awaken to see her standing at the foot of my bed."

"I see her too." Amelia paused. The knowledge that Aunt Beatrice had seen Annie's ghost, too, sent her mind reeling. "Do you know how she died?"

Calmly, with no signs of upset, Aunt Beatrice looked at her directly. In barely more than a whisper, she said, "We killed her."

Amelia's throat tightened. *We?* Her body tensed at the shock. "Who killed her?"

Aunt Beatrice shook her head.

Amelia expelled a pent-up breath and paused. Pressing too hard for information might cause distress, so she kept her approach as soft as possible. "Did you see it happen?"

Aunt Beatrice's age-marked hands tensed in her lap as she continued to stare down at them.

Amelia rephrased the question, hoping to coax an answer. "Can you tell me how you know for certain she is dead?"

Again, she refused to respond.

"Aunt Beatrice, if you know something, please tell me, or tell someone. At the very least, Regan should know. He left no stone unturned in his efforts to find out what happened. Mr. and Mrs. Simpson are suffering. Imagine not knowing what happened to their daughter. They need an answer to be at peace. If someone committed a crime, you must come forward."

Aunt Beatrice looked up at her with a tormented gaze. She wrung her hands and her face crumbled as she gnawed at her lower lip.

"Has someone told you not to speak out? Are you being threatened not to say anything? If so, I promise you that both Regan and I will protect you."

Aunt Beatrice's hands shook. Tension increased in her face and limbs; her eyes glazed with fear. Her breathing became more rapid, shallower, as if a hurricane churned inside her. She clutched her arms around herself and rocked faster and faster until she exploded into an incoherent babble, talking as if there was no time to say all that she wanted. "On the floor... alone... hurting..." Her words crowded together. Some were missing. Fragmented sentences jumped from one thing to another. "The tea... help her... you must help..." Fears tumbled out unchecked. In Aunt Beatrice's distress, Amelia could not make out one clear meaning and it scared her to see the poor woman so distraught.

"It's all right, Aunt Beatrice. Please take a deep breath. No one will hurt you. Try to tell me calmly what happened."

Aunt Beatrice's white-knuckled fingers grasped Amelia's arm. "Will it be safe? You must not talk about it."

"I promise, it's safe to tell me everything. All will be fine." To calm her, Amelia stroked her back. The woman's entire body trembled, yet Amelia's touch did little to soothe her.

"I can't keep the secret any longer. I must tell someone."

"That's very good, and I understand. You can tell me."

She pulled back from Amelia and opened her mouth to speak.

To reassure her, Amelia took hold of her shaking hands and gazed calmly and directly into her eyes. "Tell me what you know about Annie."

Her mouth clamped shut as she gave Amelia a wild,

wide-eyed stare. Her chin quivered, and she glanced at the window, as if the light would bolster her. Then the tears burst forth like water from a dam, spilling down her face. Raw anguish poured out from somewhere deep inside her soul.

Amelia pulled her into her arms as she sobbed.

After a lapse in crying, Aunt Beatrice pulled away, her lashes heavy with tears. Then she collapsed against her again. "It was so terrible."

"Whatever it is, release what bothers you."

Suddenly, Clara burst into the room, still dressed in her riding gear, crop clutched in her hand, her face crimson. "What is going on here? What have you done to upset my mother?"

Chapter Twenty

CLARA RUSHED TOWARD Amelia and glared at her with burning intensity. Her hands clenched at her sides, she exploded. "I'll ask you again. What did you do to upset her?"

Outdoors, dark clouds obscured the daylight and darkened the bedroom. A jagged bolt of white-hot lightening lit up the space. A short moment later, a boom of thunder split the air. The wind howled outside, and rain lashed against the windows.

"We were merely discussing Mrs. Simpson and her daughter, Annie."

"And you didn't think it might cause her distress? The situation has upset our entire household ever since it happened. My mother is frail. How dare you remind and discuss it with her?"

"On the contrary, I'm coming to her aid. Ever since I came to Edenstone, it's become obvious that something about Annie is bothering her."

Aunt Beatrice calmed down and wiped away her tears. "Audrey is kind and was only trying to help."

Clara's glare moved to Aunt Beatrice and then back to

Amelia. "If that were true, she wouldn't be crying like this." She strode to her mother's side and in a gentle voice, said, "Come, let me take you to your room. It's time for your nap. You'll feel much better afterward."

She reached for her mother's cane that rested against the chair and handed it to her, then took hold of Beatrice's arm and helped ease her up. She cast Amelia an icy glare, a warning she was not done with her yet, and then left the room.

Amelia steadied herself. *A Belleville never falters,* her father used to say. *You were born into a family of vigorous men and women. Full of iron, souls of steel, brave.* She rejected this small failure, determined to forge ahead, and discover the truth. The family could not heal without it.

Amelia wandered out into the hall and went up to her room. She needed time to think. Perplexed, her thoughts surged as she stared out the window, the view obscured by the rain running down the glass. A bolt of lightning lit the skies, followed by a crash of thunder. She turned away and sat on the tufted armchair.

Now, more than ever, she was convinced Aunt Beatrice knew what happened to Annie Simpson. And Clara knew something, too. Why else would she keep such a stringent watch on the poor old woman, never leaving her alone, and always preventing her from talking about it? A dark, sinister mystery lurked at Edenstone, diminishing any hope for happiness. She must speak with Aunt Beatrice alone, without interruption, and without upsetting her. The only time she could think of would be late at night when everyone was asleep, especially Clara. And it needed to be soon, this very night.

Restless, she went to the library to work on some

accounts to pass the time. As she descended the stairs, she came to a sudden stop midway on the landing. Clara sat on a chair near the bottom of the stairwell, arms crossed, mouth pinched tight, glaring at her every move through narrowed eyes.

Amelia raised her chin and resumed her descent.

Clara rose to meet her, fisted hands on her hips. "I want a word with you," she demanded in a brusque tone.

The sight of her annoyed Amelia. "And I have plenty of questions for you. Shall we go into the library?" Amelia led the way. "Please close the door. I don't want anyone to overhear us."

Like a volcano about to erupt, Clara slammed the door shut and leaned against it, her knuckles white from clenching her fists; her mouth pressed closed from an obvious effort to remain silent. Her posture exuded an acid-like hostility—smoldering, potent.

Amelia stood firm, unprovoked by Clara's display. Her arms folded; she locked her gaze on her opponent from across the room. "It has become abundantly clear to me that something serious is troubling your mother. I think we owe it to her to find out what it is so that we can set her mind at ease."

Clara's hard, staring eyes never blinked. Then she pushed herself away from the door and strode toward Amelia. "My mother is my concern, not yours."

Amelia brushed away a loose curl that had fallen over her eye and recrossed her arms.

Clara's eyes widened at the sight of the ring.

"But it is my concern, too," Amelia said firmly, before Clara could open her mouth to say something. "Regan and I will be married soon. Like it or not, I'm going to be a member of this family, and everything that happens here is my affair, too."

"Not when it applies to my mother," Clara challenged. "She is my concern, not yours."

Amelia walked around to the desk and sat. "If you truly cared for her, I think you'd be eager to learn what is upsetting her, so that you can bring her relief."

Clara placed both hands on the desk and leaned forward. "It is only in your presence that she becomes upset. You are the one causing her distress, not me. And I want you to stop pestering her."

Amelia refused to allow Clara's vitriolic tone and fiery eyes to intimidate her. "It's not pestering when it is clear something is burdening her. As her daughter, I think you should do everything you can to make sure she lives her last years in peace with nothing weighing heavily on her soul."

"There is nothing bothering my mother other than a failure of mind which occurs in old age."

"I disagree. She seems to forget things that happened recently, but her memory regarding the past is sometimes clear to her." Amelia softened her voice. "Clara, please, I beg you. I think she knows something about Annie's disappearance. Let's find out together if that's true, so we might help her. We can approach her as a family, with Regan. Ignoring the matter and doing nothing is not helping Aunt Beatrice. Don't you see that?"

Clara crossed over to the window and stared out at the rain, then after a few moments, she swung abruptly around. "No. I will not have her upset, especially not to ease your foolish unfounded suspicions." She took a menacing step toward the desk. "I will not ask you again.

Stay away from my mother," she threatened in a brazen, intimidating voice as menacing as a cobra seeking its prey.

Malice flickered in Clara's gaze, but Amelia did not flinch. It shattered all trust and confirmed something sinister was afoot, strengthening her resolve to learn the truth. "I will not ignore what has become so clear—your mother needs help."

Clara pushed her face so close; Amelia could smell the lavender scent she always wore. "You will or else…" she threatened in a voice that rose above the silence that normally thrived in the house. Suppressed rage colored her face scarlet.

Her every word fueled the fire that burned inside of Amelia. "Or else what?"

The air between them was so brittle it could snap.

A loud cough from behind them forced them apart. They both turned to look.

"Enough, Clara." Regan stood in the doorway, glaring at his cousin. "I could hear your voices from outside. What are you arguing about?"

Clara's eyes flashed at him with indigence and anger, like the lightning on this dark day.

"Ask your bride-to-be. She is the one at fault." She grabbed her skirts and stormed past Regan.

He watched her walk away in a huff, then strode toward Amelia, eyes aglow with concern the way her father's did when he was worried about her. He laid his hand lightly on her shoulder, the touch soothing. "It's worrying to come upon my cousin and my future bride having such a heated squabble. Let me guess, you were discussing my aunt?" He squeezed her shoulder and spoke in such a soft voice; his words immediately calmed her.

"Yes. Clara was supposed to be out with Phillip, so, I thought it would be an opportune time to find out why your aunt was crying the other night."

"And did you?"

Amelia shook her head. "She didn't remember a thing about it. But after Mrs. Simpson brought us tea, the subject of Annie came up. That's when she told me that Annie was killed and that her spirit also appears to her."

He stared at her open-mouthed, then slowly sat on one of the two chairs before the desk.

Amelia took the other and watched as he ran his fingers through his hair. His puzzled expression revealed his desire to flee from the conversation. To his credit, he did not lose patience with this never-ending topic of conversation. "Did she say how she knows Annie was killed?"

"I asked her several times. At first, she couldn't give me an answer. It was as if she was afraid to say anything. When I inquired if she was under some sort of threat not to speak about it, she refused to respond. I tried to coax it out of her, reassuring her, but then she became panicked and fearful. She blurted out an array of words, all mumbled, her thoughts so scrambled, I couldn't make sense of it."

"Not a word? Nothing that could lead us to an answer?"

"I did my best to soothe her, and when I did, she told me she had a secret she needed to tell me."

"And did she tell you?"

"She was about to, but that's when Clara came into the room. With one look at her mother's tearful expression, she became angry at me for upsetting her. She swept Aunt Beatrice away to her room and then confronted me. Nothing I said appeased her. That's the moment you came upon us."

Elbows on his knees, he stared down at his clenched hands. "So, Annie *was* killed. It confirms what I suspected was true, yet I've found no evidence to prove it."

"That's what she said. And she said it with such clarity, I knew she told the truth."

Regan inhaled a deep breath, then leaned back.

"What should we do?" Amelia asked after several long moments.

He frowned. "You know, I have a hard time believing in ghosts. Such talk has brought nothing but darkness and sorrow into this home. And I'm concerned you're being drawn into something that will lead to nothing. Annie's disappearance has been investigated not only by me, but by all the local authorities. Nothing was ever found to explain her disappearance. But if you are determined to find out what Clara and Beatrice might know about Annie's death, then we must get to the truth. However, Aunt Beatrice's memory is failing so fast these days, I'm not convinced we can believe anything she says."

"I agree, but whatever she can tell us, might lead to something. Knowing something is better than not knowing anything at all. We can investigate and verify what she tells us. And what about Clara? She won't let me near Aunt Beatrice alone. Maybe you should be the one to talk with Aunt Beatrice?"

"You don't think I've tried? She never tells me anything. You seem to have earned her confidence. It sounds as if she came close to confiding in you today. I think you should try to question her again, and soon."

"I had the perfect opportunity today when Clara went for a ride, but the weather didn't cooperate, and she returned home earlier than expected."

"Then you must continue to try, and you have my full support."

"I appreciate that. Leave it in my hands, for now." Amelia wanted to speak to Aunt Beatrice alone because she might need to bring up the contents of Catherine's diary to her. Regan had loved his mother deeply, and unless she had stronger proof that she had killed Annie, it was best to keep that information to herself for the time being. She didn't want to shatter his memories of her unless she had no choice.

He hesitated. "Then I'll leave it in your hands… for now," he said, emphasizing her own words.

"Yes," she agreed.

"Besides, I leave for Boston later today, and I'll forced to be away from home. There's a shipload of carriage parts arriving at the port from England. I'm afraid it will take several days to sort the delivery with the port authorities, paying the customs duty, and then recording it all in my inventory. So, I'll ask one more time. Are you certain you want to approach Aunt Beatrice alone? If you change your mind, you can wait until my return so that we can speak to her together."

Amelia hesitated, disappointed he would not be here in case matters went awry. Despite her misgivings about Clara, Amelia remained determined. She had nothing to fear from Clara. "No, I don't think that will be necessary," she answered in a firm tone. "The sooner we learn the truth, the sooner we can put the past to rest, and the better it will be for all of us. But after Clara's reaction today, I'm afraid it will become more difficult to pry her away from Aunt Beatrice. The only time she leaves her alone is when she's sleeping. I plan to visit her tonight when everyone has gone to bed."

Regan sat up straighter and leaned toward Amelia, stroking his chin. "Tonight, it is."

"And pray I don't upset her," Amelia added. She did her best to disguise the growing unease she felt about Clara and what she would discover from Aunt Beatrice.

Chapter Twenty-One

AFTER DINNER, WHEN darkness fell, and everyone was getting ready for bed, Amelia waited. Outside, strong winds swirled, contrasting with the stillness indoors. To be less conspicuous in the dark when she went to Aunt Beatrice's room, she wore a midnight blue robe over her nightdress, and deliberately left her feet bare for greater stealth. She pressed her ear against the door and listened.

"Good night, Mother," she heard Clara say. Amelia then heard the door click shut, followed by the fading patter of Clara's footsteps as she made her way to her own room. Amelia waited for a long time to be certain Clara wouldn't return if she had forgotten something.

She ventured forth into the hall, guided by the dim light of the solitary lamp on a side table, and tiptoed to Aunt Beatrice's room. Carefully, she turned the handle and slowly pushed open the door. Relieved it didn't creak, she stepped inside and closed it softly behind her. The partially open curtains allowed some moonlight into the room, enough to avoid bumping into the massive mahogany and carved black walnut furniture. Her steps light, the wooden floor smooth and silent beneath her feet, she crept to the bed and looked down.

Aunt Beatrice lay on her back, gray hair neatly braided and resting on her chest that rose and fell with slow, shallow breaths. Her features were much softer in slumber, and she looked serene. Light snores escaped her lips.

"Aunt Beatrice," Amelia whispered.

She did not respond.

"Aunt Beatrice, wake up," she said again with a gentle nudge of the woman's shoulder.

"Huh?" Aunt Beatrice muttered as her eyes gradually opened.

Amelia gave her a moment to shed her drowsiness.

She rubbed her eyes and looked up at Amelia in confusion, blinking, her eyelashes brushing against her cheeks. "Rosie, is that you?"

"Yes, it's me… Amelia."

She rubbed her eyes. "What time is it?"

"Almost eleven o'clock. I hoped you and I could talk before you fell asleep, but I wasn't able to come sooner. Would it be all right if we spoke now? To finish our earlier conversation?"

Aunt Beatrice pushed herself up on the pillows, her brow puckered.

Clearly, she seemed to have forgotten they had spoken earlier, but it pleased Amelia when she nodded.

"Good, but you must promise not to become upset. There is nothing for you to worry about. I am only here to help. You have my word." Amelia smiled at her. "After all, what are we if we don't find the courage to do what is right for others? I'll tell you what I know, and you can tell me what you know. Together we can solve any problem."

Her words seemed to encourage Aunt Beatrice

because her lips curved into a tiny smile. Amelia sat on the bed next to her and rested her hand on the elderly woman's arm. "Earlier today, you told me you have seen the auburn-haired girl, Annie. Well, I want you to know that I've also seen her."

Aunt Beatrice's eyes widened. "She comes to you too as well?"

"Yes, on more than one occasion."

"As she has to me."

"That's why it's important to talk about it. And you also believe you see her ghost, don't you?"

Aunt Beatrice pressed her lips together and nodded.

"Do you want to know what I think?"

"Yes," she murmured hesitantly.

Encouraged, Amelia was eager to reveal what she thought. "I think someone killed her."

Aunt Beatrice's gnarled fingers clutched her bed covers. "I do too," she said breathlessly.

"The only thing I'm certain about is that she appears to us because she needs our help. Her spirit is not at peace, and she wants us to discover what happened to her. I'm afraid that unless we do, her soul cannot rest. Will you help me?"

Aunt Beatrice swallowed; her hand rose to her throat as her eyes widened. "Yes, I'd like to."

"That's good. Think carefully. Can you recall anything about the day Annie went missing? Do you know what might have happened to her?"

"She was killed," Aunt Beatrice said, her eyes filling with tears.

Amelia reached out a hand to calm her. "You can tell me, it's safe. How was she killed? Do you know who did it?"

Her wrinkled hands repeatedly clutched and puckered the covers. Her eyes became fixed, glazed over, and troubled, as if she were recalling a nightmare.

Amelia attempted to bolster her. "It's all right. I'm here to help you." She spoke softly yet at a soothing volume.

Aunt Beatrice pushed herself up a little more and opened her mouth to say something. But before she could utter anything, a powerful gust outside buffeted the shutters and blew them fully open. The wind repeatedly slammed them against the outside wall.

Amelia ran to the windowpane and opened it. She battled the blustery weather to catch hold of one shutter, and then the other, and bolted them both closed. Nearly out of breath, she pulled down the windowpane.

The bedroom door suddenly swung open. Clara stood in the doorway, arms crossed, eyes darting between Amelia, Aunt Beatrice, and the window. She turned on Amelia like an enraged lion. "What are you doing here?"

"I thought I heard a noise in the hallway, so I came out of my room to check on Aunt Beatrice." A partial lie, but the only one that sprung immediately to mind.

Clara stared at her, then she uncrossed her arms, and with fists clenched, hurried to her mother's bedside. "You can go now, Amelia. I'll look after my mother now."

At the sharp command, and not wanting to cause a confrontation, Amelia left them. Once back in her room, she closed the door and leaned against it. Clara had interrupted each of her attempts to speak with Aunt Beatrice. Mere coincidence? Or was it because of Clara's tendency to be over-protective? Even worse, could it be because she was preventing Aunt Beatrice from revealing what she knew? Whatever the reason, Amelia was more determined than ever to get to the truth. It was time to confront Clara directly.

THE NEXT AFTERNOON, when Aunt Beatrice retired for her nap, Amelia sought Clara. She found her sitting on a bench facing the ocean, absorbed in a book. Last night's winds had abated. A gentle sea breeze caressed her face as she walked toward her. Soft white clouds floated in the perfect blue sky above.

Amelia steeled herself as she came up beside the bench. "May I join you?"

Clara glanced coldly up at her and hesitated, her lips thin with wrath.

Bolstered by the determination and inner strength she had summoned within herself, Amelia returned an open, friendly smile, her intent not to antagonize but to mollify.

Clara shut the book, held it against her chest, and stared out at the gentle waves. "Suit yourself."

Amelia sensed the other woman's cool attitude toward her, but refused to let it bother her. "It's peaceful here, especially on a beautiful day like this."

"Yes." Clara gave her a defensive glare, then faced the sea again.

Amelia knew she would have to tread carefully if she wanted to gain her confidence. "I'm glad to have this opportunity for us to speak. I dislike the rift that has developed between us, and I'm appalled by yesterday's argument. I hoped we could chat to put our differences aside. Do you realize that we've never chatted alone?"

"Mother's needs keep me constantly occupied. I have little time to dwell on the niceties of social decorum." Her words sounded intentionally blunt, meant to discourage any opposition.

"Your devotion to your mother is admirable. Few daughters would make the sacrifices you have."

Clara set down the book and leaned forward, her gaze never leaving the vista. "It's good that you understand that. Caring for her is the least I can do. She's easily upset and frail. As the years go by, the mother I once knew fades more and more. I'm afraid that one day her memory will completely fail, and it will be as if she never existed at all. And it makes me want to protect her even more. Even from you; if need be."

Despite the clear meaning behind her words, Amelia noted the sorrow beneath them. She had little doubt Clara loved Beatrice. It saddened her to know that in their mothers, their paths could not have been more different. Clara had spent a lifetime with hers, whereas she had lost hers years ago. "I understand how you feel."

"I doubt you do."

"A mother's love is divine. To lose it, whether it be through death or old age, leaves us all with a wound that will never heal. I lost my mother far too soon, but you're fortunate to still have yours, regardless of her current frailties."

Clara leaned back on the bench. "So very true." The iciness with which Clara had greeted her thawed slightly.

"Regan has spoken of the loss of his mother. I cannot imagine how difficult it must have been for your mother when she lost her twin."

"It devastated her. With the death of each of Catherine's children, my mother wrapped her sister in a never depleting repository of love. They were inseparable, dependent on each other."

"But the love between them wasn't enough. Things became worse for Catherine, didn't they?"

Clara pivoted her head sharply and made eye contact for the first time since they began talking. "How do you know this? Regan told you?"

"No, not Regan. In fact, I find him reluctant to talk about his family because it pains him so."

"Then how?"

Amelia paused. "I found Catherine's diary."

She stared at Amelia open mouthed. It was as if she couldn't formulate any thoughts while her mind raced to comprehend the impact of such a discovery. She closed her mouth, looked at her toes as if to stall for time to gather her thoughts, then glanced back up again. "I wasn't aware of any diary. Where did you find it?"

"Do you believe in ghosts, Clara?"

"No."

"Well, I do. The dead have appeared to me a time or two. My father, for one." And here she paused. "And Annie. Her spirit led me to the attic where I found the diary—at the bottom of an old trunk that once belonged to Catherine."

Clara's jaw clenched as she absorbed the information. Then she laughed, a dry, cynical sound. "I don't believe you. Hiding behind a ghostly presence as an excuse for skulking through the house to rummage through the private belongings of a poor woman long dead? Such a lie is beneath you, Amelia."

"It is not a lie. Annie has come to me on more than one occasion. In fact, your mother has seen her too."

"My mother's mind has become soft in her tender years. You shouldn't believe anything she says."

"I understand, but it has become very clear to me that something is bothering her about Annie's disappearance. Wouldn't it be best to find out what it is so that we can put her mind at ease?"

"Is that what you have been doing? Pressing my mother for information which may or may not be part of her faulty mind?"

"Yes, but only to help her."

"Like I've said before, her mind is faltering. Maybe it's to me you should direct your questions."

This was the opening Amelia needed. "Very well, then. Tell me what you know of Annie's disappearance."

Clara looked away again and shrugged. "There is very little to relate. One day she was here, and the next she was gone."

"Was Catherine fond of the girl?"

"Of course, she was. Annie was raised here at Edenstone and familiar to all of us. Her parents have served our family for many years."

"Did you notice Catherine's attitude toward Annie change in any way?"

"Her attitude toward everyone, even life itself, changed. After losing her third child, Catherine's fragile mind broke. Madness stole into her head like a deranged thief, pulling her deep into a dark grief none of us could rescue her from, least of all my mother who rarely left her side."

"How did the madness manifest itself? Was it simply a

vast melancholy or something more?"

Clara tilted her head, and her eyes narrowed slightly. "Why are you asking such questions? Madness is madness. My aunt suffered too many losses and lost her mind because of all the tragedies. What exactly are you trying to find out?" She scrutinized her. "You know something, don't you? Tell me what it is."

Amelia hesitated, not wanting to reveal the diary's contents, but Clara was sharp minded enough to see through a lie. She told her the truth. "Catherine wrote about terrible voices. They plagued her and directed her to kill someone as the only way to end her mother's curse." Amelia stopped short of telling her the name of the intended victim.

Clara's posture stiffened, and her muscles tightened. She clutched the book tighter to her. "I was not aware of the existence of any diary, but obviously she wrote it during the height of her madness. We can take nothing it reveals at its word. Besides, my aunt was a kind woman, and this is not in keeping with her character." She paused. "Does Regan know about the diary and that you suspect his mother was a murderess?"

Amelia shook her head. "No, of course not. At least not yet. It will be painful for him to learn such a thing. I'm waiting for the right time to show him the diary."

"A wise choice, I suppose. He was close to his mother. Maybe it's better he doesn't learn the extent of Catherine's despondency."

To Amelia's surprise, Clara took her hand, yet she felt the gesture lacked all shreds of sincerity. "I'm grateful for your concern, but you have been told everything there is to know about Annie's disappearance. Regan and the authorities did their utmost to investigate, and it all came to naught. Every member of our family has struggled to put it behind us. I think it's best if you do too. Spare my mother any further talk about it because it unsettles her. I fear it's too much of a strain on her heart. Concentrate on your upcoming wedding with Regan, instead."

She let go of Amelia's hand and rose.

"I must go. Mother will wake soon." Clara took a few steps before glancing back. "If you ever need to check on my mother, for whatever reason, I expect you to fetch me first."

Amelia watched her stride away, the wind rustling her skirts, her back stiff as she went. In her wake, she sensed Clara knew much more than she revealed and had made it clear she would not speak of it anymore.

Aunt Beatrice held the answer—if she only could recall it. When Amelia had spoken to her about it last night, she had almost revealed it. There was no choice. Regardless of Clara's warning, she would risk her ire and try again to speak to Aunt Beatrice.

Chapter Twenty-Two

WHILE EVERYONE SLEPT, Amelia lay awake staring at the ceiling and fidgeting with the pendant around her neck. Two matters were at the heart of her sleeplessness and needed urgent resolving.

First was Catherine's diary. Now that Clara knew of its existence, Regan must be told with all haste. She didn't want to give Clara the opportunity to mention it to him first. She would tell him at breakfast or shortly thereafter as soon as she could be alone with him. It was not something she looked forward to. When he learned the extent of his mother's insanity, and that she intended to kill Annie to appease voices clamoring in her head, it would cause him great pain, and would forever destroy the last memories he had of her. But Regan must be told. Pity the diary ended so suddenly. If only she could discover if a subsequent diary existed. It might confirm whether Catherine had followed through with the murder.

Second, she thought of poor Aunt Beatrice and the disturbing exchange with Clara earlier that afternoon. The concern Clara bore for her mother was one thing, but to prevent the poor woman from talking about what vexed her seemed not only odd, but cruel. It was clear Aunt Beatrice sought to tell Amelia something. Did she know who killed Annie or how she disappeared? She needed to hear her out. All her previous attempts to speak with the older woman alone had failed, but she must keep trying.

An idea sprang to mind. She cast aside her bed covers, lit the candle on the bedside table, and carried it to the writing desk to pen a note.

> *Dearest Hannah,*
> *I am writing to request a favor from you. Clara would benefit from some respite from her loving attentions to her mother. Could you invite her to join you and your brother for a small outing tomorrow afternoon? Tea at your home or a brief ride? Please do not respond directly to this note, but if you send an invitation to Clara, I shall be grateful to you and your brother.*
> *Warm regards,*
> *Amelia*

With a hopeful sigh, she folded the note, slid it into an envelope, then put the pen and paper away. The dark night sky outside her window had receded. On the ocean's horizon, the sun had already begun its gradual ascent; a canopy of gold, bright amid the fading dark indigo sky.

With rest no longer a possibility, Amelia dressed and groomed herself, eager to meet with Regan. A glance into the oval mirror above the dressing table revealed dark circles beneath her eyes. She pinched her pale cheeks, hoping the rosiness would detract from her bleary eyes.

Taking the letter and diary with her, she left to find

Mr. Simpson and encountered him at the bottom of the stairs carrying a tray of scones into the dining room.

"Ah, Mr. Simpson. Could I bother you to have this note delivered to Hannah and Phillip Wakefield?"

"Yes, Miss Amelia, it will not be a problem." He balanced the tray on his right hand and reached out with his left.

Amelia handed it to him and watched as he tucked it into the pocket of his jacket.

"I hope it's not too late to have it delivered this morning."

He nodded. "I think one of the stable lads is still in the kitchen eating his breakfast. I'll tell him to deliver it immediately."

"Thank you, Mr. Simpson."

"My pleasure, Miss."

"Do you know if Clara or Aunt Beatrice will be down soon?" Amelia added.

"Miss Clara has advised she will have breakfast in her mother's room this morning." He waited for her to precede him into the dining room.

She paused at the entrance. Regan sat alone at the head of the table, buttering a slice of toast, and engaged in reading the newspaper next to his plate. A touch of dread arose as she fought the desire to reverse her steps and flee back to the safety of her room. Her stomach churned—the aroma of coffee, eggs, bacon, and freshly baked scones suddenly unappealing. She clutched the diary a little tighter, straightened her shoulders, then strode into the room, Mr. Simpson behind her.

When Regan saw them, he put down the butter knife. His smile was like a spring flower opening to the sun. It arose from somewhere deep inside of him, lighting up his eyes.

She cringed at the knowledge she would soon extinguish his delight.

"Amelia, I'm glad you are up so early. Join me." He rose to pull out her chair. "Your timing is perfect. Eating with you is far more enjoyable."

She sat and tucked the diary next to her plate.

Regan's brow wrinkled as he squinted at her critically. "You look a little tired this morning. Did you not sleep well?" He hesitated, then frowned. "Something's wrong. What is it?"

Amelia handed him the journal and watched as he studied the delicate blue volume. How small it looked in his firm hands.

"What is this?"

"By right, it belongs to you. It's your mother's diary."

He gave her a puzzled look, then ran one hand reverently over the soft leather. "I didn't know she kept a diary." His voice softened with emotion.

"It's common for people to keep their diaries a secret."

"Where did you find it?"

"In an old trunk of hers stored in the attic."

"You went into the attic? No one has been up there for many years. Why?"

"One night, I heard someone crying. Concerned, I tried to determine where it was coming from, so I followed the sound to the attic. But the door was locked, and the weeping stopped. Later that day, after Mrs. Simpson gave me a set of the household keys, I let myself into the attic. There were no signs of anyone having been there." She touched his hand. "I must apologize to you. My curiosity got the best of me, and when I spotted your mother's trunk, its prettiness intrigued me. When I opened it, that's when I stumbled upon the diary." Guilt weighed heavily on her chest. What she had done, albeit with good intentions, could not be undone. She studied him, hoping she had not made him angry at having snooped through his mother's possessions.

But it didn't seem to bother him. Instead, he asked, "Crying from the attic? You're certain? It doesn't seem possible. No one ever goes up there."

"Very certain." She bit her lip, still intent on ensuring he wasn't upset at her. "I hope you're not angry at me for searching the attic and your mother's trunk."

"Angry? Of course not." His gaze gentled. "This is your home now. After my mother died, I didn't have the heart to go through her things, so I had them brought up there hoping to tend to it sometime later. I'm glad you found her diary."

Amelia swallowed. "You may not like its contents when you read it."

He cocked his head and his forehead puckered. "What do you mean?"

"It revealed your mother suffered from melancholy."

"Yes, we knew that."

"But what you may not know is how profoundly she suffered. She tried to hide it from everyone and expressed her dark thoughts and feelings only into her diary, which she kept secret."

Regan studied the volume in his hands and flipped open its pages. His expression stiffened at the sight of the once familiar calligraphy. His troubled eyes met hers.

"Thank you."

She gave him a tender smile before her expression eroded into seriousness. "I must warn you…" She struggled to find the words to continue.

He grimaced. "What's the matter?"

"You'll find the diary difficult to read." She gentled her voice and took his hand. "You may find it disturbing. Your poor mother's tremendous grief affected her more than anyone imagined. Thoughts that you and I would dismiss as bizarre, took root. She heard voices in her head, voices she believed were real. They controlled of her thoughts, commanding her, and caused her to tumble into madness."

Regan ran a hand over his chin.

Amelia toyed with the knife next to her plate, flipping it over and over. She grappled to find words that might soften the blow.

Regan leaned closer. "What did they command her to do, Amelia?"

She swallowed hard. "It's all in the diary. You should read it for yourself to understand it fully."

"Please. Tell me."

She inhaled a strengthening breath and chose her words carefully. "They told her how to end her mother's curse." Then, in the gentlest of voices, she added, "They told her that to stop any future children from dying, she had to kill someone… and that person was Annie."

His expression revealed he struggled to accept her words. And why wouldn't they? The sordid facts seemed bizarre. Yet they were true.

He shook his head, his gaze on the untouched plate of food before him. His face lost all color and his mouth hung open with his lips parted. "I'm having a hard time believing what you're telling me. My mother killed Annie?"

His skepticism was palpable. She understood his apprehension and looked at his clenched hands. Her heart broke for him. "The voices in her head told her to kill Annie to end the curse, but the diary abruptly ends, so it's not known if she followed through."

He inhaled a deep breath and stared out the window.

So deep was his consternation, Amelia doubted he even noticed the view he was staring at.

Regan reached for the bell next to his plate and rang it.

In a few moments, Mr. Simpson appeared in the doorway.

"Instruct the driver to unhitch the horses, Simpson. I won't be going to work today."

With a nod, the man left to carry out the order.

Regan sat so still, so quiet and forlorn. Torment flashed in his eyes, as if long buried memories, and dreams of what could have been, and what should have been, taunted him with savage intensity. Words and regrets haunted the living long after losing a loved one. Regan would be no different.

He drew a long breath and set the book aside. "I'll read it after breakfast."

"I can see you're struggling. Please, don't wait on my account. Read it now if that's what you need to do."

His eyebrows rose. "You're certain you don't mind?"

"The sooner you read it, the better. There's a lot for you to come to terms with. We can talk later."

"I'm grateful." His voice simmered with unbridled emotion.

Her heart fluttered. But the knowledge that the diary

would forever alter how he viewed his mother, distressed her. Would he unintentionally blame her? Regardless of the risks, it was right of her to bring it to his attention, and she must trust in him not to condemn her for doing so.

Amelia watched him shove back his chair and quietly leave the room with the diary clutched in his hand. Her appetite diminished, she nibbled on some toast, left the rest unfinished, then spent the rest of the morning strolling in the garden and sitting on the bench facing the ocean. Anything to keep from envisioning his distress when he read the horrific events in the diary.

When the sun was high in the sky, she went indoors as it would soon be time for lunch. First, she peered into the library. Regan was neither there nor in any of the rooms on the main floor. The only place he might be was in his bedroom, likely still reading.

Despite her heart hammering, she kept a casual gait as she went to take her seat at the dining room table. The tick tock of the hallway clock was the only sound. The silent house seemed as if it had buried its secrets deeper within its walls. She kept glancing at the door, hoping Regan would walk in at any moment, but the minutes passed, and she remained alone.

Soon she heard Clara's and Aunt Beatrice's chatter in the hall. Their voices became more discernable as they approached.

"Watch your step, Mother. The rug is uneven. I don't want you to trip."

"My eyesight is perfect. I'm more than capable of watching where I step. Really, Clara, you must stop fussing over me all the time. It's quite humiliating." Aunt Beatrice now stood in the doorway and smiled. "Well, hello. Good day to you, Loretta."

"Good day to you both," Amelia responded as the two took their seats.

Luncheon comprised baked beans, corned beef on rolls, and sauteed cabbage. Aunt Beatrice carried most of the conversation with trivial comments about her plants, the latest fashion, and the aches and pains that come with age. Clara kept silent except for the occasional glance at Amelia between mouthfuls of food, her tension palpable.

Amelia glanced repeatedly at the door, expecting Hannah's invitation to Clara, which should arrive any moment. She breathed a sigh of relief when Mr. Simpson finally carried it in with the tea and cake. She watched Clara open and read the note before tucking it next to her plate.

"I forgot to mention, Clara, I'll be away from home most of the day tomorrow," Amelia said, disguising the guilt she felt at telling the lie. But there was no other way around it if she wanted to speak with Aunt Beatrice alone. "I'm going into Boston to fit a gown I recently ordered."

Aunt Beatrice clapped her hands with joy. "I knew it. It's your wedding gown, isn't it? Do tell us about it."

"It would ruin the surprise," Amelia said. Another lie, another necessary one. She must keep up the ruse. Clara needed to believe she would be gone for the entire day, otherwise she wouldn't accept Hannah's invitation.

"Is everything all right, Clara?" Amelia asked. "You look pensive. Is it the note?"

"Hannah has invited me to tea tomorrow afternoon, but I must decline."

"But why? I'm certain Mrs. Simpson will keep Aunt Beatrice company while we're both away."

"I'll be well, Clara," Aunt Beatrice said. "You should go. Besides, I always nap in the afternoon. Anyway, I could use a few hours without your incessant hovering. You'd think I was a child."

Were Clara's thoughts visible, they would be like an explosion of uncertainty. Amelia did her best to disguise her anxiety as she awaited her answer.

Clara looked at her suspiciously, but Amelia tried to assuage it by sipping tea as if she had no care in the world.

"You are certain you don't mind, Mother?"

"How many times must I tell you I don't need you flitting over me all the time?"

"Very well, it's only for a few hours. I'll go."

Some tension left Amelia's body. "I'm sure you'll enjoy yourself," she said. "Everyone deserves a well-earned respite, especially you for tending to your mother so well."

The matter settled; they finished their lunch.

Amelia retired to the library to work on the company ledgers while Clara took Aunt Beatrice upstairs. Tomorrow she hoped to question Regan's aunt at length without interruption and prayed her memory wouldn't fail this time. The bond between twins was strong. Did she know for certain whether Catherine killed Annie? If she did, could she recall the event?

Certain she was close to solving the mystery of Annie's disappearance, she became absorbed in her work.

When the hall clock struck four o'clock, Amelia set aside the ledgers and went to her room. Soon it would be time to change for dinner. She swung open her door and stopped, drawing a sharp breath.

Clara stood before her open wardrobe, rummaging through the contents of her armoire, shoving garments aside, and leaving them rumpled and in disarray.

Chapter Twenty-Three

"WHAT ARE YOU doing in my room?" Amelia demanded.

Clara yanked her hand out from beneath a pile of folded shawls and spun around, her expression stiff with defiance.

Amelia crossed the threshold and stood before her; hands fisted on her hips. "I'll ask you again. What are you doing here?"

Clara smoothed out her gown. "Looking for Mother's fan."

Amelia glanced around. Everything was in place except for the items in disarray inside the armoire. "Why would I have it?"

"Mother came in here earlier to look at the tree outside your window. She believes there's a bird's nest in it and your room is closer to it than hers."

Amelia brushed past her, knowing full well Clara was lying. "And she supposedly misplaced her fan inside my wardrobe?"

A sneer formed on Clara's smooth face. Her gaze bored straight into Amelia's. "Your maid, Sarah, might have spotted the fan and put it away."

"Did you find it?" Amelia strode even closer and stood firm opposite Clara's unwavering stance.

Clara took a step back. "No, I didn't, but I'm sure it's here somewhere."

"You are lying."

Crimson tinted her cheeks. "I am not."

"Of course, you are. It isn't Aunt Beatrice's fan you are looking for, is it?"

Clara hesitated; her expression taut.

"You refuse to answer me?"

Clara clenched her hands. "Don't be ridiculous."

"Now that I've told you about Catherine's diary, you want to find it. Admit it."

Clara glanced at the door beyond Amelia's shoulder. "Doubt me if you wish, but I was searching for Mother's fan, nothing more. She is so forgetful these days and can't remember where she leaves her cane, her reticule, or fan. I apologize for having disturbed you." With a swish of her skirts, she dashed past Amelia and hurried away, her footsteps echoing across the hall.

Amelia closed her bedroom door and leaned her back against it, letting her tension ease, glad the diary was safe in Regan's hands. She glanced at the armoire and the disarray inside. Why would Clara go to such lengths to gain the diary? The only plausible answer that came to mind was she must be afraid of something the diary might reveal. And if Catherine had indeed murdered Annie, where was the body? Was Clara involved somehow? Clearly, she knew more than she admitted. Consumed by such questions, she set about tidying the mess Clara created.

Afterwards, she crossed the room and flopped onto

the bed. Her thoughts reverted to Regan and the diary's revelations. She longed to go to him, embrace him, and soothe away any anguish he might feel, but he needed time to absorb the truth. To distract herself, she tried to read, but ended up with the book across her lap as she stared out the window.

At the sound of the dinner bell, she went downstairs. The first to arrive for dinner, she took her place at the table, eager to see Regan.

Simpson entered with a bottle of wine and poured some into her glass. "Mr. Lockhart sends his apologies and wishes me to tell you he cannot join you for dinner this evening."

She looked sharply up at him. "Did he say why?"

"Only that he has a pressing matter which requires his attention. The ladies are dining in their rooms."

He set the goblet down, bowed his head, then left the room.

Unnerved about Regan's absence, Amelia reached for her goblet and sipped the fragrant, richly flavored burgundy wine. Her thoughts swirled with uneasiness. She fought the urge to seek him out. He needed time, was all. She must wait until he came to her.

Clara's absence displayed her wish to avoid her and keep Aunt Beatrice away too.

Alone at the long table, Amelia had no appetite, despite the rich aroma of the beef barley soup, corn cake, and vegetables Simpson served.

Only the tick-tock of the hallway clock and the crackle of the fire broke the complete silence.

Simpson came back in to clear the dishes and frowned when he noticed she had not touched her meal. "Not hungry, Miss?"

Amelia pushed her chair back from the table. "The meal was lovely, but unfortunately, I seem to have no appetite this evening."

"Not to worry, Miss. Later, if you wish, I'll ask my wife to bring a tray up to your room."

While he gathered the dishes, she went into the hall to retrieve her shawl from the cupboard and stepped into the cool night air.

By the light of the waning moon, she sat on the edge of the fountain, dipping and swirling her hand in the cool water. In the distance, the waves ebbed and flowed against the shore in a soothing rhythm. A briny aroma lingered in the breezeless night air. The surrounding ambience often brought her peace, but not tonight. Too many unanswered questions left her unsettled.

She glanced up at the windows on the upper level of the house. A light glowed behind the drawn curtains in Regan's room. She saw them shift and glimpsed him look out. He stood for a moment until the drape fell back, then she lost sight of him.

Soon, the mansion's front door opened. Regan strode toward her, his pace slow, the gravel along the drive crunching beneath his soles. When he drew near, he picked a twig from the ground. He sat next to her, snapping off its small branches, one by one. He leaned forward and rested his elbows on his knees, jaw twitching as he stared at the ground.

Wrapped in silence, it seemed an eternity passed.

She respected his reticence and waited.

Regan turned to her; his expression tortured. "I can't remember her voice. I try—but it's gone."

Amelia heard the knell of loss in his own voice and put her hand on his arm.

His shoulders hunched together as if he wished to disappear inside himself. "I didn't realize her mind had deteriorated so much. If only I'd known."

"How could you? Years passed between each child's death; her decline into madness was gradual and probably difficult to notice. You were a young boy when you lost your first sister, and an adult by the time you lost your father. She confided her deepest thoughts to no one, except into the diary she secreted away."

"I'm grappling with the fact my mother killed anyone, let alone poor Annie, a girl on the verge of womanhood whom my mother knew and loved. The Simpsons have lived in this house and served our family for decades. They have always been like family to me." He reached for Amelia's hand. "The diary ended so abruptly. It's highly likely she might have hidden another somewhere."

The touch of his hand comforted her. "On that point, we are in total agreement. I've searched but haven't found it yet."

"Maybe Clara might know of a second one. She helped me pack away some of Mother's things when she died. For all we know, she has it already."

"I'm not sure. Clara has been acting strangely toward me lately," Amelia said. "I spoke to her the other day, and when I mentioned I had found your mother's diary, she appeared shocked. Then, earlier today, I caught her rummaging through my belongings. When I confronted her, she said she was searching for a fan your aunt left in my room. I'm convinced she lied. There's no doubt in my mind she was searching for the diary, and the only reason she didn't find it was because you have it."

Regan shook his head as if bewildered. "That's certainly strange behavior, and it's not sitting well with me." He gripped a fisted hand. "Have you learned anything from Aunt Beatrice?"

"Every time I try to question her, she becomes so distraught she can't speak, or Clara interrupts us and puts a stop to my questions. I'm hoping to try again tomorrow. I asked Hannah to invite Clara to tea so that I can speak to your aunt alone. The only reason Clara accepted was because I lied and told her I'm going into town to have a gown fitted. I don't enjoy lying to her, but it's the only way I can speak to Aunt Beatrice without her being present."

"That's good. Don't feel bad. You had no choice. Clara never leaves her mother's side. I would prefer to join you but cannot because of an early morning meeting with an important client who will depart for England in the afternoon. I'll hurry back as soon as I can. You'll have to tell me about it then."

"I'd prefer that you joined me, but since you can't, I'll go it alone. I pray everything goes well."

THE NEXT DAY, after Clara left for tea with Hannah, Amelia hurried down the hall where she found the door to Aunt Beatrice's room ajar.

Regan's aunt sat in a wing chair next to the open window from which the sunlight shed warmth and light over her shoulders. With her eyes closed and head tilted back, Aunt Beatrice listened to Mrs. Simpson's soft tones reading to her from a matching wing chair.

Amelia rapped on the door. "May I join you?"

Mrs. Simpson glanced up from the book.

Aunt Beatrice sat up straight. "Annabelle, how delightful. Do join us. You're a tad late, so we began without you."

Mrs. Simpson winced at the memory lapse and offered Amelia an apologetic look. "I was reading to Mrs. Yates to pass the time. Will you be leaving for your appointment soon, Miss Amelia? Is there anything I can help you with?"

"The dressmaker rescheduled my appointment for another day. So, I'm free to spend time with Aunt Beatrice."

Aunt Beatrice clasped her hands and raised them to her chest. "What a wonderful idea. I'd enjoy that very much."

Mrs. Simpson left the book open, presumably to keep her place, then set it upside down on the small table between the chairs. "Then with your approval, I'll leave you to your enjoyment and go down to the kitchen to make dinner."

Amelia nodded and made her way to the chair Mrs. Simpson had just vacated.

"Thank you again," Mrs. Simpson said as she left the room.

Amelia settled in the wing chair and adjusted her skirts. "It's such a lovely day. I'm pleased to spend the afternoon with you."

Aunt Beatrice smiled at her. "What shall we do, my dear?"

"Sit and chat while we enjoy the warm sunshine."

"It is pleasant, isn't it?" Aunt Beatrice leaned back and shut her eyes.

"That's the second time I've seen you rest your head since I've come into the room. Are you tired today? Did you not sleep well last night?"

Aunt Beatrice snapped open her eyes. "How did you guess?"

"Sometimes I have trouble sleeping, especially after my father or Annie appear to me," Amelia said cautiously.

A muscle twitched in the older woman's chin and she grimaced, clasping her hands tight across her stomach.

"Aunt Beatrice, tell me the truth. Annie comes to you, too, doesn't she?"

"Yes, she does. On some nights, I wake and she's standing next to my bed."

"Does she say anything?"

Aunt Beatrice nodded, her hands twisting in her lap.

"You can tell me what she says," Amelia urged softly. "Talking about something that is bothering you might allow you to sleep better."

After a brief hesitation, she said, "Sometimes she begs me to find her. Other times, she urges me to speak the truth."

Amelia reached over and took hold of both her hands to calm her, stopping them from fidgeting. "The truth? Do you know what happened to Annie?"

She pulled her hands from Amelia's grasp and chewed her bottom lip.

"You can tell me. Regan and I will help, no matter what."

Her muscles tensed and she arched her back, her eyes flitting to the door as if seeking escape.

Amelia leaned forward. "It's all right. You can tell me what you saw," she said in little more than a whisper.

The woman swallowed. Her lips quivered and voice shook as she spoke. "Annie was on the floor, her body shaking hard. Froth came out of her mouth. I tried to help Annie, held her in my arms... but she died."

Amelia's heart twisted and blood raced through her veins at the revelation Annie was dead. Finally, the truth was coming out. Myriad questions raced through her mind, but she had to proceed carefully to draw out answers without upsetting the dear woman. "Was anyone with you?"

"Catherine. She watched Annie writhe on the ground. Oh, Juliette, it's all my fault." Aunt Beatrice thrust her head in her hands and burst into heart-wrenching sobs.

Amelia rose and kneeled before her. "That can't be true. Why do you say that?"

"Catherine... black flowers..." she cried incoherently.

At that moment, Aunt Beatrice's gaze shifted to something behind Amelia.

Before she could turn around to see what it was, a blow to her head brought crushing pain. Then the world turned black as she tumbled into oblivion.

Chapter Twenty-Four

REGAN'S MEETING TOOK longer than expected. Eager to arrive home, he snapped the reins of his phaeton carriage to keep the gelding at a fast trot. The revelations in his mother's diary kept him distracted the entire day. He struggled with the belief his mother killed anyone, but especially young Annie with whom she had a bond. Guilt at his failure to recognize her dreadful decline, and aid her in overcoming it, gnawed at him. Although Amelia suspected his aunt might know something about what happened to Annie, because of her failing memory, he held little faith in anything she might tell her.

The sun hovered low in the sky as he jerked the conveyance to a stop in front of the house. A stable lad who sat waiting on the edge of the fountain, jumped up to grab the horse's bridle.

Regan tossed the reins to him and hopped out of the phaeton. "I drove faster than usual. Cool him well. He'll be thirsty and give him some oats with his hay. He's earned it."

"Yes, sir." The lad stepped up into the conveyance. With a click of his tongue, the lad urged the gelding into a slow walk and drove to the stables.

Regan hurried inside. Encountering no one, he raced up the stairs to his room. With haste, he changed his clothes. He fastened his watch-chain across his brown silk waistcoat, then looked in the mirror. What he saw disappointed him. Dark circles beneath his eyes and a paler than usual complexion confirmed how little he had slept. Hopefully soon, he would have the answers he needed to set his mind at ease. He turned away and went down to the dining room.

First to arrive, he settled on his chair and reached for the decanter to fill his glass. He swirled the Bordeaux to aerate the liquid, and after inhaling the rich fragrance, tossed back a quick swallow before releasing a satisfied breath. It was good to be home. The unresolved mystery of what happened to poor Annie had been a constant source of anguish, and he was keen to learn anything his aunt may have revealed to Amelia.

He glanced at his watch and frowned. It was half-past six o'clock; dinner was late. They had likely postponed dinner because they expected him to be late coming home. He sipped more wine and waited.

At the sound of women's voices, he glanced up. When Clara and Aunt Beatrice walked into the room, he rose to pull out their chairs.

His aunt's expression blossomed. "Regan, you're home. I'm so happy you arrived in time to dine with us."

He kissed her cheek and helped her into the chair. "I hate missing supper with my favorite ladies."

"Pshaw! Flattery will get you everywhere, nephew."

He pressed a hand over his heart and grinned. "I seek nothing more than your love, Aunt."

"You shall always have it, my dear." She sat taller in the chair and clasped her hands on her lap.

Next, Regan helped seat Clara, but received only a pithy 'thank-you' in response. He returned to his seat, picked up the decanter, and offered to fill Clara's glass. When she declined, he presented the Bordeaux to his aunt.

"None for Mother, please," Clara interrupted with a raised hand. "She always suffers the most dreadful headaches the day after drinking wine, especially the red ones."

"Don't speak on my behalf, Clara," Aunt Beatrice scolded. "I am not a child. If I desire wine, then wine I shall have, and there's nothing you can do or say to stop me." She raised her empty goblet to Regan.

He hesitated.

Aunt Beatrice scowled at him and raised the glass higher and closer to the decanter. "Fill it, what are you waiting for?"

Clara remained silent; her expression hardened.

He shrugged, then poured, but only partially filled the goblet.

"Thank-you," Aunt Beatrice said with a self-righteous tone and took a long sip. With a smile, she set the glass down to await the meal.

Regan drained the contents of his goblet, relieved she did not complain about the scant amount he gave her. He glanced over at Clara, who glowered at him.

He listened politely to Aunt Beatrice who chattered on at length about herself—the novel she was reading, a new shawl, the discomfort of arthritic hands, toes, and more. Every so often, he glanced at Clara. How odd for her to be so quiet and let her mother carry on without stopping her or correcting her. She seemed pre-occupied, barely making eye contact with either of them, rarely glancing up.

Throughout, he tried to concentrate or show interest, but the horrific disclosures in his mother's diary played heavily in his thoughts, vexing him, keeping him unsettled. And where in the blazes was Amelia? What was delaying her?

A movement in the doorway caught his attention, but it was only Simpson who wheeled in a trolley with the main course. Worried, Regan sat back.

Simpson set plates of haddock with sauteed vegetables before them. He placed a covered dish in Amelia's spot, a sure sign they expected soon her. Before Simpson walked away from the table, Regan stopped him. "Please find out what is keeping Miss Belleville."

The man nodded and withdrew.

"We may as well eat," Aunt Beatrice said, taking up a fork and knife. "My father, your grandfather might I add, could not abide tardiness. He never let a meal grow cold waiting for someone who was late. And I believe we should do the same." She stabbed a chunk of potato with her fork and ate it.

Reluctantly, Regan grabbed a roll from the breadbasket. "Do either of you know why Amelia is so late this evening?"

Clara snapped open her napkin and settled it neatly on her lap. "She told me she was going to Boston for a fitting at the dressmaker's today."

He turned to his aunt. "Have you spoken with her today?"

Aunt Beatrice frowned and shook her head. Her eyes clouded with confusion as she opened her mouth to answer.

Before she could say anything, Clara spoke up. "Neither one of us has seen her all day. She must have left before we woke up." She reached for her mother's hand and squeezed. "Isn't that correct, Mother?"

"Uh, I'm not sure," Aunt Beatrice muttered. "I don't recall when I last saw Andrea, but she must be here somewhere. Oh dear, why can't I remember?" Then her expression relaxed and brightened somewhat. "I suppose you are right, my dear. She must have left before I woke. Who can blame her for wanting to leave early to see all the fascinating sights in Boston? If she's anything like me, she probably lost track of time among all those tempting little stores, windows decorated with the loveliest fans and shoes and hats in the latest French fashions." She savored a piece of haddock. "Mmm, delicious."

While she droned on about various shops, some of which no longer existed, Regan and Clara dined in silence, only broken by Simpson's reappearance.

Regan raised an expectant eyebrow.

"So sorry, sir, but Sarah and my wife cannot find Miss Belleville anywhere."

The knot in his gut swelled. He couldn't dispel the growing premonition that something was terribly wrong. He knew her plan, that she deliberately lied to Clara so she could remain home and question his aunt. The growing sense of alarm looped around in his mind until there was no room for anything else.

"I'll send someone out to the stables, Mr. Lockhart. Maybe she just arrived," Simpson offered.

Regan thrust away his plate. "No need. I'll go." He turned to the women. "Please excuse me." After tossing his napkin down, he strode to the doorway, then glanced back over his shoulder. "Have the house searched again, Simpson."

"Don't you think you're over-reacting, Regan?" Clara said dismissively. "Amelia's merely late, nothing more. Why worry?"

Regan glared at her before stalking out.

He rushed to the barn. All the carriages were there, her horse and tack too. As planned, she had not left the estate. Saddling his stallion, he cantered in the darkness toward the graveyard. The gates were closed; nothing stirred among the graves. Regan swung around and took the path beside the trees that led around the meadow and the perimeter of the estate. Not a sign of Amelia anywhere.

Having exhausted all obvious possibilities, he trotted his stallion back to the stable and left him with the stable master. Dread consumed him as he ran to the house. Fear owned him, pressing down on him as if it were an invisible gale. Inside, he glanced into the dining room at the cleared table. He assumed everyone had retired. Regan raced up the stairs to the upper floor where he encountered Clara leaving Aunt Beatrice's room.

She raised a finger to her lips. "I had a terrible time getting her to sleep. You've unsettled her with all this talk about Amelia's whereabouts."

"Have you found her?" he asked.

She shook her head. "We searched every room. She's not here, Regan."

He ran a hand over his face and paced.

"It's best to prepare yourself, Regan."

He stopped. "Prepare myself. For what?"

"Haven't you realized it yet? Amelia has left you. She

seemed unhappy here. After you returned her dowry, there was nothing to keep her here. You must face the truth. She's broken off your engagement, and Mother is heartbroken about it."

He studied Clara, who stood calmly before him. She never glanced away or batted an eye. Clara thought Amelia went to Boston for a fitting, so why would she make such a statement? Nothing could be further from the truth.

"You're wrong, and God help you if you're hiding something from me." He brushed past her and strode away. He sensed her gaze on him as he entered Amelia's bedroom.

In the vacant stillness, worry seeped into his flesh; a paralyzing poison that rendered him immobile. At a loss over what to do, he studied the room for any clue, but everything was tidy and in its place. Shoulders slumped and with heavy steps, he passed through the doors linking their rooms. Once in his bedchamber, he poured himself a full glass of brandy, and downed it in one gulp. The slow heat burned through his body but did little to dispel his fears. He stood at the window, staring out at the landscape for any sign of where she might be. As the last rays of sunlight faded into the horizon, the world became dark and still and hopeless, and with it, so did his spirits.

INTENSE POUNDING IN Amelia's head wrenched her slowly to consciousness. Her body trembled in the cold, damp air. It took a while for her to realize she was in a small, dark room. She groaned, and through the narrow slit of her eyes, took in her surroundings. In the gloom, four thick, gray stone walls surrounded her. She lay beneath a thin blanket that smelled of stale sweat and dirt on a makeshift bed—a mere plank of wood on legs, with a straw mattress. She saw a cracked chamber pot was partially protruding from beneath it. Dank water pooled in the center of the old stone floor. Shelves lined both walls on either side of an old wooden door. Near the ceiling, a crack in a timber-barred window let in an almost unperceivable shaft of light. A sudden flash of fiery light and a stunning crash followed it, rattling the bed and walls.

She moaned with pain and forced herself to sit. At the effort, her head throbbed harder. With her hand, she checked the back of her skull where most of the pain emanated from and discovered an inflamed lump the size of a goose egg. When she pulled back her hand, her fingers came away with traces of blood on them. The stench of mold and decay soured her nostrils and throat. Bile rose in her stomach. A powerful wave of nausea caused her to break out into a sweat. She pulled out the chamber pot and vomited, then wiped her mouth with the back of her hand before reclining to appease the pain. Where was she? How did she get here? The last thing she remembered was talking with Aunt Beatrice, who told her she had seen Annie die. That's when someone or something struck her.

From beyond the closed door, footsteps echoed in the corridor, drawing closer.

Fear sparked in her gut as blood raced through her veins. Paralyzed with terror, she waited.

The footsteps stopped. She heard the rattle of keys and the click of the lock's tumbler.

The heavy wooden door, grown moldy and soft with years of dampness and neglect, creaked slowly open.

Chapter Twenty-Five

AMELIA SUCKED IN a deep breath. Her pulse clamored in her ears and cold sweat dripped down her back as she blinked in disbelief.

Clara stood in the doorway with a tray balanced in one hand. The dim light from the corridor cast her shadow on the cell floor.

Amelia jerked herself up to a sitting position. It caused so much pain, she had to hold her head in both hands.

"You're awake." Clara spoke with calm ease, as if keeping someone locked up in a dingy stone room was normal.

Outside, a fierce gale thrashed against the small window. With it came incessant rain, a wall of streaming water lit at intervals by bold, bright lightning flashes. Amelia's rage flowed with the speed of a deathly waterfall. "How dare you keep me locked up here."

Clara tucked the key into her pocket and stepped inside, shutting the door behind her. She strode toward Amelia and set the tray down on the bed and gazed down at her with cold-hearted hostility and gloating. "You must be hungry. There's some bread, roast chicken, and water."

"I'm not." A simmering rage boiled inside her, but she resisted. Her inner voice warned her to keep her wits sharp.

Clara's lips formed into an ingenuous sneer, her face a callous, controlled mask. "You will be. I suggest you eat and drink," she said with obvious irritation.

Amelia took one quick glance at the door, then darted past Clara.

Clara yanked her back by the hair and threw her onto the ground.

Amelia toppled over. Her head struck the stone floor. Pain seared through her skull. She yielded to it, unable to think or bring a thought to completion. Instinctively, she curled into a primeval fetal shape as the powerful throbbing radiated in her head. Stars flashed in her eyes as the walls and room spun. Her stomach roiled once more.

"You won't be going anywhere. I'm afraid you're here to stay. At least for a while." A hint of victory was clear in Clara's rising smirk; the joy of an enemy after winning the battle.

"Regan will miss me," she groaned. "He's looking for me…" Too difficult to speak, she waited a few moments, letting the dizziness and nausea ease. When the worst of it passed, she asked, "Why are you doing this?" Her battle with Clara had only begun, and she must keep alert.

"You left me no choice."

With great effort, Amelia swung her legs around and pushed herself slowly up into a kneeling position. Ignoring the pain in her head, she reached for the bed and pulled herself up onto it. The exertion brought on a terrible throbbing, but she denied herself the relief of laying down. Through blurred eyes, she gave Clara an unflinching stare.

"There is always a choice."

"Yes, that's true. Unfortunately, you've made some wrong ones."

Amelia rubbed the back of her head. Her fingers felt the wetness at the blood still seeping from the wound. "What do you mean?"

"You made the mistake of asking far too many questions and should have let a sleeping dog lie." Anger flashed in Clara's eyes.

To keep from upsetting her, Amelia changed tactics. "Why am I here?"

"You lied to me about going into Boston. When the weather turned bad, I returned early from Hannah's house. It's a good thing I did. That's when I caught you questioning Mother, pressing her for answers, upsetting her. To shut you up, I struck you on the head with a heavy vase. While you were unconscious, I dragged you down here." She gestured at the cell walls. "Charming, isn't it?"

Amelia pinched her lips to smother the barrage of furious words she wanted to shout. She stared at her nemesis with disgust.

"All houses built during the Revolution were constructed with plenty of secret passages and places to hide in case the occupants came under attack. Years ago, I discovered a trapdoor in the floor of my room. It opened to reveal a set of stairs leading down to this cellar. I doubt anyone knows the stairs or this room even exists."

Amelia took a deep breath to calm the outrage boiling up inside her. "How long have I been in this filthy, pathetic cell you're keeping me trapped in?

"Not long. A little more than a day."

"You won't get away with this. It won't be long before

Regan finds me, and when he does, you will pay dearly for what you've done."

"I doubt that. He's already been searching, but he'll never find you. He hunted for Annie for weeks. If he knew about this underground room, he might have found her. Good thing that he didn't."

"Annie?" Amelia asked. "You know what happened to her?"

Clara crossed her arms. "Of course, I do. Very little happens at Edenstone that escapes me."

"You didn't know about Catherine's diary."

She unfolded her arms and leaned closer, sneering. "You're right, but I will find it and when I do, I'll destroy it."

Amelia held her position and glared back at her. "You killed Annie." Disbelief echoed in her voice. She was trapped in a room by a woman who had killed before. The realization increased the sense she needed to tread carefully; the urge to escape pressing hard upon her. Clara was more than capable of killing her and leaving her body to rot. She had to find some way out of this nightmare.

Clara scoffed and went to the window where she looked up at the pouring rain. "You're wrong. It wasn't me who killed Annie." She swung swiftly about, then leaned against the wall. "My poor Aunt Catherine. After so much tragedy, little by little, she lost her grip on reality. At first, we believed it was mere melancholy. How could we have known she heard voices in her head? When we did, it was too late."

"Too late? Too late for what? Are you telling me it was Catherine who killed Annie?" Amelia shivered in the cold. She yearned to lie down and warm herself beneath the woeful and filthy blanket, but kept sitting to keep Clara engaged.

"Of course, it was my Aunt Catherine who killed Annie, not me." Clara's eyes grew distant, recalling the memory to mind. "Mother and I went to check on her one day. When we entered the bedroom, we found Annie laying on the floor in a terrible state. Froth seeped from the corners of her mouth and her body was convulsing. Mother and I rushed forth to help, but she died so fast. We could do nothing for her." Clara's voice held no emotion, her expression showed no sympathy.

How could she not have seen Clara's callousness before? She pushed away her fears that she may never get out of here alive and tried to keep her talking. "What happened to her?"

Clara sighed. "I suppose there's no harm in telling you. Catherine poisoned her with the petals from some black flowers she somehow gained."

The poisonous black flowers. Amelia's heart skipped a beat, and she drew a sharp breath.

"While Mother and I fussed over poor Annie, Catherine stood oddly still, watching without emotion. I grabbed her by the shoulders and shook her and demanded an explanation. The cold, detached look on her face made me shudder. She muttered something, but I couldn't make out what she said. That's when I noticed something clutched in Annie's hand: a milk bottle of Laird's Bloom of Youth for the complexion. The label promised to bleach the skin to a milky white appearance and could remove a suntan and freckles. Annie hated her red hair and freckles, so Catherine poisoned the contents, gave it to her, then calmly watched her die."

"Why would she do such a thing?" Amelia already knew the answer, but she wanted to learn what Clara might know.

"She told me the voices in her head made her do it."

"And what of Annie's body? What did you do with her?"

"I needed to protect Aunt Catherine, to keep anyone from finding out, to save her from the gallows, so when there was no one in the corridor, I dragged Annie's corpse to my bedroom, and then pulled her through the trapdoor and down the stairs to this very room. In fact, she lay right there, on the same bed and beneath the same blanket you're now lying on."

"But she was dead—"

Clara interrupted her, "I see that patience is not one of your virtues, Amelia." She shook her head with malevolent amusement. "Yes, she was dead, but I needed to dispose of her body, and I had to wait for the cover of darkness."

Amelia shivered at the iciness in Clara's eyes. With sudden terror, she was coming to understand the full depth of her cunning deviousness.

"With Annie's body temporarily hidden, I hurried back to Aunt Catherine's room. On her writing desk, I found a diary. I thought it was the only one, but it seems you stumbled upon an earlier one." She glowered at Amelia.

"So, I was right to believe you were searching for the diary when I caught you in my room."

"Of course. For the good of the family, especially for Mother's sake, there could be no evidence of Catherine's madness or crime. You can imagine how distraught she was after witnessing Annie's death. The diary revealed how the voices told her to murder Annie, and how she mixed deadly, dried hellebore into the face cream. When Annie came into her room to make the bed, Aunt Catherine offered her the cream. And of course, Annie accepted it, eager to make the freckles on her face disappear. The diary revealed Catherine acquired black hellebore to cure herself of the voices, the madness, the despair."

Amelia inhaled a deep breath to calm her growing alarm. "So, permit me to ask you again; what did you do with Annie's body?"

Clara pushed herself away from the wall. "It's a good thing she was so slight. In the dark of night, I wrapped her body in a blanket then dragged it to the little well you discovered behind the graveyard and dumped her in it."

Amelia stared at Clara as if she saw her for the first time—a cold, calculating, callous woman. She shivered with disgust. It galled her to know how Annie's parents must have suffered at their daughter's disappearance, and Clara, with the ability to set everyone's mind at ease, did nothing. The haughty look reflected on her face sent another icy shiver down Amelia's spine. Clara lacked humanity and had a stony heart, a trait likely inherited by her cruel grandmother. "And you were foolish enough to believe no one would discover the secret of Annie's death?" Amelia asked. "The truth always surfaces."

"I didn't know that then, but I realize it now."

"And what about poor Catherine?"

"Poor Aunt Catherine. It turns out, Annie's murder was not enough to appease the voices. They returned even stronger, more persistent, urging her to kill someone again."

Her mouth sagged open, and she took in a sudden

intake of breath.

As if freed from the burden of keeping secrets, Clara seemed eager to tell all. "One day, as I walked past her bedroom, I heard her talking with someone. When I glanced into the room, she was alone. That's when I realized she was arguing with the voices in her head, repeating my name, and uttering the words kill, death, die. I concluded correctly that the voices were telling her to kill me."

Amelia's blood ran cold as her instincts warned her Clara was about to reveal something even more unspeakable.

"But I could do little because the search for Annie continued for weeks. I had to bide my time while I kept vigilant and monitored my aunt closely. It gave me time to think, to plan, to come to terms with what I knew I had to do."

Words jammed in her throat. Amelia swallowed. "Oh my God, you killed her," she rasped.

"Yes, of course. I had no choice."

"How?" Amelia asked breathlessly, horror jammed in her throat.

"Late one night, when everyone slept, I brought her tea laced with arsenic; the bitter taste well disguised with ample sugar. I held the chamber pot for her when she vomited. After that, she moaned and struggled to breathe as her heart slowed until it finally stopped. She was old and mad, so it would be easy for everyone to believe she died alone in her sleep. After I arranged her body in the bed to make it look as if she died peacefully, I took the chamber pot, emptied it into the rear garden, and returned to bed. That's when I realized I had done her a great mercy by freeing her from the torments of madness. In the morning, poor Mrs. Simpson discovered her body."

"How your mother must have suffered. First Annie, and then the loss of her twin."

"She did, unfortunately. Mother was extremely distraught. She was never the same after that. Her memory declined sharply. She began hearing Annie's cries, convinced Annie's ghost haunted her. At first, I shrugged it off as part of her mental decline, but when you saw Annie's reflection in the mirror on your first night here, it was more than Mother could bear."

Amelia listened with repugnance to the torrent of horrific words. She could not tear her gaze away from Clara's cold, calm demeanor, and soulless eyes. She yearned to cover her ears, to not hear any more of the hellish tale. Her entire body numb with fear, and dumbfounded, she struggled to make sense of what Clara had done. Her actions were out of character with the Clara she believed she knew.

"Oh, please, spare me that look of disgust on your face. It was kill or be killed. And if it had not been me, it could easily have been someone else in this house; my mother, Mrs. Simpson, perhaps even Regan."

"You'll never get away with this."

"I already have. After Aunt Catherine's funeral, peace returned to Edenstone. Everyone simply disregarded any of her ramblings, blaming it on her failing memory and dementia. But then you arrived and began asking too many questions. I watched you, and even tried to stop you from digging for answers, but you persisted."

"So, it was you I sensed watching me, or heard skulking behind doors."

"I'm surprised it has taken you this long to come to the realization."

"Regan will never forgive you for murdering his mother."

Clara threw back her head and laughed. "Regan will never know. Do you remember that letter you wrote to your lawyer asking him to release you from the betrothal arrangement with Regan? I intercepted it and showed it to Regan. He was aware you wanted to leave him. But instead of sending you packing, the fool returned your dowry and encouraged you to stay. I had not expected that. So, now, it will be easy to convince him you've broken off the engagement and have left him."

"He'll never believe you. He won't stop looking."

Clara scoffed. "No one will find you. Look around, there's no escape, and I have no intention of letting you out alive." She paused. "You must be hungry. Better if you ate something."

Clara stared down at the plate of food. Of course, the food. That's how Clara meant to kill her. With poison. Blood raced through her body as sweat drenched her skin. Silent screams rang through her mind. Her fingers curled into a fist, nails digging hard into her palms. "I won't eat your poisoned food."

"You are over-reacting, my dear. Trust me. You will eat."

Amelia shoved the tray, scattering food into the wretched pool on the floor.

"Suit yourself. Eat what I bring or die a slow death from hunger and thirst. Either way, you will never leave this room alive." Carefully spoken, without drama, her words had an air of finality to them. Clara turned on her heel, opened the door, and left.

After the slam of the door, Amelia heard the click of the key turning in the lock, followed by Clara's fading footsteps down the corridor. She couldn't move a single muscle, not even to scream. Absolute horror paralyzed her. The more she thought about escaping, the more discouraged and utterly terrified she became. She struggled to breathe, fear choking her. All she wanted to do was curl up into a ball and wait for someone to save her. But no one would. A desperate cry for help forced its way up and out of her throat, and tears coursed down her cheeks. The thought that she would die in this forlorn place was too much to contemplate.

She cursed Clara with more venom than she had ever felt before, and with a range of profanity she had not known she possessed. When she purged all the malice and fervor and outrage, she sunk her head in exhaustion and cried the last of her tears. In its place came an unfathomable fury. Her knuckles turned white from clenching her fists too hard. She gritted her teeth, then growled like a trapped animal. Her body burned with a slicing, potent animosity. She was alone, trapped in a vortex of evil. Regan could not come to her aid. She must help herself or perish. In desperation, she studied the walls and floor for a way out.

Chapter Twenty-Six

ANGUISH TWISTED IN Regan's heart, its intensity so harsh, so all-consuming, he believed he would die. In his bedroom, a third glass of brandy in hand, he stopped pacing and yanked back the curtains to peer out at the storm. The tempest obliterated the usual tranquility of the lawns and garden.

Ah, Edenstone's beauty. An estate lauded far and wide. But these appearances are deceptive. Behind the facade of elegance, misfortune lurked and plagued his family—his first fiancée who drowned, his grandmother's curse, the deaths of his three young sisters, Annie's mysterious disappearance, and now Amelia vanishing without plausible explanation. He swiped aside the curtains again, hoping for some clue, something that would make sense. But the vista yielded nothing.

The curtains fell back. He ran his fingers through his hair and resumed pacing. His thoughts roiled, his guts churned, his mind a confused muddle. Amelia's disappearance crushed him. He needed answers, and he wanted them now.

He downed the strong brandy, then hurled the glass

into the fire. He flung open the bedroom door, then dashed into the hallway. The hall lamps stood as silent sentinels, which shed the only light. The clock downstairs struck five, slow and resonant. When it fell silent, the howl of the wind returned to overpower the nocturnal silence. The blustery weather reinforced his belief Amelia had not left of her own accord but was in danger. The thought that she might be hurt or cold was more than he could bear.

Regan drew a deep breath and went down to the library. Perhaps there, he could clear his head and form a plan. His heart beat so fast, it felt as if the air was being choked from his lungs.

The library was dark, devoid of daylight and warmth. He halted in front of the large windows and stared at the violent storm. Confusion rose within him. How could this have happened? Amelia was here on the estate somewhere, he knew it. He sensed her presence and must find her before it was too late.

Despite the early hour, he must do something, anything, or lose his mind. Simpson confirmed he and the others had searched the house from top to bottom, and he trusted in the man's impeccable thoroughness. He needed to organize a search party. He hurried out into the hall, grabbed his coat, hat, and boots, then braved the storm as he went to the barn to saddle his horse.

Just as he had done once before, after Annie Simpson had gone missing, he would ride to all the neighboring estates to ask for their help to search for Amelia.

AMELIA DOZED FITFULLY, then awoke to utter darkness and the sound of thunder. The pounding in her head made it difficult to keep her eyes open. Darkness persisted, unmoved and unaltered. The stagnant smell of wet dirt worsened as rain seeped in through the edges of the crumbling tiny window frame and various cracks in the wall. She lost track of time and didn't know whether she had slept for only an instant or a day or more.

The storm raged without pause until, at some point, the last of the thunder rumbled and the occasional flashes of lightning waned. But the rain continued to fall, even though the violent wind had partially died down.

Amelia wept at the hopelessness of her situation. When she exhausted her tears, she dried her cheeks and steeled herself. From somewhere deep within, strength and courage stirred. She must take matters in her own hands, otherwise she would perish in this forsaken hole in the ground. With difficulty, she sat up and looked around. She must find a way out. The sole window was too small.

Rising slowly, she stood, but the room spun about, and her vision blurred. She braced her hand against the cold stone wall until the dizziness subsided. She took a deep breath and bent to pull the bed away from the wall and dragged it to the middle of the cell. The lack of light made it difficult to see, so she ran her hands over the wall behind it. The stones were solid, and she found no chips or cracks in the grout.

On her knees, she ran her hands over the flagstones on the ground, moving from one corner of the cell to the other. Her hand brushed against something cold and metallic. She grabbed hold of it. A spoon. Obviously from the meal she had tossed on the floor. At some point, while she was unconscious or asleep, Clara must have returned to clean up the mess, but had missed the spoon. It gave her hope as a plan slowly formed.

She crawled over to the wall where her bed had been and chose a brick close to the floor. With a firm grip around the spoon, she scraped at the surrounding grout. Her spinning head throbbed. Dizziness and nausea made the painstaking work difficult, but she persisted and made slow progress. The old grout fell off little by little, and using the spoon as a lever, the brick came loose. She dropped the spoon and with both hands, freed it from the wall.

Whispering her gratitude, she clutched the treasure to her chest and fought back tears of relief. She rose to her feet, then pushed the bed back into place. Exhausted, she lay down; the brick tucked safely beside her, hidden beneath the blanket. She let out a deep breath, closed her eyes, and waited.

REGAN RODE FROM estate to estate, gathering men as he went. Word spread quickly, and despite the weather, every available man from Winthrop came to his aid. He could see the concern on their faces at having to ask for their help to search for a missing woman once again. What must they think of him? They divided into several small groups and spread out in all directions, searching all roads, ditches, and structures in the vicinity.

As the dismal day progressed, Regan's hopes faded. Gloomy skies turned even darker as the afternoon grew late. After several hours, the men regathered; cold, wet, exhausted. No one found any sign of her. Amelia had vanished without a trace.

He had no choice other than to stop the search and let everyone return home. As they took their leave, each man stepped forward to pat his arm or back, speak an encouraging word, or promise to return in the morning to resume the search.

His heart heavy, Regan rode home. Time was his enemy. With each passing moment, the chances of finding Amelia diminished. He turned into Edenstone's front lane and rode straight into the stable. He slid down from his horse, his muscles stiff and aching, his clothes soaked through. A lad rushed forward to take the reins from his numb hands.

"Extra oats and then blanket him well." Regan pulled his hat down over his face, hunched his shoulders, then went back out into the heavy rain. Lured by the warm lights shining from the house's windows, he ran across the lawn. At the front door, he stomped his feet to rid his boots of mud. Then he stepped inside, just as the clock was striking six, the dinner hour. He had been searching for Amelia for over twelve hours.

Simpson rushed from the far end of the hall to help Regan out of his wet coat and took his hat. He raised his eyebrows but did not speak.

Choked by despair, Regan managed a slow blink and a shake his head.

"I'm sorry, Sir," Simpson said as Regan headed toward the stairs.

As he passed the dining room, he noticed the unset table and unlit room.

He glanced back at Simpson. "Where is everyone?"

"What with all the upset, the ladies declined to come down for dinner. You must be exhausted. I'll have a tray sent up right away. Would you also like a hot bath drawn?"

Regan shook his head. "Something warm to eat would be welcome. As for the bath, I'm exhausted. It'll have to wait." Regan gripped the bannister and went upstairs.

In his room, Simpson had already laid out his nightshirt, robe, and slippers. Regan stripped and donned the nightclothes. He poured himself a brandy and drank it, relishing the welcome warmth as it burned down his throat into his belly. He filled the glass again and slumped into the wing chair.

A warm fire crackled in the hearth. He downed that second brandy and rose to fill his glass yet again. He needed to feel the effects of the drink to help calm his nerves. When he returned to the chair, he stared at the private door that led to Amelia's room.

He conjured a vision of her, her beautiful face, the sound of her laughter. From the first time he saw her, she ignited a primal need to protect her. And he had done so, barely leaving her side while she grieved over the loss of her father, her home, and all its contents, and then he had welcomed her wholeheartedly to Edenstone. Ultimately, despite all his efforts, he had failed to keep her safe. The realization shook him to his core. After setting down his glass, he rose and strode to the connecting door. He swung it open and stepped inside her bedroom.

A fire burned in the hearth, a sign that Sarah and Mrs. Simpson expected her return. The sight soothed him at first; the dim firelight, the comforting bed with its turned down covers, the book she had been reading on the bedside table.

Regan walked to the bed and sat on the down-filled coverlet. As he looked about, the room's emptiness haunted him. His fingers extended; he ran his hand over the silk pillows where she rested her head. His throat clogged with emotion. He loved her deeply and could not imagine his life without her. *Where in the blazes are you, Amelia?* Something corrupt and malicious was afoot. Feelings of helplessness threatened to surface, but he refused to let them affect him. No matter what, he was determined to never give up until he found her. He prayed she would be alive.

His thoughts settled on Clara. He had no doubt she knew something. He pushed himself to his feet and marched to Clara's door and knocked. There was no answer. She must be with Aunt Beatrice, so he moved to the next door and knocked.

"Enter," the frail, familiar voice said.

He swung open the door. Aunt Beatrice sat in the wing chair next to the window, reading by the light of a solitary candle. She glanced up and smiled.

"Have you seen Clara?" he asked.

"Yes, of course. She is with Alexa in her bedroom helping your bride to choose a gown for the ball."

Regan swallowed. There was no forthcoming ball, and the women were not in Amelia's room discussing fashion.

"Don't worry, my dear," she added. "I'm sure they're nearly finished, and you'll see them both when they come down to dinner."

Was she confused again? Or had Clara put that excuse in her mind? His alarm intensified. He returned to Clara's door and pounded on it. "Open, Clara. Please, I need to speak to you."

No answer.

He tried the doorknob, but the door was locked. "Clara. Open the door, damn you," he shouted. He shook the crystal doorknob.

Regan ran to his room, flung open his wardrobe door, and grabbed the ring of household keys from the top shelf. Then he raced back to Clara's door and used the master key to unlock it.

Stepping inside, his mind stuttered for a moment. The Aubusson carpet in the center of the room was folded back. It revealed an open trapdoor. His heart thumped. Sweat drenched his forehead. Hands clenched into fists, he peered down into the cobweb lined hole. A decrepit set of wooden spiral stairs led down into the dank darkness.

He grabbed the candlestick on the bedside table, lit the candles from the fire in the hearth, then placed his foot carefully on the first step. It held. Cautious, silent, and slowly, he went down the rickety stairs.

Chapter Twenty-Seven

AT THE SOUND of the key being thrust into the lock, Amelia pushed herself up to a sitting position. A wave of dizziness engulfed her. She closed her eyes to let it pass, slid the brick to rest against her right thigh, and covered it with the blanket.

The door swung open. Clara carried in a tray of food and set it down at the foot of the bed.

Amelia noticed she had forgotten to close the door behind her. Just as Amelia was about to look away to distract Clara from the fact it was open, Amelia's heart skipped a beat. Regan stepped out of the shadows into her view. When he saw her, his face lost all color and his lips parted. Eyes wide, his expression of surprise changed to one of fury. He gave her a powerful look, raised his index finger to his lips, then stepped silently out of sight. Disappointment seized her, but then she realized he wanted to listen or was waiting for the right moment to sweep in. Amelia played along.

Blood raced through her veins. She held herself still and fixed her gaze back on Clara. Her ordeal would be over soon, but first, she would make Clara repeat what she had done so Regan could hear it firsthand.

"I've brought you dinner," Clara said, resting her fists on her hips. Her lips rose into a horrid grimace. "You must be hungry by now."

The aroma of roasted meat turned her stomach. Her throat was so dry, she could barely swallow. "I'd rather starve than eat your poison-laced food."

Clara stared down at Amelia with a scowl that made her shudder. "Suit yourself. I've been told that starving and dying of thirst is a terrible way to depart this life. Eat the food and it will be much easier."

"As easy as death came to Catherine when you poisoned her?"

"Yes, just like that, and Annie too. It didn't take either of them long to die. It will be the same for you." She spoke cheerily, as if poisoning someone was normal, and as simple as a conversation during an afternoon tea.

"You cannot get away with this, Clara. Regan is searching for me. It's only a matter of time before he finds me and discovers what you've done."

Clara tossed back her head and let out a cruel, mocking laugh.

Disgust at Clara's melodramatic behavior swept through her.

"Regan will never know about Catherine. In fact, he has yet to discover what happened to Annie." She leaned over and pressed her face close to Amelia, who shifted to avoid the closeness and the feel of the woman's breath on her face. "He will never find you, either."

"So, I am to die here, at your hand. What do you intend to do with my body? How will you dispose of me without help?"

Clara straightened and strode to the wall where she leaned against it. "The same way I got rid of Annie's body. It wasn't easy, but I managed because she was a slight girl. In the middle of the night, I dragged her body out to the rear of the house where I had a horse waiting. With a rope, I hitched her body to the creature and then rode to the graveyard where I tossed her into that well you found."

The impact of the revelation almost knocked the wind out of Amelia's lungs, yet she held herself firm, without reaction. "Please, Clara, let me go, I beg of you. I'll not tell Regan you put me here. It will be our secret. We can go on as before, as if this never happened."

"How stupid of you to wish for the impossible. I'm afraid I'm decided." Clara stepped over to the tray and raised the lid off the plate. The sight of roasted chicken breasts, asparagus, and wild rice let off a tempting, rich aroma, but it only stirred up her nausea. Amelia fought back the urge to vomit.

"Eat, Amelia. Let's be done with all this. It's over, and you know it."

"No."

Clara replaced the lid and took a step back. "Suit yourself. A day or two more won't matter. It takes three to six days to die of thirst."

"How long have I been here?"

"Not long, really. A mere two days."

Two days—an eternity.

"What have you told Regan? Surely he has asked when you last saw me."

"You made that very easy for me. What a fool you were to offer to break the betrothal if he returned your dowry. And he was no less the fool by restoring it to you. I told him that now that he returned your money, you left him."

"He would never believe that."

"Oh, in time he will." Clara looked around the room with disgust. "I've had enough being stuck here in this pathetic little room with you. I've better things to do. So, I encourage you to eat. You never know how long it will be before I can return with more food and water."

She turned her back to Amelia and stepped toward the doorway.

Amelia slid her hand beneath the blanket and grasped the brick, hoping she wouldn't need it. She rose from the bed, her body weak and trembling with fury.

Just as Clara was about to pass through the doorway, Regan stepped out of the shadows and blocked her way.

"Regan!" Clara gasped; her voice shrill with shock. "Look, I've found Amelia. I was just coming upstairs to tell you."

Regan's eyes narrowed and became cold and hard. "You lied, Clara. About everything. You killed my mother, and I'll not let you get away with it."

Clara attempted to run past him, but Regan grabbed her by the waist and yanked her back. She struggled to free herself, but he held her firm. Her fists clenched; she pounded his chest while kicking wildly at him with her legs. Through gritted teeth she bellowed and groaned, but Regan held steady and she couldn't rid herself of his grip. She exuded an acid-like animosity—scorching, cutting, potent. Her face was red with exploding rage. She thrashed about with a feral madness, attempting to bite him, terror echoing in her voice as if she were a trapped animal.

To help Regan, Amelia swung the brick and struck her

on the back of the head.

Clara tumbled to the ground, motionless.

Amelia thrust herself into Regan's arms. Before she could draw a breath, her body melted into his. His heart thumped against hers, filling her with relief. He folded his hands around her, pulling her tight to him. Her body shook as she unleashed a flood of tears.

He pulled slightly away and wiped her tears with both thumbs. His touch brought more respite than her heart could bear. His gaze took her in, assessing, concerned. Then he kissed her with a forceful passion, trying to ease away her troubles, catching her tears between their lips. When the kiss ended, Amelia wanted to speak, but all she could rasp was, "Hold me, Regan. Never let me go."

"Exactly my intentions. But I need to get you upstairs, summon the doctor, too. I need to know you're not harmed." Relief and concern mingled in his voice as he lifted her into his powerful arms, clutching her tight against him until her body stopped trembling and her heart's cadence slowed.

"But what of Clara?" Amelia uttered as a renewed terror rose inside her. "We have to check on her. What if I killed her? We can't leave her here."

Regan turned to look at Clara's crumpled body on the ground at his feet. "She's still breathing, so she's likely unconscious for now. I'll bring her up as soon as I get you into your bed. And if she awakes in the meantime, it will do her good to see what it feels like to be locked up like an animal."

Trusting herself to his protection once more, she rested her head against his chest as he effortlessly made his way down the passage and up the spindly stairs.

The blood drained from her face when she saw the stairs led up to a trapdoor and into Clara's bedroom. So that's how Clara brought her down into the cell.

He crossed the room and carried her out into the hall. He leaned over the bannister and bellowed. "Simpson. I've got her. I found Amelia. Summon the physician right away."

He carried her into her bedroom and laid her gently on the bed.

Regan reached for the pitcher and poured her a glass of water. She struggled to swallow and choked when the liquid forced its way down her parched throat.

He took back the glass. "Slowly, Amelia. Take your time. Your body needs time to adjust. There's plenty of water."

When the coughing spell passed, he handed her the glass again. She sipped the rest, then laid her head back on the pillow in relief. Regan refilled it and set it beside her on the nightstand. "Give it a few moments, then try drinking a little more." He sat on the bed next to her, his gaze never leaving her face. His breathing had softened, the pensive look melting into a smile as soft as the morning light. In that moment, their souls united in a profound love.

Pounding footsteps up the stairs and down the corridor heralded the Simpsons, Sarah, and Aunt Beatrice. They crowded the entrance, their expressions a mixture of relief and worry.

"I've sent the stable lad to fetch Dr. Morris," Simpson announced.

"Thank you," Regan said.

"Where did you find her?" Mrs. Simpson asked as she rummaged through a trunk and pulled out an extra quilt, which she spread over the bed.

"In a cellar accessed by a hidden trapdoor in Clara's room. I'll tell you everything soon, but not yet. For now, let's make sure Amelia has come to no harm." He paused. "Mrs. Simpson, Amelia will need some food, preferably something light like soup. And Sara, please stay with her. Don't let her out of your sight," Regan commanded. "There's something I have to attend to."

"Gladly, sir." With a swish of her skirts, Mrs. Simpson swept back out into the corridor with haste.

Sarah opened the wardrobe to retrieve Amelia's night clothes.

Regan rose, but Amelia stopped him with a grip of her hand. "What are you going to do?"

"I need to bring Clara up. The physician should see her too. I promise I'll be back shortly, after I make sure she can do no more harm to anyone under this roof."

The expression on their faces revealed their shock. They must be told, but not now. Amelia was glad that no one asked questions, for the time being. There was much for her and Regan to discuss before they revealed the truth to them.

While they left to attend to their tasks, Sarah helped Amelia undress and wash with a cloth and water.

"We were all so worried," she said. "Mr. Regan was relentless in searching for you. He had the entire house, the estate, and all roads and homes in the vicinity searched."

"I'm sorry to have put you all through such an ordeal."

"The only thing that matters is that you're now safe and home again." Sarah searched her face questioningly.

"I know you want to hear what happened, but I can't talk about it just yet. It's best to wait for Regan. I have to speak with him first."

"I understand, Miss. You are pale and look sickly. Food, a bath, and sleep will restore you. Let's get you feeling better first."

Soon Mrs. Simpson appeared with a bowl of soup, rich in vegetables, chicken, and chunks of potatoes. Anadama bread slathered in butter and a cup of warm milk was also on the tray. Nothing ever tasted so good, and Amelia delighted in every spoonful and bite.

Once she finished eating, Sarah and Mrs. Simpson prepared her bath.

Amelia lingered in the warm bath until it cooled. Sarah helped her dry off and don a nightgown that carried the fresh scent of lavender.

Exhausted, she returned to bed to await the physician and Regan. What was taking Regan so long? Had Clara somehow revived and done something to him? Her fear reignited, she was about to climb out of bed and rush back into Clara's room and down the trapdoor again, when Regan came back into the room with the doctor in tow. He stood stone-faced while the physician examined her. He listened to her chest, and checked her limbs for bruising, then declared her fit and well, urging her to rehydrate with plenty of water and to eat light foods until her body became re-accustomed. He left a small brown bottle of laudanum on her nightstand. "Rest. A regime of plenty of soup, fresh bread, and fruit will restore you. I don't expect any problems, but should the need arise, please summon me." He smiled down at Amelia. "You gave us all a scare, young lady. But you are in the best of hands here. A day or two of bed rest is all you need."

"Thank you, Dr. Morris," she responded with a wealth of gratitude.

He picked up his hat and Regan led him out of the room. The two spoke in hushed tones in the hallway just beyond her door. Amelia tried to listen but could not make out a word. Then the voices faded down the hallway. She had little doubt Regan was asking him to check on Clara.

Amelia noticed Sarah waiting in the room's corner. "You can go too, Sarah. I need a few minutes alone with Regan, and then I intend to sleep. I'll see you in the morning."

With a smile and curtsy, Sarah left her too.

Before long, Regan returned. Amelia sat up against her pillows and obediently took a spoonful of the laudanum Regan held to her lips. She was too weak to speak much. But when he smiled down at her, his expression was cheerful, but calm.

"What of Clara? Please tell me she's still alive." Amelia asked. Already, the laudanum was taking effect, calming her, and bringing on drowsiness.

"She's safely tucked in her bed. Dr. Morris has already seen to her. She's alive, but still unconscious. He says she'll make a full recovery. In the meantime, I've had the trapdoor nailed shut, and after the doctor left, I locked her in her room." He wiped a wayward curl from her forehead. "Everything is under control. She can't go anywhere. You're safe, I promise."

"What are you going to do with her, Regan? She killed your mother."

At these words, the light disappeared from Regan's eyes. In a choked voice, he said, "I need time to think."

"Surely you're not contemplating turning her into the authorities. She'll be charged criminally and might hang for her crime."

He frowned, his expression one of torment and indecision. "Not now, Amelia. This is not your concern for now. The most important thing is for you to get some sleep and we can talk about it when you're feeling better."

"Yes, when I'm feeling better," she murmured as her eyes fluttered a few times before closing.

She felt his lips kiss her forehead.

With the comforting certainty that when she awakened, whether by sunlight or lamplight, he would be nearby, she let sleep sweep her away.

AMELIA AWOKE TO the sound of Clara's screams coming from the hallway. Bright sunlight shone through a crack in the drawn curtains. Ignoring the headache, she jumped out of bed, grabbed her robe, and hurried out of her room. Her face drained at the sight of two brawny men dragging a combative Clara toward the stairs. Regan walked behind them. He glanced over his shoulder at her when he heard her footsteps.

She ran to him, and he put his arm around her, pulling her tight against him.

"What is happening?" she asked.

When Clara heard her voice, her flailing intensified as she screamed, "Amelia, help me. Don't let them take me." But the two men continued to pull her down the stairs.

Amelia looked at Regan. "She is being arrested?"

He shook his head. "No, I did not have the heart to

turn her in. She is being taken to The McLean Asylum for the Insane in Boston."

Amelia's throat jammed as horrendous visions of abuse came to life in her mind.

"Amelia, help me, please." Clara's tear-streaked, crimson face exuded terror as they reached the bottom of the stairs. "I promise not to hurt you. Please."

Regan gave Amelia's hand a squeeze. "Say nothing. Trust me."

Amelia swallowed and fell silent as she watched the orderlies drag Clara down the hall. Amelia and Regan followed them, silent and disconsolate.

Clara's screams faded as the trio passed through the front door and the men pushed her thrashing body into an awaiting black carriage emblazoned with the crest and title, McLean Asylum. With a flick of the reins, the driver set the horses into a brisk walk and they disappeared down the drive. Clara's terror-stricken face peered back at them, her fists pounding on the rear glass.

The sight of her distress sent a shudder down Amelia's spine. "What will happen to her?" she asked Regan.

"She is my cousin, my childhood friend. I didn't have the heart to turn her in to the authorities and see her hang, even though she deserves it for murdering my mother and hiding Annie's body, and for almost causing your demise too. Sending her to the McLean Asylum was the most humane thing I could do."

"I suppose it's far better than having her arrested and facing trial. But an asylum? I've heard terrible things about what goes on within such places."

"This asylum is different. It sits on a wooded hill on the outskirts of Boston. It's luxurious, with impeccably maintained grounds and elegant interior. In fact, it looks more like a prestigious college rather than an insane asylum. The physicians there believe that the mentally ill benefit from its tranquil, idyllic setting, and they follow a gentle regime of moral treatment with the intent to heal. There she will receive the finest care. In the winter she can skate. In pleasant weather she can ride horses or go for lovely walks. When indoors, there are other activities. She can learn to paint or access a well-stocked library. There is even bowling and croquet. Her room will be well-furnished with its own fireplace, small parlor, and a private bathroom. It's the best I can do for her and far more than she deserves." He clenched his fists. "I'm trying really hard not to hate her for what she's done to my mother, to you, to this entire family."

"But for how long will she be held there?"

Regan peered down at her with eyes softened by pain. "For the rest of her life."

Chapter Twenty-Eight

AT ALL THE commotion, Edward and Mary Simpson and Sarah rushed out the door to see what was happening. They arrived a few moments before the carriage drove off, their faces drained of all color, mouths agape.

Regan squeezed Amelia's hand before he turned around to face the trio. He cleared his throat. "Mr. Simpson, Mrs. Simpson, please make yourselves comfortable in the drawing room," Regan said. "I'll join you there in a few moments. I owe you an explanation. I'm sure you're eager to hear what I have to say."

Their countenances white, they nodded and tiptoed into the house.

After a quick glance from Amelia, Sarah spoke. "If you need me, Miss, I'll be upstairs preparing your gown for the day." She also hurried past them.

Once they were alone, Regan tipped his head closer to Amelia. "It's time to tell them the truth about Annie. If you are up to it, would you join me?"

"Of course, but I'm worried about Aunt Beatrice."

"To spare her, I instructed Mrs. Simpson to put a sleeping draught in her chamomile tea last night. I suspect she won't wake up for a while."

Relieved, Amelia sighed in response to Regan's thoughtfulness. It gave them some time to think about the best way to approach the poor woman. Amelia hoped Aunt Beatrice's failing memory would prevent her from suffering very much over the loss of her daughter.

Regan took her hand. She inhaled a deep breath, and together they went to the drawing room.

※

IN THE MID-MORNING light beneath a cloudless sky, and the air fragrant with the scent of flowers and pine-needles, Amelia gathered with Regan and the rest of the household around the well in the graveyard. Stone faced; Simpson clutched his wife to him as she sobbed. Sarah rubbed Mrs. Simpson's back to comfort her. The Reverend conducted a brief memorial service and when he finished, offered his condolences, and drove off to give them their privacy.

Several weeks passed since Clara's departure. Guilt consumed Regan at the knowledge it was his mother who killed Annie Simpson. He did his best to have the poor girl's body retrieved from the well, but because of how much time passed since her death, the immense depth, and the danger it posed to send a man down to retrieve the bones, Regan turned the well into a beautiful memorial instead. A white marble slab sealed it forever shut. A simple plaque on the side read, *Anne Simpson, beloved daughter of Edward and Mary.* Hired gardeners planted colorful flowers in the bucket that hung from the pulley beneath the newly restored gable. Workmen replaced loose or damaged bricks. The black hellebore, roots, stems, and leaves had been dug up and beautiful rose bushes planted around its base where they would bloom in place of the uprooted poisonous flowers. Regan ordered the conservatory and various places in the house and on the estate searched for remnants of the poison. Not a trace of the deadly plant remained.

In this place of final endings and loving words, where the earth welcomed back her own, Amelia found tranquility, and a connection to those in Regan's family who had passed on. She reached into her pocket and held the locket. Through her tears, Mary smiled as Amelia dropped it into her palm. "It's long past the time to return this to you," Amelia whispered.

"Thank you, Miss. Were it not for you and Mr. Regan, we would never have known what happened to our Annie, may she rest in peace. And we can be at peace now. We can mourn her loss, and you've honored us by giving her this place in the Lockhart family graveyard."

Regan stepped forward and slid his arm around Amelia's waist. "I cannot bring Annie back to you, but I hope this small gesture will help to ease some of your pain. On behalf of my family, please forgive me for what happened to your daughter. It was the least I could do for all that you suffered."

"You must not blame yourself," Mr. Simpson said. "No one could have foreseen what happened. You have suffered enough losses. Our daughter is finally at peace and we can grieve and remember her here at her grave. We are grateful to you both. We can now look to the future and hope for better days."

"You're a good man, Simpson," Regan said before

turning toward Amelia. "Come, my dear, let's leave them to their privacy."

Amelia nodded. To see loved ones committed to the soil seared a memory into the minds of those left behind. It also brought closure and healing. To hearten the grieving couple, she walked back to the house with Sarah.

BRIGHT SUNSHINE WRAPPED Amelia and Regan in a blanket of warmth as they ran out of the church amid cheers and applause and gently tossed grains of rice from those in attendance.

Regan helped her into his most elegant carriage, a barouche emblazoned with his business crest: Lockhart Carriage Company. The top was down, and white ribbon and roses decorated the back and sides. As Regan took his place beside her on the blue velvet seats, Amelia glanced at the friends and family gathered on the front steps of the church.

Aunt Beatrice waved her handkerchief at them with a new nurse by her side, an efficient, kind, and patient woman of middling years whom she liked. And although Aunt Beatrice often asked about Clara, in her mind she believed Clara merely went to visit someone and would soon return. Grateful that her failing memory shielded her from grief or pain, Amelia hoped the coming years would bring her peace and simplicity.

Phillip stood next to his sister, Hannah. Beneath his slight smile, Amelia knew Clara broke his heart. Since childhood, he loved Clara. She wondered how different Clara's life would have been if she had married him.

Mr. and Mrs. Simpson held hands, their expressions serene and joyful, past burdens lifted from their shoulders. Although they suffered the loss of a child, Amelia hoped now that Regan allowed them to retire with a healthy pension and a nearby cottage, they could spend the rest of their days surrounded by their love for each other.

William Finnerty stood off to the side, a triumphant grin on his face. Amelia whispered, "Thank you," to him. "You and my father were right all along. I'm glad Regan has retained your legal services for his business and our personal affairs."

In response, he gave her a nod and the widest of grins.

And then Sarah, with tears of joy in her eyes, blew a kiss to her. Amelia blew back one of her own.

Amelia and Regan waved to them all as the driver set the horses into a trot as their carriage drove away.

"Are you happy, Mrs. Lockhart?" His eyes looked deeply into hers as he smiled as softly as the morning light.

Her body relaxed in the warmth of his gaze. "There is nothing you could do to make me happier."

He raised her chin with his fingers. "That's where you're wrong. There is much more to come. In fact, I have a wedding gift to give you."

"I only need you, Regan."

"And that you shall have, my love. But what kind of husband would I be if I didn't do everything in my power to keep my bride happy?" He held her face in his hands, pulling her to his chest as he gazed at her. Alight with passion, his eyes blazed like candles in the dark. A small but teasing smile crept upon his face.

Goosebumps lined her skin, not from the cold, but from anticipation.

She had not realized how her love for him had grown, and the depth of which she loved Edenstone, with its tranquil, beautiful setting on the shore that soothed her soul when beset by grief and indigence.

He pressed his lips to hers in a kiss so steeped with passion and the promise of everlasting love, it took her breath away.

When they finally pulled apart, they laughed.

Despite the bumpy ride, they sipped champagne, spilling only small amounts, and indulged in fine cheese, bread, and fruit during their journey. No matter how many times she asked where he was taking her, Regan only grinned in response.

But as they traveled, the landscape soon became more and more familiar to her. The road they took was the one to North Chelsea, her hometown. She kept glancing at him questioningly, but Regan continued to play coy, keeping his silence. She swallowed the lump in her throat as they drove past her father's shoe warehouse, a hive of activity with deliveries coming and going. Amelia could not help but wonder about the new owners. It appeared they had made a great success of it.

When the carriage stopped in front of her former house, Amelia struggled to push away the barrage of emotions threatening to surface.

Barely able to speak for the anguish, Amelia crushed Regan's hand. "Why have you brought me here?"

In response, Regan reached beneath his seat and pulled out a folded parchment he placed in her hand.

"What is this?" she asked.

"Open it and see." He kept an expectant gaze on hers.

With trembling hands, she unfolded the document and

read. Mouth agape, through eyes flooded with tears, she stared at Regan, unable to speak.

"My first gift to you. Your home, and your father's business, are yours. You are sole owner."

"But how, why...?"

"I could not bear to see you lose everything that mattered. I purchased everything from the bank and put it solely in your name. I sent my assistant, Henry Townsend, to come to your house on the day before you left to record the possessions you wanted to keep. Remember? I kept it all a secret, wanting to surprise you with it on our wedding day. Have I made you happy, Mrs. Lockhart?"

Still choked with emotion, all she could do was nod.

Her bridegroom swung open the carriage door and stepped down. He held out his hand to her. "Come. Let's go inside."

Her legs trembling, she allowed him to lead her to the front door. Regan reached into his pocket and pulled out a beribboned ring of keys and handed it to her.

Overcome, she stared down at them in her palm.

"Well, go on. Open the door."

Her hands shaking, she slid the key into the lock and turned it. The familiar sound of the click made her heart flutter.

Regan swung open the door for her.

Inside stood an overjoyed Mr. and Mrs. Seeton. When she ran to them, they embraced.

Amid laughter, they pulled away.

"You came back?" Amelia asked.

"We never left," Mr. Seeton said.

"These are our new positions. Mr. Regan kept us employed here and increased our wages and asked us to keep it a secret from you."

Amazed, Amelia glanced around. All was just as she had left it, immaculately clean and in order. "Everything is here?"

"Well, not everything," Regan said. "I moved the portraits of your parents to Edenstone, where they now hang in the drawing room with all the other ancestors. Our ancestors now."

She ran into his embrace.

"I love you, Amelia. I will defend you with my life, comfort you in pain, and dance with you when times are good."

"And you have done that and more, my love."

Mr. Seeton cleared his throat, then he and his wife discreetly disappeared down the hall toward the kitchen.

"They insisted on preparing a special meal for us," Regan said. "We'll stay tonight, and, in the morning, we will go to Boston to catch a train to New York for our honeymoon where I will indulge my wife with her every desire."

"All I want is right here, with you." Happiness bloomed in her heart and soul. She closed her eyes to savor the moment, joyful because her love for Regan would thrive for as long as they lived.

With her arm entwined with his, they walked into the dining room to share their first meal as husband and wife.

Anadama Bread

This bread earned its name from a local fisherman in Rockport, MA. He was frustrated with his lazy wife because she always served him steamed corn meal mush and molasses for dinner. Tired of the same old fare, he mixed it with bread flour and yeast and baked it saying, "Anna Damn Her." The bread was so delicious and became so popular, his neighbors called it Anadama Bread.

INGREDIENTS
2 (1/4-ounce) packages active dry yeast
2 cups warm water or milk (110°F-115°F)
3/4 cup coarse yellow cornmeal, plus extra for coating the pan
1/2 cup dark molasses
6 tablespoons unsalted butter, at room temperature
1 teaspoon salt
5 1/2 cups bread flour

PROCEDURE

In a large bowl, stir the yeast in the warm water and let stand for 10 minutes.

Beat in the cornmeal, molasses, butter, and salt. Add the flour, one cup at a time, blending well after each addition, to make a moderately stiff dough.

Turn the dough out onto a lightly floured surface and knead for 6 to 8 minutes until smooth and elastic; add a little flour, if necessary, to prevent sticking.

Transfer the dough to a large bowl greased with vegetable oil and turn the dough to coat with the oil. Cover with a slightly damp towel and let rise in a warm, draft-free location for 1 to 1 1/2 hours, until approximately doubled in size.

Punch down the dough.

Turn the dough out onto a lightly floured surface and divide it in half. Cover and let rest for 10-15 minutes.

Lightly grease a very large baking sheet with butter, then sprinkle with cornmeal. Shape each half of the dough into a ball. Place the balls, smooth sides up, on the baking sheet. Flatten each into a 6-inch round loaf. Cover with towel and let rise for 30 to 45 minutes until almost doubled in size. Meanwhile, preheat the oven to 375°F.

Bake for 25 to 30 minutes, until the bread is golden and sounds hollow when tapped on the bottom. Remove the bread from the baking pan and cool on a wire rack. Serve warm, if possible.

Joe Frogger Cookies

Joe Froggers are rum-laced molasses-spice cookies originating from Marblehead, Massachusetts. The "Joe" part of the name came from a man named Joseph Brown, an African American slave who earned his freedom after serving in the Revolutionary War. He opened a tavern where he served the ale and his wife, Lucretia Brown, did the cooking. These cookies were her specialty, and she baked them in an iron skillet. The cookies earned their unusual second name of "Froggers" because when the batter hit the pan, it ran in all directions and formed the shape of a frog's body and legs. This, and the fact that a frog pond existed next to the tavern, gave birth to the name Joe Froggers. Recipe yields 4 dozen cookies.

INGREDIENTS

1/3 cup plus 1 tablespoon hot water
2-1/2 tablespoons dark rum
3-3-1/2 cups all-purpose flour, plus more for work surface
1-1/2 teaspoons table salt
1 teaspoon baking soda
1-1/4 teaspoons ground ginger
1/2 teaspoon ground cloves
1/2 teaspoon ground allspice
1/4 teaspoon freshly grated nutmeg
1/2 cup (1 stick) salted butter, softened
1 cup granulated sugar
1 cup dark molasses

PROCEDURE

In a small bowl, combine hot water and rum. In a larger second bowl, stir 3 cups flour with the salt and spices. Set aside.

In another large bowl, cream together butter and sugar until light and fluffy, about 4 minutes.

Add the water and rum mixture to the creamed mixture and beat well. Add one-third of the flour mixture and stir, then stir in half the molasses, scraping down the sides as you go. Repeat with an additional third of the flour mixture and the remaining molasses. Finally, add the rest of the flour mixture. If dough seems too loose, add the extra ½ cup flour.

Divide the dough into two balls, cover with plastic wrap, and chill at least 45 minutes and up to overnight.

Preheat oven to 375 degrees and grease two baking sheets or line with parchment.

Break off walnut-sized pieces of dough and roll into balls between your palms. Arrange the balls on the baking sheet approximately two inches apart. Put some granulated sugar into a bowl. Press the bottom of a drinking glass into the sugar, then press it onto each ball of dough, flattening it before baking. Bake the cookies until they have set but still seem soft in the middle, about 10 minutes. Cool on wire racks.

For My Readers

When you buy a book from an author, you're buying more than just a story. Authors put in so much time and energy and so many hopes and dreams, anticipating they have created something to entertain readers and that they find enjoyable. It is my sincerest hope that I kept you entertained and that you enjoyed my story. For authors, feedback is important. I would be most grateful if you would consider leaving honest feedback to help guide me in writing future books and so that others may read your words and make that final decision to purchase the book too. Thank you so much.

For anyone who wishes to contact me directly with questions or feedback, I'd love to hear from you. Visit www.mirellapatzer.com to connect with me.

Acknowledgements

I would like to thank the fabulous authors of the HisFicCrit Critique Group, all talented authors who read and edited every chapter to ensure it was the best it could be: Anita Davison, Maggi Anderson, Julie Howard, Rosemary Morris, Colleen Donnelly, Susan Cook, Ursula Thompson, Katherine Pym, Diane Dahlstrom Parkinson, and Lisa Elm.

Lisa JM Yarde-Bim and Jeanne Kalogridis who have been a constant friends and supporters in my writing career, whose own writing talents and achievements have always been a great inspiration to me.

And then there are those who picked me up and helped me through the difficult times. Marge Ruggles, Sandra Falconi, Paddy Cush, Ersilia Ward, Elvira Jackson, Myong Crich, Brad Braaksma, and Jeff Hawryluk.

And of course, my daughters Amanda Braaksma and Genna Hawryluk. Your constant love and support lift me up always.
Finally, my grandchildren, Joseph Patzer Hawryluk, Gabriella Hawryluk, Chloe Hawryluk, and Charlee Hawryluk. You bring immense joy and laughter into my

life. I am grateful to you all.

Books by Mirella Patzer

The Prophetic Queen
Orphan of the Olive Tree
The Contessa's Vendetta
The Novice
Dangerous Betrothal

Manufactured by Amazon.ca
Bolton, ON